The Devil's Red
Daemon Moon
Copyright ©

NOTE: JN Moon is a British Author.
The following is therefore written in British Grammar.
Just like Bram Stoker's Dracula.

Edited by Samantha at <u>Proofreading by the Page</u> Facebook
Cover art by <u>Manuela Serra</u>

<u>Wolf Moon.</u>
A lone alpha. A community shattered by a bloodbath.
A love born from the ashes...
Grab your FREE Copy Wolf Moon
www.jnmoon.com
Facebook: Author JN Moon
Newsletter JN Moon

Dedication

To my late parents; my mum who told me to never give up and always follow your heart and my step-dad who loved books and encouraged me to keep writing.

To my brother, Simon Knott for believing in me and his ideas that contributed to this story.

Huge thanks to my coach, Janita. I really appreciate your help.

When I looked around, I saw and heard of none like me.
Was I, then, a monster?
Mary Shelley
Frankenstein.

Break Out

Hell. For over two thousand years I had been imprisoned here and now? Now, it was time to leave. The clanking of metal on metal jolted me as a huge demon, his body a mass of muscle and armour, was lumbering towards me, each footstep thumped on the ground.

White paint smeared around his face, raven skin scorched from Hellfire, his beady eyes stared menacingly beneath his large over brow. Sharp dirty teeth jutted out, some broken from fighting. I braced, not wanting to smell his stench.

Rattling the keys, he placed one in the lock, it grated as he twisted then threw the door open. In one swift movement his hand shoved me in the chest. "You're to be moved down to the lake, your unholiness, Satan!" he sneered, twisting his neck so that his face was almost in mine.

I could taste fear—copper in my mouth—as my body lunged, crashing into the bars of my enclosure. My prison.

Bronze light from Hell's infernos spilled across the cell, illuminating shadows that flittered menacingly in the dark crevices of the cavern where my cage was placed. All around me, that familiar stench of charred fat and meat that was stuck in the back of my throat.

Burning flesh...

My breath caught. I was shaking as sweat broke out all over me. A violent sensation ripped through me, and I knew that my soul had merged back into me. In that instant, I convulsed, rasping, clutching my stomach. In my mind's eye, I could see my brothers, their faces distorted, bodies crippled and tortured. A bolt of pain flashed through me: I could feel their agony. Trying to regain my senses, I staggered backwards as the foul stench of demon breath swept over me, hot and fetid as it grabbed my neck, spitting obscenities.

Dazed, I stumbled forward into the demon, slipping on the blood daubed on the floor where I had painted sigils to perform a ritual to retake my stolen soul. Now, anger whipped through me like fire. Gasping, I shoved the beast out of my way, snarling as I grabbed at his sword as he snatched at my wrists.

Another convulsion. I wheezed and doubled over into the demon as another vision of my brothers flashed before my eyes. Michael. His face contorted in agony, I heard a hammering, metal on metal. Michael's arms outstretched, a clinking as Michael jolted, screaming. I knew in my soul, fallen as it was... he was being crucified! My brother, the archangel. I had to get out of here; I had to escape.

Swallowing down bile, I held back a gag, wide eyed back into the present. Frantically, I glanced around. The sword hilt slipped out of my bloody palms. Sounds in the distance of wailing grew louder, the constant cacophony of tortured souls. I clutched at the rusted bars that had imprisoned me, this cage slick with my blood and the gunge that oozed on the walls and the floor.

For once the door was open. I had to get out. Wriggling to unlock his grip from around my wrists, I stepped back, kicking my foot straight into his groin. Yelling as he doubled over, moaning, I managed to liberate his heavy sword. I swung it back, my arm shaking, my stomach knotted. It struck the demon.

I took his head. And my freedom.

Outside the cell I sprinted along a ledge, the cries of Hell all around me and demons swooping low in the distance, their black wings beating hard. Beneath me, fire leapt and brimstone bellowed, and the taste of charred flesh stuck in my mouth again, the smell heavy with blood and fear.

As I turned a corner, I came face to face with another demon, his face part-animal, part-human leering into mine. Mouth opened, he bellowed a guttural roar in my face. Stench of human flesh hot on his breath. I retched, bracing, then winced as his sword slashed at my side. My flesh split, a piercing pain. Gulping I dodged to the side of him as his sword swept towards me again.

This beast towered high above me, red paint on his face exaggerated his sharp, extreme features. He sneered, baring his teeth. I crouched fast, holding my sword up to block his as metal chinked on metal, he pushed harder. Toppling back, my arms splayed. I panted trying to regain my footing. I was rusty at fighting, that was obvious and he took the advantage driving forwards.

Hefting my sword, legs wide, I waited for his onslaught, my jaw clenched. At the last moment as his feet thundered on the ground. I side stepped, thrusting my sword into his side. I heard a clamour of steel on steel as he easily blocked my sword.

"You are to be moved... angel!" He spat, "Lower your weapon or die!"

Maybe, but I doubted a demon could kill an archangel. Only another archangel could do that. Still, I wasn't going to wait around to find out. As pain smarted through my side, I spied a shield and stumbled towards it. Snatching it, I leapt up with all my might into that sweltering heat as white-gold flames licked at my wings. Stretching them out, for a moment pain throbbed through them, then a slow easing as my blood pumped through them. Sighing, it felt so good, the relief. I hadn't been able to open them for eons.

Now I was ready to fight my way out of the furnace of Hell.

He was hot on my tail, his vast wings pounding below me, but I was lighter and flew faster. Burning, the acid in my muscles was hot and I needed all my energy for what I had to face next. Not one demon, but dozens.

Scrunching my face against the oppressive heat, I soared higher. My only benediction was that my singed wings no longer had feathers like my brothers. Mine are leathery—now ripped—torn from the many fights, having to constantly maintain my place as Guardian of Hell. But the demons, led by the upstart Paimon, one of the Kings of Hell had locked me up. And even with my power as a fallen angel, I was unable to fight them all off. I had tried, and ended up here in this dirty, tiny cell.

Soaring higher, vast craters spewed lava, a molten river surged below me. I flew past the charred ridges of mountains.

Therian demons armed with swords came into view. Swallowing hard, my lips curled back in disgust. Racing, my heartbeat pounding, my chest tightened as did the grip on my sword hilt. I braced, waiting for their onslaught. Distorted and hideous, they flew at me.

Faces part ape, part human, their mouths revealed vast razor teeth, huge muscular limbs and talons that could tear me in two. There was a flash of steel, a chink of metal, and rustling and swirling. Their swords poised, silver tipped spears and claws. The demons grabbed me, attempting to pull me back down into the fiery pits as they grunted and roared in outrage.

I got it, they really didn't want me to leave. They'd sooner kill me than allow me my freedom. But I had to get out.

Gulping in air and pushing all my energy into my wings, I fought hard to escape, sword in hand, cutting through the monstrosities that I was meant to govern. My left arm braced, my fingers burned, clenching the shield as I stopped the incoming slashes from swords that bounced from it, my arm aching with cramps. I hadn't fought like this for eternity, but I had no choice.

Michael and Gabriel were being tortured. I had seen my brothers in my visions, felt their agony, their anguish, their terror. And even though they had left me here for over two thousand years, I'd rather die than let them suffer. I'd take the blade from every sword in Hell if I could save them. So, even with the might of Hell against me, nothing would stop me.

Snarling with hate, I thrust my blade through the belly of an incoming demon; it spat poison that stank of decaying flesh. As its gnarled wings thrashed, I felt a breeze sweep over me. Any draft, however slight, was welcomed in this sweltering hole.

My blade crunched through the beast's ribs and got lodged there. I cursed loudly and braced my foot against its body, tugging on my sword's hilt fast before it could pull me down with it. To my relief, the blade came loose, and the demon gurgled and spewed black blood as it plummeted down to the torrent of lava below me.

A macabre noise echoed loudly throughout Hell. I shuddered hard.

In the distance horns bellowed, their sinister bass reverberating right through my fallen celestial body. I winced as loose rocks tumbled from the cliff faces around me.

My muscles were on fire; my body ached. I roared, making one last push to the surface, charging fast, my stomach flipping at the speed of my ascent. Demons crashed into me, grasping at my wings and my feet.

I didn't look down.

I could already hear them, thousands of monsters wheeling to grab me, their master. The horns resounded, loosening more rocks. I dodged the rubble which threatened to trap me.

Flying between the mountainous blackened overhangs on either side of me, the passage was almost too narrow for my wingspan. I gulped, sword in one hand, shield in the other.

Unable to wipe the sweat from my face, it stung my eyes, blinding me, but at last the faintest breeze touched my skin. This time it didn't smell of sulphur or burnt flesh. Surging with hope, I took another breath, spiralling up I spied a glimmer of light above, I fought to get out.

I had to get out.

Suddenly the light above me darkened. I narrowed my eyes, looking up, trying to see what shadow had appeared there. It moved. It was flying fast.

A mighty demon, skin coal-red, scorched from the flames of Hell, its body a mass of muscle and plate armour, its sword glinting in the flames.

Shit, shit, shit!

Roaring, my voice guttural, I yelled at the monster. "Demogorgon, back off, or you will know what it is to be on the wrong end of my sword!"

He tilted his massive head, grinning, his array of teeth catching the light. Lunging forward, wings beating slowly as he hovered alongside me, he squeezed us in the tight crevice of mountain ridges that spanned Hell's sky.

Demogorgon's sword lashed towards me. I blocked his blade as it smashed onto my shield, my back shoved against the rock face, forcing my wings to splay open, scratching and cutting as they scraped on the stone. Biting past the pain, it took all my strength against this colossal monster to hold him back. Pushing into me, his breath rancid, he sneered, then pulled back his sword, jostled it in his hand, then took aim at my shoulder. As he did this, he pressed his shield into mine, the gap now even tighter, and unable to move fast enough I howled as I watched his sword bear down into me.

Silence lingered around me. My eyes watered, he was a blurred vision of death before me. I swayed as shock bolted through my limbs. His mouth curved up, his head shook as he slowly pulled his weapon from my shoulder and I felt myself fall, heavy, tumbling. Muted sounds vibrated through me, then gasping deeply survival kicked in.

Thrusting his sword as he came towards me, I plunged downwards, flying perilously close to the rock edge before gasping, leaping fast, pulling in my wings with my feet against the cliffs. I sprung past him and soared higher, rocketing to the exit, only opening my wings at the last second.

The cool air fanned my skin. There was a sudden flush of sweat as hot and cold melded. I squinted as my eyes became once again accustomed to the rays of daylight.

I hadn't been in the sun in two thousand years.

Nephilim Nation

Finally flying free, I landed on soft grass, the sweet scent of leaves and foliage filling my senses. I glanced back fast.

Behind me I could still hear the demons' roars and the echo of the trumpets. Sword in hand, I waited, bracing for Demogorgon to appear. Demogorgon had been my nemesis for a thousand years. I hated him with a vengeance. For some reason that demon made my suffering his reason for existence it seemed. Vile, evil creature of Hell who detested Heaven and especially angels.

I fell to my knees, my arm now searing in pain, clenching my teeth battling back a cry. Panting, my eyes scanned the landscape. As the earth filled around the hole, a grasping hand pierced through the soil, then was lost.

I bent over, my chest rising and falling heavily. As utter relief coursed through me, I dropped both my shield and my sword. With one hand resting on the ground, I wiped the sweat from my brow before standing tall and taking in my surroundings.

Earth.

I both loved and despised the place. This was where it had all begun. My downfall.

Trees dotted my view. Birds scattered, their cawing forcing a forgotten smile. I'd arrived in a tiny park. Manicured grass, rows of neat flowers, pinks, blues, yellows—colours that had become only a memory until now. Their fragrance forced nostalgia on me. I had only smelt the horror of Hell for millennia.

I picked up my weapons and strode forward. Somewhere on this planet, my brothers' lives were in danger.

My muscles eased as I walked, my breathing lighter now that my death was—at least temporarily—postponed. Clean air filled my aching lungs. There would be time for rage and further battles to free my kin, but for now I was grateful for the balm of nature.

Something stirred. A sound. Weak and fearful. Frowning, I stood still, listening hard, trying to identify the noise. What was it?

Whimpering seemed to come from a rosebush of all things. I tread lightly over, wary that some malevolent monster might be waiting. Almost panting now, my fingers gripped the handle tightly. I scanned the bush, noticing the tiny red buds that dotted it.

Crying and shivering under the hedge, a puppy looked up at me.

A puppy! Shaggy black and white patches, his soulful eyes were wet, fearful. He shivered hard, backing away but the sound, his whimpering cut through my core. If I'm honest, it pained my heart. How you go from killing demons to helping a puppy almost in one fell swoop was new to me. But in that moment, in that instant, something happened.

A fire melted my frozen, angry heart. My chest trembled at that, such an unfamiliar sensation. I felt bewildered by an intense compulsion to protect, to comfort. Instinct had me averting my eyes to the ground, my hand low and slow, moving just a little forward toward the shivering dog. I barely recognised my own voice, almost a whisper...

"Are you afraid of me, little creature? You should not be!"

Although, to be fair, most earthly creatures cower in my presence.

"I will help you," I said.

I edged back, sheathing my sword I'd stolen from Hell in my belt, and placed the shield down. Stepping lightly forward, I crouched on the ground before the puppy. In Hell we have Hell hounds, and I had enjoyed playing with the pups, their innocence, their unconditional love and even cared for a few. But in time they grow and become obedient to their masters, as is their destiny, and all become cruel and vicious. But this, this was no Hell hound. This pup was earth-bound, filthy and terrified. His eyes were wide and rolling, and I could see his ribs.

"Whatever are you doing here, Hound? It's all right, you have the Devil's attention now, and I'll damn any who try to harm you. Come."

Carefully keeping my eyes on the ground to show I meant no threat, I noticed the little creature's tail wag as he mustered his courage and slowly crept forward.

"Hello! Good boy, yes, that's right. Come here. Hell, you're starving, what disgusting human dumped you here? Yes, that's right, come to uncle Lucifer. I'll smite the bastard who abandoned you!"

As he wriggled closer still, I lay down, caught in the moment of one of my father's better creations, and let the dog climb onto me. Another smile. That's two in as many minutes. I smiled again for the third time, stroking his rough fur, my hands resting on his ribs. Turning my head as the pup now sniffed me, he climbed onto my chest as I laid there; I noticed a black canvas bag. So, someone had dumped him.

It was strange. My anger that is usually legendary—not that I'm proud of that—had to be kept in check so as not to frighten the helpless beast before me. And odder still my compulsion to help it. Tenderness whipped through my veins like warm bubbling water and I smiled. I noticed this as my cheeks burned; I hadn't smiled for a long, long time...

"I need to get you some food, Hound. And water. Oh, yes... and a flea collar!" I brushed the parasites off my face, glancing skywards. "Thanks, Dad, for inventing them!"

I sat up slowly, allowing the dog to gain some confidence in me. I needed to help him. Dog. Yup, my dad's favourite, but dog, aptly named, is an anagram. But you knew that, right?

Scooping him up, he nestled his tiny black and white patched head under my chin. His fragile frame almost fitted into my hand. I leaned over to the canvas bag, checking it for other dogs, and scanned the surrounding bushes. Nothing. So, with my dog under my hand, resting against my chest, my other hand clasped the shield, and whispering to him, I looked for the exit.

The park was tucked away down a cobbled side street. The place was unfamiliar to me; two thousand years ago everything felt and looked much different. I shook my head. I had no concept of time in Hell, except that I'd been there too bloody long. But it felt good to be here, the crisp clean air, the scents and nature filled my limbs with an ease I hadn't known in eons. I realised then in that moment how I'd lost hope, after a thousand years of being stuck in Hell. Of course, I'd tried to escape many times, but with hundreds of demons guarding the exits, it had always ended the same way. Me being caged and tortured. After a time, the demons would let me out of the cage, and guard me heavily for a while. I was forced to punish the wicked. And now, right now I would be lying if I thought it was just luck this time that got me out of Hell. It wasn't, something or someone else was at hand here, had aided my escape. Who that was I knew I'd find out. After all, everything has a cost and the price of freedom from Hell, well it would be high, wouldn't it? Getting out, escaping, was the third strange thing that happened to me since my fall into Hell.

But weirder than escaping was when the self-proclaimed King of Hell had ripped my celestial soul from me.

I remember it as if it was only yesterday. I've rarely felt the fear of death.

A force had bolted through me, sucking the life out of me. Winded, unable to breathe, I'd staggered helplessly, fear clutching my heart. Dizzy and disoriented, slowly my breathing had returned. Then I had fallen into a trance slumped against a wall in one of Hell's caverns.

After some time, I'd realised that I wasn't dreaming but I was actually viewing life, seeing the world above through the eyes of another. My soul was in the body of another being. It took a long time before I could gather the energy, the will to move and break out of that spell. But when I did, rage consumed me. The travesty that a lesser demon had the audacity to steal my soul. The soul of Lucifer Morningstar and had summoned it into the body of a vampire, of all the damnedest things.

And I really, really hate vampires.

And that someone was a pagan deity, Bael. Bael, father of the Princes of Hell, seven of the deadliest demonic beings created. Their legacy is one of turmoil, horror and destruction.

Bael wanted his sons back, and as I am a supposed prince of Hell, though I dispute that, he wanted my soul. Not me per se, obviously I would have refused. Firstly, I am an archangel, secondly, Hell would freeze over if I bowed to a lesser being, a pagan king!

So, Bael's bright idea was to use my soul and shove it in another creature, a vampire that he could control. But I wasn't the first to be used in this manner, so I was told. Bael had instructed some vampire creatures to infect a mortal. Which they did, but the mortal man was ignorant of his demonic ancestry. But that's all I knew. Hell is awash with rumours, especially from above.

But when my soul had been cast into another's body, I had a glimpse of the world above and I learned a great deal. This era, the twenty-first century, was unrecognisable from the time that I fell. Humans had advanced, far from the days of fighting over food and living in the muck. Their languages had evolved. They had built cities, and most had left religion behind. As for the immortals, centuries ago they hid in the shadows waiting for unsuspecting victims and fed from them like the parasites that they are. But now, now the dead lived better than the living and existed in plain sight along with humans.

You learn a lot in Hell—mostly stuff you'd rather not know—and I'd learned a little about chaos magic from a bored wizard-come-demon. Vetis, the red-headed, burly wizard-come-demon got his name, he informed me because before his descent into Hell he took a particular delight in corrupting the holy. It was because of his earth-bound life of sin and mischief the authorities of Hell had unusually allowed him to become part-demon. The normal punishment in Hell for a wizard being horrific. At a spritely one-hundred and thirteen years old, Vetis was a rare demon. He had the gift of making all who encountered him laugh- no mean feat in Hell! When he realised it was futile trying to corrupt me, he taught me a little chaos magic. Then I set about casting a spell that led to the death of the imposter who'd rapaciously inhabited my soul.

Let me tell you, having your soul in another body, seeing the world from someone else's eyes is useful, but also terrible. Everything that vampire had seen in the world, everything he had touched, experienced, I had, too. Yes, everything. I'll just let that sink in!

It disgusted me they had thrust my divinity into a vampire's body. Bael was long dead, killed by his own progeny. Perhaps it was a good omen for me.

I felt the puppy shiver against my chest, pulling me back into the moment. I needed earthly things. Contacts, shelter, and a phone. This was the part of mortal life that irritated me.

As I stepped through the wrought-iron gates of the park, I stopped and shuddered. Earth. For its beauty, I had to endure its inhabitants, my father's proudest creations. I had to tone down, blend in! Me! I concentrated, using the little divine magic I had to hide my huge crimson wings from human eyes. A tingling sensation rippled through me, taking in air deeply, I cast a quick glance over my shoulder. Done! But looking down at my body, the dirt on my blackened skin, I looked like I'd been to Hell and back!

A chill shivered through me, Pulling my leather jacket around my chest, I strode forward, chin up as my matted long raven-black hair fell around my shoulders and the pup nestled his tiny head under my cheek.

I quickly realised I was in England, of all places. *England!* That meant one thing. Grey skies and rain, incessant bloody rain! Why couldn't Michael and Gabe be captured somewhere warm, like Greece or Italy? Cold, I stepped up my pace, my hand around the pup who was nestled inside my jacket. Incessant cawing and screeching overhead of seagulls, looking up I watched as they dived and soared from the rooftops. Dozens of them. A flurry of pigeons huddled lower down on window ledges, no doubt taking shelter from the huge winged predators. Birds, I hadn't seen them for so long. There was so much I had forgotten.

Stopping abruptly, I sensed something. Taking a slow breath, I quietened my mind.

The Nephilim live here. Good, my fallen kin.

The Georgian city of Bath is nestled within a valley, the streets lined with neat and antiquated buildings. Honey coloured columns adorned doorways and neoclassical arched windows. Although a small city, the affluence of the buildings is prolific. They towered high, almost looking down on the smoggy traffic. Heaving with humans, Bath is the home of many supernaturals, as most prefer ancient cities, sticking to the oldest areas which felt most familiar. And Bath dates back pre-Roman.

Letting my senses guide me, I could detect others.

Being the most powerful archangel, they all bent a knee to me. In theory, anyway.

Other kin were here. I knew that feeling that they emitted like a frequency. My eyes narrowed as I surveyed the area.

Grigori, the Watcher angels. Not fallen, still pure, sent by my father to oversee the mortals and kill those not born unto God. That's vampires, demons and anything else Dad despises.

A wry grin on my face, I stepped up my pace, glad that the Grigori knew of my arrival. I could imagine their little flurry of wings. They're a pompous lot, full of their own self-importance, thinking they're top of the hierarchy here on Earth.

What the bleeding hell Mike and Gabe were doing here, only Dad knew. I headed out of the city along the dirty, congested road. A prickling sensation stung my skin. I sensed the Nephilim were somewhere on the edge of this little city. They leave a signature in the air, just as magic does. It's subtle, but I know the signs. I scanned the sky before me and, sure enough, I saw faint thin trails of their white-gold light.

The scent of the surrounding humans was spicy and sweet, intoxicating. Although I'd sensed everything when the meat-suit had embodied my soul, I hadn't experienced this personally. In Hell the only stenches were of fear, death and other smells that I'd rather forget. Earthly colours moved me. That pale blue sky, the soft golden light as the sun peeked behind the swollen grey clouds, and the shades and hues of mortal's clothing.

I raised my brows at them as I caught them staring, the underlying fear in their expressions being in the presence of something they didn't understand. They sensed my power. No change there. Good.

Here on Earth, humans automatically cleared a way for me as I walked. In the past I had pitied them, their existence weak and fleeting and filled with fear. Back then disease and poverty were rife, but now... now the world they had built was almost mesmerizing. Pausing for a few seconds, I gazed at the surrounding shops. Everything and everyone looked and smelt so clean. Various scents, musky, sweet, floral mixed around me. Two thousand years ago the smell in a city was revolting, especially to us sharp-sensed angels.

How humans had evolved!

I wondered for a brief moment, had I been wrong? When I had been created, my father had instilled in me—in us—that we were perfection, so the prospect of being wrong felt disjointed and uncomfortable. I had wondered why he had created flawed beings, but seeing humans now, seeing how they'd advanced, their development made me wonder if I had been wrong to stand against my father. Had he known all along that humans, even with their flaws, would bloom and become so much more...

My fall from grace two thousand years ago that had enraged my father so was in part because I couldn't believe that he had abandoned us for humans. I mean, really? Had I been wrong to question him? But that sense of abandonment, of loss, had crippled me, and cast alone in Hell, isolated and rejected. I wasn't about to forgive that.

But I realised I had been angry for two millennia. And now? Looking down at the fragile creature sleeping on my chest and its complete trust in me, the supposed Devil, I swallowed hard. Most saw me as evil, as against God, and indeed I had disagreed with my dad. But I was his son, his creation. Isn't it natural for a father and son to disagree?

As I strode, I gazed at the bright window displays of shops, at the humans who passed me, their tangy aromas, their eagerness, their desire to live. And I wondered if maybe my father had known that all along. Known that they would evolve...

Yes, this time was preferable, but my brothers' lives were foremost. I doubled my stride. Clutching my dog tighter, I launched myself into the air and unfurled my wings. Flying above the cloud-line, I sensed the house where my lesser kin lived. Only a few mortals saw me. Clenching my teeth, my heart thumped fast as my mind searched my memory of a spell that I hadn't used in over a thousand years. I whispered the incantation so they would question what they saw. I hadn't used much magic for a long time and for some reason I always braced when I used it. A part of that I think was my questioning whether or not I still had the ability to wield it. Chaos magic is different, but invisibility spells are harder. Easier to mesmerize someone into believing they imagined you, rather than trying to go full out concealed.

The hound raised his tiny head, barking, and a slight tremor rippled through him. I held him tighter, to reassure him. "Hey, don't worry, little dog. This is how I travel, I won't drop you. Hold tight!"

Descending slowly, so as not to give the tiny dog a heart attack, a few mortals stared open-mouthed. I shot them my best attempt at a smile and winked, but judging by their reaction that didn't go down so well. I mumbled the spell again, making them disbelieve their eyes.

When I'd been on Earth before, mortals usually bowed reverently to angels. This time they just stared, but at least they smelt better.

The house I sensed where the Nephilim lived in was nondescript. In the past, nothing less than a gilded palace would do for their kind. The Nephilim had been larger than life, grandiose. Their egos were the stuff of legends, as were their parties. The Nephilim Nation, they called it: a proud and arrogant race who had the power and the righteousness to pull all that off. Dad had punished them because they had taught mankind the secrets of the universe—metallurgy, science, medicine and magic. He'd flooded the earth to punish the Nephilim and humankind for accepting these half-angel, half-human hybrids. Obviously, that didn't work. I was glad, not in a spiteful way, but I liked the Nephilim, liked their cocky attitude. You never knew what they'd do next.

But now it seemed here in this time, this era, that they lived in a bland small house in suburbia. This was a far cry from their glorified origins. What the hell stood on the other side of that door, I could only wonder. I placed my shield on the floor, clutching the pup who shifted slightly under my hand. I hammered on the door until it opened.

I didn't have to wait long. A slack-jawed Nephilim warrior opened the door. His hair was crimson, which made me grin. And he was dressed in leather trousers and a grey T-shirt with an unusual picture on it: a winged man wearing a trench coat, I believe they call it. How odd, what did it mean?

He stared at me incredulously with wide eyes and furrowed brows, shifting with a nervous energy.

Slowly, deliberately, I extended my hand, waiting for him to do the same, but his gaze fell to it. He didn't move, so I cleared my throat, hand still outstretched as I eyed his hair.

"Be not afraid. There is no need to fear me." Then, shooting him my finest smile, my gaze rested on his hair. "Red. I like it. Did you colour it yourself?"

Doubt flickered through his face. He rolled his lips before making eye contact until his gaze fell back to my outstretched hand.

"I see. Afraid of taking the hand of the Devil. I understand. And I welcome such infamy. But I'm surprised to see a Nephilim who has hair the colour of blood, very maverick. Most of your kin are very conformist and you must infuriate my father." I took a breath. "You dare to be deviant. I respect that, shows strength in your character." I winked and nestled the dog onto my shoulder, "Still, I can't stand around making idle chat. I have come here because I need help. My brothers are in great danger. I just battled my way out of Hell to get here, and I need to find them urgently. And..." I tilted my head down, "This animal needs some food. I found him on my way here, abandoned."

The angel nodded madly, spluttering, "Lucifer? Really, I thought—"

Throwing my head back, I smiled, retracting my hand. "Ah, you thought I was that pathetic vampire, that meat-suit, Jack. I know you met him, I saw you through his eyes." I lowered my voice. "Unfortunately, I saw everything through his eyes. May I come in or shall we stand here on the doorstep all day?"

Nodding, he stood aside, and I strode into his small home. I had expected a castle, a mansion perhaps, or one of the fine Georgian town houses. It shocked me that one of such legendary heritage lived in such a tiny house.

The puppy looked about and I watched as the Nephilim closed the door, then I set the little dog down, his tail wagging weakly as he went off to investigate. Waiting for him to show me in, he strode through to a small room, still wide-eyed as he glanced from me to the puppy who was sniffing at his boots next to some chairs.

I broke the silence. "You can thank Bael for that nonsense of Jack. Bael used Jack's body to host my soul. So, you're Aaron then, the wild one?"

Aaron stood up taller, but he couldn't hide that he was still dumbstruck.

"Someone has taken Gabriel and Michael. You will help me find them."

Aaron tossed his head back, not used to being subordinate, "You are asking for my help. Let's do this as equals, partners."

I laughed and held his stare, "We are not equals. You are a half-human hybrid. I am an archangel. Lucifer, Satan, whatever." I wanted to test him. Pressing my lips together, I held his gaze. Would he bow to the Devil, or rise to the challenge?

Aaron stared back defiantly. I wet my lips while I sized up the rogue warrior before me with his brazen hair and attitude to match. I already liked him. He had the Nephilim spirit I admired.

"Technically, you are higher, I guess, but no one gives a shit about that anymore. No one here on Earth. We've moved on, Lucifer. You're two thousand years out of date. But I'll help you, though I doubt a lowly half-breed like myself is any match for someone or something that has taken your brothers. You sure you can lower yourself to work with the likes of me? I am, after all, hated by your father, not that you're on good terms with him. I'm no pure blood angel."

"I will try to tolerate you, Aaron, I really will." I laughed, raising my eyebrows, "That was a joke. You're very serious, aren't you? We do have them in Hell, jokes. But hey, I like you, Nephilim. You have the heart of a warrior and the spirit of a rebel. No harm done, I just wanted to see what you were made of."

Aaron was refreshing. Nephilim are often, like Grigori, pompous, loud, and full of air. I glanced around Aaron's human home and nodded. It was snug—if I was being polite—and homely. No Nephilim Nation found here. I was almost relieved.

"So, I'm surprised... I had thought you would live in a more grandiose place?"

He indicated we sit down. Macabre black and red paintings of angels fighting hung from cream walls, which reminded me too much of Hell. Small fabric seats were placed around a glass centre table where we sat. Curiosity got me and I grabbed at the cushion, its soft texture strange against my thumb and finger, and frowned. "You live like them. Do you like them? The mortals?" Before Aaron could answer, I waved my hand and continued, "No matter, I don't have time to socialise. Each second my brothers' lives hang on by a thread."

Aaron smiled. He leaned forward and touched me on the arm which made me jolt. I'm not accustomed to being touched. He looked at the dog who was sniffing the Nephilim's floor. "I don't have any dog food, but I have meat and water. What's his name?"

"What? Oh, I don't know. I just found him." The puppy barked, and he wagged his tail meekly. His ribs showed through his rough fur, white with patches of black, two of which were around his eyes, making him look like he was wearing a mask. He wobbled. I leapt up, then crouched before him, supporting his weakened frame.

Aaron's voice, though quieter, still bounced lightly around the room, "Hello little pupster. Look at you. Do you want some chicken? Come on then, come on..."

I watched as the dog followed the wayward warrior out to the adjoining kitchen, his tail flapping frantically—the dog's that is, Nephilim don't have tails. I sat back down, my body melting into the incredibly soft furniture. I had a mind that if I hadn't needed to rescue my brothers, I could sink into that chair for the rest of eternity. In fact, had I had a chair like this in Hell, I may never have bothered to leave. I leaned back, lowering my lids.

Aaron came padding back in with a plate of chicken and a bowl of water, a slight frown on his face. I opened my eyes and sat up watching as the dog ate.

He indicated to the puppy, "What will you name him?"

"Aye? No, I can't have a dog, no. You must care for him. You're already better at it than I, you have a home, food. Me, I have a sword, a shield and a score to settle. I can't be taking a puppy around with me. What if he got hurt?"

He raised his brows. "You're not what I expected. Lucifer, the Devil, Satan. I expected you to be full of anger, wrath, arrogance and pride. I wasn't sure if you were evil, but then again, you're not good, either, are you?" His eyes darted back to the puppy.

I lifted an eyebrow, "What makes you say that, you're not sure if I'm evil?"

Shrugging, Aaron's lips twisted, "You're a fallen angel. Certainly, you have your faults." He shot me a lopsided grin, "Pride obviously! But evil? Still, at least you don't have horns and a tail." He leaned towards me, his voice rising, "Or cloven feet!"

You'd better hope not Aaron.

Shaking his head he patted the pup, who growled guarding his food. But it was such a feeble attempt and Aaron soothed it by muttering softly before looking back at me. "I mean, Satan's puppy?"

I sucked in my cheeks, thinking before answering him. "I am angry, wrathful, perhaps a little arrogant, but that you can blame on my lineage along with pride. But he," I pointed to the dog, "I can hardly vent rage with that tiny creature beside me, now can I?" Taking a deep breath, I wondered how it was that as soon as I left Hell, I found this creature. For angels, at least, there are no coincidences.

It felt in that moment as if someone else was talking through me, I rarely thought much further than my own needs. I didn't need to.

Aaron ignored my answer, "Where did you find him?"

"I broke out of Hell, landed in a park in your city. Imagine! Though I know Hell has many gateways, they're usually guarded by Cerberus or various Hell hounds. Anyhow, my lucky day, no Hell hounds, just this little chap."

He eyed me squarely. "Cerberus seems a fitting name, maybe he'll grow into a Hell hound?"

I laughed. "No, he's earthbound. But Hell hound pups are charming for sure. Look, Aaron, my brothers are in great danger..."

"Yes, well, that figures. We've been having some strange concerns with the weather, not to mention demons. Acacius is right now investigating something he thought was bringing about Armageddon."

I grinned, "And you're not with him? Were you dyeing your hair?"

He spluttered a laugh. "I left Acacius about an hour ago if that's okay, your unholy lordship? Look Lucifer, the real Lucifer, I am glad to help but I have to eat, too. Being a half-breed and all, I've done twenty hours straight of chasing down a rogue Baba Yaga, and I'm famished. Which in itself is a feat as they eat human flesh, you know, and you'd think that would put me off eating. The Baba Yaga eat the flesh of humans, whilst the human is alive. And that is enough to make anyone feel sick."

I screwed up my face, "Did you catch it?"

"Her, yes, and I took her head." He suddenly yawned, then stretched out his arms. "So, Lucifer, a dog. Do you think your dad sent him, I mean he had to, surely? You're not all the evil monster history has made you out to be, are you? Lord of Darkness, Lord of Flies? Terror of—"

I cut him off, nodding, "Forget it, I've heard it all, trust me. Evil depends on your perspective, Aaron. You're surprised ol' Nick helped a dog. I am an angel first, remember, and an archangel at that. I'm still angry at being punished for simply stating what I believed, but me keeping the dog? It's not possible, Aaron. I cannot be responsible for a puppy."

He leaned forward, "Kind of the point though, huh? Dog, your dad's favourite. And you said yourself how you've had to keep your anger in check since finding Cerberus." He leaned back, eyeing me, then Cerberus. "In this short time since you came here to my home, I've seen a side of you I'll wager none have ever seen. That is no coincidence. The Devil and his dog... Look, Cerby is happy, you'd best let him outside to do his ablutions, then we'll eat. You do need to shower, though, because you smell worse than the flesh-eating shape shifter I just killed. Then we three will plan how to rescue your kin, if that's even possible. Oh, welcome home by the way, nice to meet the real you."

"Heaven is my home, though I've spent longer in Hell." I pointed to the dog, "It's Cerberus, not Cerby."

He raised his brows, lips curved slightly into a grin. "You're not as tall as I'd thought you'd be."

"Really? You are as insolent as I knew you'd be."

Cerberus stood by the glass back door, his tail wagging. I hauled myself away from that chair of paradise and, after a look from Aaron who gave a nod, opened the door and surveyed the small and neat garden.

Watching him bound onto the grass barking, tail frantic, lifted my stoic heart. Such a tiny creature, so weak, vulnerable. Maybe Dad had placed him before me. Dad loves his lessons, but then I'd heard nothing from my family... maybe it was wishful thinking. Cerberus chased his tail, whizzing around and around in circles, and I heard laughter rumble through my ribs. Something dark and bitter inside me dissolved. It was the hopelessness that I had carried for two thousand years. And I knew then in that instant that I would actually do anything for this creature...

"Um, Cerberus has..." I pointed to the lawn where Cerberus had left a poo.

Aaron chuckled. "I have a hand spade, I'll bury it. You'll need to get some doggy bags, you know, for picking up his business."

I picked up my dog, careful that his bottom didn't rub onto me, and eyed Aaron as he pointed the way to the stairs. It didn't faze me, cleaning a puppy. I'd smelt worse in Hell, seen worse in Hell, and though I'd admit it to no one, done worse down there.

Cerberus trembled as I cleaned him, so I whispered to him about how I was going to avenge my brothers with his help, then I called to Aaron who leapt up the stairs silently.

Cerberus shivered a little. I realised then that I could sense his emotions.

"He's scared, the two of us here in this little bathroom, but I'm thinking, can I wash him? He's filthy, though not as bad as me, but..." I looked at the immaculate bathroom, the white bath.

A warm smile, "Of course, budge over." His huge frame bent over the bath, dropped the plug in and ran a mix of water, hot and cold.

"Just let me grab a towel, no offence pup, but you're not having our best towels." Aaron stopped and eyed me. "We're not squeamish. Killing evil-doers, we get pretty filthy. We have towels for that."

He left us alone and I washed the frail creature who quaked in my hands. It was strange. I'd spent thousands of years in a hole of torture, death, depravity, and had been so filled with revenge and anger that it had almost consumed my soul. Yet here I was only hours after escaping Hell, kneeling down over the bath and cleaning a puppy who trusted me. It was... humbling. For a moment a flashback to my youth when we were first created, and I played with my brothers, my father and mother watching over us, smiling.

"Why, Cerberus, why was I punished so violently? I still don't understand. Still, I'll rescue my brothers and they'll have to redeem me, have to. There!"

I held him up to my chest as he squirmed, wet and slightly more relaxed, and I grabbed a towel and gently dried him off. Pulling the plug, I watched as the dirt and fleas swirled away down the plughole. I carried Cerberus downstairs and placed him on the floor. A new zest whipped through him. After eating, drinking and a wash the puppy bounded around, his yelps matching his vitality as he explored Aaron's home.

"Drink?" Aaron offered.

"Yes."

Aaron poured two large drinks. Handing me one, he sat back down opposite me, his ankle resting on his knee. "Tell me what you know."

"I had a vision of my brothers and I saw, no, I felt a... wrenching in my gut. I saw my brothers' faces contorted in pain. Their cries rang out, piercing. I felt their pain, their torture."

I looked earnestly at Aaron, then took a large swig of the drink. Spluttering as the liquid burnt my throat, my eyes red with flames, I yelled, "What the hell is this?"

Grinning like a gargoyle, Aaron chuckled. "Whiskey. Drink it, it's good for you. The Devil's drink, it'll boost you."

It wasn't unpleasant once you got used to it. It's what I'd imagine what drinking lava felt like. And I hadn't done that, because who would? Still, I would not be undermined by this cocky upstart. I downed the drink.

Aaron looked mildly concerned. "I didn't think you needed to eat or drink."

I rubbed my chin. "On Earth I need to take nourishment from time to time." Despite the whiskey he had given me, I was still parched. I had, after all, been fighting demons. "Do you have any water?"

He said nothing but sat there still smirking like a fool, so I got up, staggered and fell back into the chair.

"What the hell!" I yelled. Of course, I knew about alcohol, but before I fell, I'd never tried it, never dabbled in many mortal sins. My belly groaned, a heat whipped through me like flames, my muscles softened.

Aaron smiled. "Surely you've drunk alcohol before?"

"I've been in Hell, in case you forgot. It's not exactly on tap down there," I spluttered, coughing as my throat turned into Hellfire. "There is no time in Hell, only illusion." Trying to remember what I'd been saying as the liquid swam around my head and my body, I eventually mumbled, "I felt this pain, I saw my brothers in my mind's eye, I left. I knew then that they were in trouble, I hadn't seen, nor heard anything from them since I fell. It took time to fight my way out. But whoever has them is powerful, old, I cannot sense them here on Earth, but I could find you easily, they are being hidden." My words spewed out all over the place like my mind, cluttered and confused.

Obviously, I knew what the effects of alcohol were, I'd just never had it before and now I had downed nearly a full glass of strong liquor. I wish I'd started with something less potent.

My head swayed lightly. I needed water, but there was no way I was about to show a Nephilim he could out-drink me, Ol' Nick. So, I stood up slowly and purposefully placed my hand on the back of the chair and surveyed his mortal home.

I knew what everything was because of Jack, my soul's last host. But touching things, smelling them, was entirely different. Especially now, with a belly full of whiskey. Carefully placing one foot in front of the next, I made my way to the kitchen. I filled the empty glass with water. It sparkled in my hand, pure and clean. Standing in Aaron's comfortable home, I was struck by just how much time I'd wasted stuck in that shit hole.

Filthy, cruel and dark, that was Hell. Not like this. I heard birds chirping outside; the sun gleamed through the glass and bounced and danced through colourful stained-glass ornaments hanging in the window, casting a rainbow of colours through the tiny room.

This Nephilim may be bold, brash and a fearsome warrior, but I could see from these details in his home that he knew the beauty of life. Outside he'd placed a table in a tree, the birds fed there, and for some odd reason that made me feel better. Maybe I'd just seen too much of the opposite, I had actually forgotten anything of beauty. Of love... I was cold, hard and untouchable. But in that, I felt safe.

As I said, I wasn't used to drinking.

I shook my head. So much had changed, and I'd been stuck in Hell for two thousand shitty years just because I disagreed with my dad. And the irony of it was that I was his favourite son, first born, perfect. Wasn't I, after all, born in his image? So how could I be wrong...?

My chest rose and fell deeply as I tried to calm the fury in my mind, I didn't want to wreck Aaron's home. He is kind and I, well, my wrath is legendary.

Cool liquid refreshed my mouth, my body. I had another glass of water as Aaron stepped in quietly. I felt his anxiety; he'd been watching me from the other room. I sensed his tension.

"You need a shower. If that's what Hell smells like, bloody heck, that is definitely punishment enough. And look at the stain on my chair. Seriously, you can't just wander around like that and not get noticed. And, by the way, don't fly in front of mortals. I'll explain later, but humans have advanced a lot since you were here and they... well, never mind. Come here, let me show you."

Oh, too late.

I clenched my fists; I knew what a shower was, but I wanted to get Gabe and Michael, not ponce around. But he was right. He smelt woodsy and earthy. Clean. And... something else, a scent I remembered from long ago. Ah, frankincense. I'd noticed the mortals hadn't stunk on my way here as I did. Hell isn't known for its cleanliness. I smelt of sewers and blood. Of death. I followed him up the stairs and stood like a child as he showed me how to operate the shower.

Jack had done this, showered, and I'd sensed his pleasure from it. So, stripping off, Aaron took what was left of my clothes—mostly blackened rags—except my tattered leather jacket, which I grabbed, narrowing my eyes as he went to take it, then I stepped under the flowing water.

It was like a baptism. The filth swirled away, layer after layer of dirt that had ingrained onto my once celestial skin, I scrubbed with soap until my skin was sore. He'd shown me the shampoo. As I opened the bottle, it smelt sweet, another reminder of my past.

The scent was like fruit. I hadn't smelt fruit for so long I'd forgotten all about it, sweet and uplifting. I poured a handful into my rough palms and rubbed it into my matted and filthy hair. I used the conditioner, too, which if I'm honest seemed ridiculous, but necessary to untangle the thousands of knots. As I combed it through, I stepped carefully around the shower as bits of coal-black demon flesh washed out of my hair. I put my hands on the shower wall to steady myself; the water I had drank had diluted the whiskey somewhat, but my mind was still foggy. A grumbling noise made me look down. I needed to eat.

I got out and used the towel he'd left. My skin gleamed like it had when I'd been in Heaven. My body felt lighter, my hair soft.

Aaron had left some clothes for me. Black jeans, a red T-shirt and other items. I liked the red T-shirt; it matched my eyes. There was also a toothbrush. I'd seen these through Jack. I never realised how mint could feel so good in your mouth. I'd thought them ridiculous before, but now...

After washing the filth of Hell from my body, my limbs thrummed with energy, pulsating passion of revenge and just... life. Whoever had my brothers would regret it. I felt reborn, and ready to fight for my kin.

I sprung down his tiny staircase where Aaron gave me boots that pinched my feet. Scrunching my eyes and focusing on the toe of the boots, I made them morph to fit me. Magic comes at a cost, but it was worth it. You can't fight well with sore feet. Cerberus looked better, too. He yapped and bounced around me, again stirring something that I'd lost, something deep. Happiness. Crouching down, I rubbed his tiny head, then placed my hands on either side of his thin body. Closing my eyes, I had little celestial grace in me, but what I had I channelled into him.

Warm golden light oozed from my palms into the little creature, his eyes fixed on mine, and it travelled slowly through him. Before my eyes, his coat gained a lustre, a shine, and I could feel his heart warm, healing. Then I rubbed his head, "So, what, you want to be the Devil's dog, do you? Well, that should help protect you Cerberus, though it's life on the wing you should know."

Cerberus barked, then chased his tail around and around. I glanced up to Aaron who was sizing me up, smiling. Next, he handed me something hot to eat. I tilted my head, intrigued.

"It's called a pasty," he said. "It's great. Basically, it's a pastry filled with meat and vegetables. I'm guessing you're not vegetarian?"

Ah, I knew about this. Jack had talked about vegetarians. He had lived in L.A.; the mortals had a range of diets. It intrigued me. In my time on Earth before the fall, many mortals ate only fish as their source of meat, thinking dad would approve of that. I think they thought it holy to eat fish. I re-call something written in Leviticus. Still, I doubted dad had thought much about it. Who knew? Jack had experienced a lot of emotional reactions to diets, as had the mortals Jack had spoken to.

I looked Aaron in the eye, arching my brows. "I'm veg-an."

He flustered, turning red, "Oh, really, I see. I'm sorry I haven't…"

I laughed and slapped his shoulder. I took the pasty and took a huge bite, talking through the food in my mouth, "I know, the Devil, right? You assume I'll eat your children?" I laughed. After swallowing it I said, "I rarely eat flesh, after Hell I'm not keen. But I appreciate this."

Cerberus lapped at my feet, "You've just eaten. Aww, here you are." I broke away some meat from the pasty and fed it to him. I ended up giving my dog all the meat, whilst I chomped on the vegetables and pastry. Guess I'll have to be vegetarian then. Vegetarian Devil… hum.

My stomach growled, I hadn't needed to eat in Hell but bloody Heaven, this was good. He then handed me a cup with hot liquid, I knew this, too, though I'd never tried it myself.

"Coffee, you'll bloody love it. I added sugar and cream, you know, as you're the Devil," he winked.

It seemed it wasn't only humans who blamed me for sin-ful or tempting pleasures, and I wondered constantly why they did that, maybe because I had stood up to Dad, their God…

Though, I guess it was because they believed what had been written about me. That it had been me, in the guise of the serpent in the garden of Eden, tempting Eve to eat the forbidden apple from the tree of knowledge.

That wasn't me, actually. I was with Lilith. Whereas Eve had been made from Adam's rib and was subservient to Adam, Lilith was made by my dad from dust. Lilith was in fact Adam's first wife and left him, refusing to lay beneath him. And let me tell you, Lilith was definitely not submissive. Rolling my lips as I thought about Lilith, Adam's first wife, I chuckled at that thought. To say she had ignited passions was an understatement. Before her, I hadn't even known such desire had existed. I'd left her after a time, but then when I had wanted to go back to her, well Hell is not tolerant of pleasures so they kept me away, though I tried for eons to find her...

Ah, sins of the flesh.

With a sigh, I ate the pasty, sharing it with my four-legged friend, and watched as Aaron pulled out an enormous case from underneath the floorboards. Dust puffed up as he did so. Cerberus's shrill barks echoed around the room as we watched Aaron place the long wooden studded box on the centre table. As I sat there eating and slurping the coffee, he opened the box with great reverence.

Gleaming there before me, its large handle wrapped in crimson leather and a slightly curved blade, the holy sword, Heaven's Sword.

I dropped the pasty on the table. Could it be *the* sword?

Aaron picked it up with veneration, then kneeled before me. I swallowed hard, holding back a laugh as he did so, rather than splatter him with half-chewed pasty.

Yapping at my feet, Cerberus danced about. He could feel the energy of the sword, as could I.

I took it and was startled as I heard a gasp behind me. Turning my head, another Nephilim stood by the back door, and as my fingers clasped that soft red leather hilt, my wings pushed open, knocking over cups and ornaments. Cerberus, in his puppy voice, howled.

The sword's blade fired into a brilliant blue flame, its light illuminated the walls and ceiling.

Energy buzzed through my body, pumping. My arms and hands shook from raw power. The other cried, "Aaron, what have you done? You've given the power of Heaven to Lucifer!"

Yes, yes, he had, hadn't he? I'd never had this before.

My lips widened as the blue flame lit my face. I braced remembering the last time I had seen this sword. Michael's sword. He had brandished it against me, we had fought as he, with the power of our father, cast me into the flames of Hell. I shuddered.

It was ironic that the weapon used to punish me for eternity in Hell was now in my hands to help the one who sent me there...

Aaron stood up, wide-eyed, his face animated and glanced again at the Nephilim, then to me.

So, the Devil takes the holy sword, Michael's sword. Surely now anything, everything is possible. I furled up my wings. "I'll clear up the mess. It happens, you probably know that."

Aaron bellowed, laughing, "Indeed it does happen. Our wings can burst open at the most awkward times." He turned to face the blonde-haired Nephilim, then back to me, "Lucifer, this is Acacius. Acacius..."

I nodded at him, narrowing my eyes.

The flames of the sword licked my hands but didn't burn or scorch my skin. "Aaron, how did you come by my brother's sword?"

"I found it. We'd come back from killing demons, and I saw a blue light coming from the park. Drawing my sword with Acacius, we investigated. When you arrived, I assumed you knew this. That is why you're here, isn't it, to rescue Michael? We've been guarding the sword, knowing it would be dangerous in the wrong hands."

I drew a deep breath, my eyes narrowed, but I could tell he told the truth.

Nodding, I said, "Come then, no time to waste."

The Nephilim who stood in the doorway, his jaw clenched, eyed me with suspicion. He had a cherub face and long white hair that fell to his waist, and a heavy silver cross hung over his white T-shirt. He looked pious, but I smelt something from him. Sin. It conflicted him. "Will you join me, Acacius, to free Michael and Gabriel from their captors? Or will you stand there in judgement of me and let them die?"

His eyes narrowed, his gaze looked me up and down. "The archangels Michael and Gabriel are captured? Who could do this, who has that power to capture two archangels?"

"You'd be surprised. There's enough bloody voodoo, grimoires and magical icons on this planet that I suspect only Dad knows, and why doesn't he help? Useless! It's probably a test. It usually is. Well, I don't care for tests, but whoever has my brothers, I want their head. I'm thinking of putting it on a spike."

"Where do we start? And what are your plans when you find who or what is responsible? Take their head, use their power, unleash terror on them?" Aaron's eyes were wide, his chest puffed up. "I think if we could harness their power, well, we might clear the slate clean of a lot of evil on this planet."

I spent a moment thinking. "I always find church a good place to start, don't you?"

Acacius gasped. Rolling my eyes, his reaction is the very reason my temper is known. Irritated, I lowered my sword and turned to face him, "Look Nephilim, you may think yourself above me, all pure and virtuous, but remember you are not. I can taste your guilt, your sin. It radiates off of you like a cheap cologne. Conflicted in your carnal passions, when you believe you should remain chaste? You are part human, you should not judge yourself so harshly. You smell of sex, and from the colour of your face, that's the least of it. Now, churches are homes to my father, so, you can lose your judgement."

He clenched his jaw; his gaze fell to the ground as his face burned beetroot red.

Ah, I know that look, that guilt... Kinky, huh? I kept that thought to myself, a slight smirk. However tempting it was to prise it out of him, it would wait for another time.

"Good, then we are all agreed. Let's go." I put the flaming sword in my belt, leaving the one I'd found in Hell on the floor. I didn't bother with the shield, I already had a sword now. And a dog. Not enough hands...

Stooping, I picked up the fallen cup and ornaments and placed them back on the coffee table.

"I cannot join you," Acacius's voice strained as he leaned against the door frame. "I only came back to grab a grimoire, I have an urgent fight."

"What could be more urgent than rescuing my brothers?" I demanded.

Pushing himself away from the doorframe, he pulled himself up, standing tall. Clenching his fists he fixed his gaze on me. His ego, being Nephilim, was large. I guess that's why we get along.

"A pack of vicious werewolves have been killing humans in West Wales, I am needed urgently. Lucifer, I beg you would help. With you, we could be done by nightfall, then all three of us could search for Michael and Gabriel. Maybe Joseph would come, too?"

"Absolutely not," I replied. "I've wasted enough time already washing my hair with..." I glanced at Aaron, then decided no one should know about hair conditioner even with its amazing smell. "Never mind. You go, save your mortals. I didn't fight a legion of demons on my way out of Hell to kill mangy werewolves. Come, Aaron. Come, Cerberus!"

Aaron stood frozen, his eyes imploring Acacius.

"Bloody hell, you, too? Really?" I looked down at my dog and huffed, "Hum, I feel like a dad now. I have to save my brothers and protect this little creature at the same time. Come on Cerberus, come here." He ran around everywhere but near me. I zipped my jacket half way, then chasing Cerberus, calling him I eventually scooped him up, placed my hand between my dog and the zipper and I pulled it up over him, just his head poking out. He barked in my face, so I tucked my chin over him.

"You have a dog?" Acacius blurted. "Is that from Hell?"

I shot him a grin. "No. I found him when I got out of Hell, here in your dirty little city. Someone had dumped him. Aaron said he's a sign from God, you know the anagram and all? Thanks, Aaron, for feeding him, and the water. And me. I won't forget it. Now, Cerberus and I are going to church."

Cerberus barked again. "That's right little dog, church. Now you be good, okay. Just because, and especially because you are Satan's dog. They'll expect great things from you."

I strode out of the house without Aaron, ignoring his earlier advice to stay under the radar. As the cool clean air brushed my face, my wings burst open, Cerberus barked again, and I took off up into the air. My hands tingled as heat spread across my chest. Wide eyed, I felt a wonder being on the wing again. Whatever happened, I promised myself I would never stay in Hell again.

Holy Weapon

Aaron appeared below me then joined me on the wing high above the cloud line.

Shouting across, he asked, "What church do you seek?"

"The nearest one?"

He nodded and within minutes he pointed. "Down there, we should land out of sight."

A priest ran out of the place as we landed behind the church, young and pale, black robes hoisted around his legs, eyes like saucers. He acknowledged Aaron. My presence seemed to worry him. Good.

"Aaron, who is this? I've never—"

Aaron went to speak, I thought, no. "I am the archangel, Lucifer. I have escaped Hell to rescue my brothers Michael and Gabriel. I need holy water... Please." I spoke as I walked, striding towards the back door as Cerberus yapped and barked.

The priest trembled. "Lucifer?"

"Holy water?" I prompted.

"Lucifer... with a dog?"

"The very same, Reverend."

"Are you allowed in... a House of God?"

Aaron put his hand on the mortal's shoulder. "Father, he is the first-born son of God, he is an archangel. Now, do you not think if his Father hadn't wanted him to escape from Hell and rescue his brothers he would be here?"

The priest's face was confused. Aaron gave me a brief nod. "Wings."

I closed them, waiting impatiently by the door. The priest suddenly seemed to grasp the importance of the situation and hurried to catch up with me. "Who could possibly have your brothers?"

Something strange happened then. In that instant, as I saw my father's servant literally shake before me, I felt, what, sorry for him? He was actually terrified of me. Scornful and cold comments from immortals are one thing, but from humans, I pitied him.

"Reverend, I do not know who has them, only that with every conversation, every moment of judgement from every single creature I encounter, that I am losing time. I am hoping the holy water will help me locate them. Aaron, we need the Armadel grimoire, I sense it's hidden nearby in a holy place."

Aaron's voice was hoarse, "I'll have to call Acacius, only he knows where it is."

"Find out its location, it could be useful. Reverend, do you have a silver pin? This should point me in their direction. With the Christian grimoire, I should be able to locate more precisely where they are. I am sure they're in England. Unfortunately."

"W... why unfortunate?" The priest stumbled over his words, his face now whiter than snow.

I gestured upwards, my sword still flaming. "Rain. I'm not a fan, you see." I shivered. "And it's bloody cold. Silver pin?"

"Y... yes, right away. Holy water's..."

"That's all right, my man, I got that bit." I strode through the ornate chapel. I could see it was timeworn, but it felt older. Its age seemed to wrap around me like a dirty shroud, I sensed something bad about this place. They often built churches over pagan sites, so there's that.

Like all the buildings in Bath, it was built with that honey-coloured stone, each brick outlined by centuries of dirt and decay. The altar was small, stone and obviously original, I guessed medieval. Sitting majestically above it, a round intricately carved stained-glass window, its light illuminating the altar. Complex stone lattices arched on the ceiling above me, and from the small arched windows, mottled light flooded in revealing ancient coloured floor tiles.

I nodded to a few people who sat perched on the pews. They looked startled, their eyes wet with fear.

I stood by the font waiting for the priest, while Aaron stepped outside and called Acacius.

I wondered if Acacius would have to land, or whether he'd take the call on the wing? That couldn't be easy. Jack, my soul's previous host, had a hands-free phone set. Maybe the Nephilim had those, too.

The taste of copper wet my tongue as I realised I'd bitten my lip too hard. This mortal world captivated me, distracted me, after my sentence in Hell.

Glancing back at the parishioners, I watched them scurry. Maybe I was too much? With my leather jacket, black hair that fell down my back and tattoos and crimson wings tucked behind my back. It didn't help that since my fall I had crimson eyes. I could literally smell their fear.

Back in the day my wings were white, pure, almost glacial, with a hint of silver that glistened under the light of the sun or the moon. But that all changed when I fell. They burned tattoos of dark magic on me in Hell, and ironically, I'm probably more righteous now than I was before I fell. I learnt a lot down there.

The priest waddled back in, holding the pin between his forefinger and thumb like he'd just found the Holy Grail. I shot him my best attempt at a smile, but he literally trembled at that, so I thought I'd leave smiling for now. I nodded to the font where he dropped the pin in with great reverence. I had to bite my lip again. More blood on my tongue. I'd have to work on the smile thing... I guess it's not every day a priest meets Lucifer.

As the pin fell in the water it floated, I used my free hand, my left hand—ah the Devil's hand, and muttered a Sumerian witch spell over it.

A chill ran through the little place, darkness spilled like smoke blocking the sunlight through the medieval stained-glass windows. Glancing up as the light disappeared, I noticed then the windows had pictures of my pious brothers—badly depicted, I might add. Michael would never stand like that Gabriel looked about right, though. Pretentious.

The pin spun furiously.

"They're closer than I expected," I said. "Someone or something is trying to cloak them in magic."

Aaron came back in, eyebrows raised. "Did it work?"

"Perhaps ten miles," I replied. "Maybe less. Did you get the Armadel?"

"Acacius stashed it in the eaves of Bath Abbey."

I turned to the priest. "I assume you know the Reverend of the abbey? Good to get him on my side, you understand."

Trying to overcompensate for his worry, he nodded crazily.

Aaron patted the man on the arm. "Thank you, Edward, let me know of any unusual events, however trivial they may seem. A darkness is afoot to hold two archangels."

The priest's mouth hung open as I walked past him, thanked him and then strode out into the small garden, broke open my wings with Cerberus yapping, and we took flight.

I had no need for directions as I could see the abbey's spires from where I flew.

Amber rays melted over the tiny city as night crept forward. I revelled in the cool spring air and I breathed deeply.

Had I not needed to rescue my brothers, I could've flown for hours, catching the descent of birds as they flitted around one more time before roosting and the whispers of insects that were following suit. Power surged through me.

The colours merging under the sinking sun; the aromas exhilarated me. The world had changed beyond recognition since I was banished and now the glittering yellow and white lights of the city below pitched my mood with a determination that victory was to be mine. I would rescue my brothers, and Heaven would have to redeem me.

I landed lightly on the roof of the magnificent medieval abbey, alongside the tower where a worn-looking door stood between me and the answers I was seeking.

Ignoring the temptation to kick it in, I whispered a spell, and the lock clunked open with ease. Something tempered me. Maybe because I was starting to give a damn about mankind and maybe because I had Cerberus tucked inside my jacket. With that thought, I gently pressed my chin on Cerberus, his head against my chest I realised he was sleeping. Must be the celestial grace. No dog would be used to flying otherwise.

Furling up my wings, I turned the handle to find the tower empty.

Damp narrow stone steps twisted tightly down, and I descended lightly with Aaron behind me.

The further down I went, something alerted my senses... vampires?

A thick coppery scent filled my nose. Blood. Lots of it.

Stepping up our pace, I growled instinctively, glancing behind at Aaron, who frowned.

That's when we saw the bodies laid strewn alongside the pews, emaciated, the colour of the stone.

Holding up my sword, Aaron drew his from the scabbard sewn into his coat, the speckled coloured light from the massive stained-glass windows glinting off his blade.

An oppressive weight seemed to lock in the air, my shoulders instantly heavy and tense and the flash of the feeling of being back in Hell. A foreboding in the place, menacing.

Silence fell fast. We were too late.

Opening his wings, Aaron flew up to the eaves. I watched his face scrunch up as he hovered there, massive white feather tips pressed against the abbey ceiling and dust sprinkling down like tiny flakes of snow, glittering in the light.

Unlike the church, the abbey was lined with white stone pillared archways that towered up towards Heaven. The elaborate ceiling was interlaced with intricate carvings of stone, that wound in and out of each other. A massive arched stained-glass window dominated the nave. A chill ran through me. It was cold in here, and not just the temperature. Something was wrong in my father's house.

"It's gone! It's bloody gone!" His voice was frantic and echoed throughout the abbey. Landing next to me, he spluttered, "I don't understand, Acacius warded it with spells!"

Aaron pulled out his phone whilst I pointed to the bodies and smote them into ash. A bright arctic blue flame shot out. I said a silent prayer for the mortals, willing their souls to ascend, but really, I did not know whether they would. I am damned, after all. Still, you've got to try.

After Hell, nothing shocked me much, except the nagging pain in my stomach of my brothers.

Running back up the tower steps, I stepped out onto the roof and looked out across the city.

Somewhere near here, in this place my brothers were being held captive, but how the hell would I find them?

Finally, I sat on a wall that ran along the edge of the roof, Cerberus sleeping, tucked safely in my jacket and my hand over him, as I watched the mortals below. They were completely unaware of the dark underbelly of life that coexisted alongside them.

"I need to go," and as if on cue, the whole city illuminated as a mighty flash of lightning blazed throughout the sky and the world shook as thunder echoed throughout the tiny city.

Aaron's mouth hung open in a perfect circle of horror. The buildings around shook. I braced, angry, wrapping a hand over Cerberus who yelped in fear.

His eyes full of concern, Aaron whispered, "Brother, what is it?"

But I couldn't be still, yet with the pup in my care I had no choice but to temper my rage, "That!" I swung my legs around and got up, pointing with it to the sky. "That, the thunder, the lightning, the ground shaking is a sign that my brothers are being tortured... Enough, I must find them!" I stepped lightly towards Aaron. "Aaron, please take Cerberus back home with you, I will not risk both of your lives. And I will not, not under any condition, have you fight along-side me." I grabbed his wrist, staring into his eyes. "You are a brave warrior, I see that. Whatever has my brothers is prob-ably more powerful than me. I know you'll try to disobey me, you have honour. So instead consider this, the world can live without a few archangels. But it cannot live without the Nephilim. Plus, Cerberus has been through enough already in his short existence, knowing you and he are safe, I'd be grateful. So..."

"You know-"

"And yet, I could pull rank, I don't want to."

The lightning thrashed again, mocking me it seemed, and my anger wanted to erupt from me. I pointed to nothing in particular and a smite of arctic blue fire furled out. Bound tight, my muscles felt like a spring ready to explode, I held the temper, the fury when below I spied creeping fast to a building for cover, vampires... bloody stinking rotten vam-pires.

Lightly covering Cerberus's head with my palm, I whispered to him to sleep and his tiny eyes seemed to fight me, but then closed. Maybe my dad had put him before me, without him I wouldn't have bothered to control my temper, probably resulting in the collapse or destruction of something. I am not known for my patience.

I swept down lightly, Aaron hot on my tail, calling to me, "Stop, Lucifer, stop! They're friends!"

King of Hell

I landed in front of the undead, whose faces were an odd shade of blue, of fear.

Their shadows loomed behind them on the buildings, elongated like eerie shadow puppets hiding in the cobbled side street.

Sneering, my wings outstretched behind me, beating slowly. I drew my sword as the two blood suckers bared their fangs. To me!

"I hate your kind, Godforsaken evil..." I spat as they dared to stand defiant.

"If you care at all about your redemption, vampire, you will kneel before me and beg my father for forgiveness, to embrace your souls, Hell is for eternity."

One of them stepped forward, his leather coat sweeping around him, a furl of black curls falling to his shoulders, stained crimson lips and porcelain skin, "What do you know of Hell, demon? I am the King of Hell, you should bow, no, kneel before me!"

Throwing my head back, my laugh echoed around the old buildings, the sound bounced off the walls. "There's a special place in Hell reserved for your kind, as you are about to find out!" My hair whipped in my face, wet as a gale stirred and rain started lashing down. My free hand covered Cerberus's head, I followed the vampire's gaze as he noticed my hand move to protect my dog. The blood sucker's head would adorn... well, somewhere! We both jumped, startled as a crack of lightning emblazoned the sky. It was all very dramatic.

I wanted his coat, though. Still, I stepped forward, sword pointing to his neck as the undead stepped up to match me.

Aaron shouted, "Lucifer, stop! He is a friend; he and Nathaniel here were not the ones who killed those people in the abbey. He is who he says he is, and he may help you if you stop acting like a dick! This is my city, these are my friends!" His voice reverberated around, causing a slight shudder in the walls of the surrounding buildings. Cerberus shivered, I narrowed my eyes at Aaron.

"Everyone has gone insane. You, friends with vampires. Has the world gone completely mad? You are part angel- this means nothing to you? Aaron, you have fallen far my friend. Hell, even now, waits with open arms for you and you will regret it. I promise you that! Your only salvation is to take their heads, now..."

Aaron sighed and lowered his sword, "Look, times have changed since you left. Yes, we Nephilim work with underworlders, some of them at least. These two have fought alongside me to defeat greater evils. They do not kill and they only take from the evil, the dispossessed. You need to lower your weapon, let us speak, discuss this calmly."

Clenching my jaw and my anger, I lowered the flaming sword a little and spat, "Speak then, convince me if you can! But if my soul is damned further, I will know who is to blame!"

The vampire in the long leather coat spoke first, eyeing me up and down, his face confused, pure white eyes like I'd never seen "How can this be Lucifer? Jack is Lucifer. But you..."

I cut in, "We're losing time. My brothers, Michael and Gabriel, are being tortured. Look vampire, your friend Jack was a body that inhabited my soul. Bael's magic, but Jack met with a timely accident and now my soul has returned to me, and to be frank, I'm surprised his body held my soul for as long as it did. Now I'm back and someone or something has my brothers. The storm," I pointed up, sneering... "That is a sign that my brothers are being tortured. When an archangel is suffering, there are consequences and these consequences effect your planet, fire and brimstone, storms, rogue vampires. If I can't help them, well, it could start the apocalypse. It's a fine balance. Now you are up to speed, my only question to you and your fanged friend is can you help me find them? I am tired and beyond angry and ready to kill the next creature that pisses me off!"

His jaw clenched as I spoke, then he nodded and extended his arm. "You're Lucifer? And you have a puppy?"

I raised my brows, a slight nod.

"Why? Why do you have a puppy?" His voice shook.

I couldn't help it, I chuckled. "Everyone needs a dog. How is it you don't even know that?" I knew obviously that this was a ridiculous answer, but I didn't feel like I needed to explain my life to a bloodsucker.

Tilting his head, he narrowed his eyes. "No, I did not know that. We had a cat." He shrugged and looked to his companion.

Then he stepped closer, I raised my sword. "No closer, fang boy, or your head comes off! No one is hurting Cerberus. Understand? Or I'll drag you and your boyfriend straight to Hell myself. And I doubt you have seen the darkest, most terrifying places in Hell."

Putting his palms up, frowning, a slight sheen glistened from his brow. I didn't think the undead could sweat. Huh.

"No, of course I wouldn't hurt him, I'm not a fiend. I just wanted to look. I love dogs." He shot Aaron a look, Aaron whose smile tugged at his lips.

"So, you are Lucifer, the actual fallen angel. And you're trying to find your brothers? Is that why we've been having crazy weather, we've seen strange shapes in the shadows... something's coming... I knew it!"

I huffed. "Well, can you help or shall we stand in the storm whilst Cerberus dies of exposure and my brothers die of torture?"

Narrowing his eyes, lips pressed tightly together, then he glanced at his vampire friend, then back to me. "Sure, if you can shut your mouth hole, then I'll help. Lucifer..." He shook his head and started walking. "Follow me. Thought you'd be taller though..."

Bloody vampires! The lengths we go to for family. It had better be worth it.

We had to walk since they have no flight and I wouldn't want to carry them, especially with Cerberus tucked in my jacket. But in minutes we were outside a huge town house just off the centre of the city.

Its grandiose architecture loomed high, the complete opposite of Aaron's small place. Vampires are vain creatures, it seems.

Inside, the tiled monochrome floors, soft designer furnishings and obscure art work lent more to the opulence than outside and the heat of the place and the scent of cinnamon, orange and spices in the air hit me.

"Down here." He showed as we followed the two fanged creatures into a basement.

I shot a look at Aaron who oddly looked at ease, relaxed.

The cellar was large, warm, and held an intricate pentacle painted in red on the floor. Instinctively, I bent down to touch it. "It's paint," the other vampire said.

I felt no malice here. How was that possible? But my brothers' lives were in the balance, so I let them proceed. Unzipping my jacket, I let Cerberus down, placing him gently on the floor. "Do you have some water, he may need a drink and I need to take him out for five minutes."

"Sure, back up the stairs, the first door on your right, the kitchen is through there. You'll have to come back down here, though, the backdoor to the garden is through that alcove." He pointed behind him.

"Come on Cerberus, come on!" I pitched at my dog, who bounded past me back up the steps. Walking past the vampire's living room, it was awash with old books, cracked spines embossed with gold writing, but the modern furniture was minimal. An enormous fireplace with stacked logs ready for lighting and the surrounding mantelpiece showed off the decadence of the Georgian period when it was built.

Cerberus sniffed around whilst I eyed their high-tech kitchen, rummaged for a bowl in the cupboards, then filled one with water and placed it before my dog.

He lapped up the water as I crouched over him, stroking his back, his hair now shining black and silver white.

He finished, looked me in the eye, barked and then shook himself, the water from around his mouth splattering on my face. I refilled the bowl, and we went back down to the basement where I took Cerberus outside to have a wee.

Worry tugged at my face. It would be safer if Cerberus were with another, a kind, strong immortal. But he seemed to have chosen me, so until I could find such immortal, I would keep him safe. I mused to myself; I hadn't, when I thought about, really had to think of any other being for a millennium. Not since Lilith...

I surveyed the lawn. A long rectangle with its borders awash with buds of crimson, canary yellows and blues, the flowers were crammed in. The slight nip of ice in the air, springtime held a crispness in the wind. A stone footpath led up the end, and beside the large wooden back gate, a trowel and various gardening tools made me wonder if these vampires dabbled in gardening. This question was answered as I walked through the place. A small patch of herbs, lavender, rosemary, basil amongst others filled my senses, and I made the connection. They practised magic. Of course, they grew herbs to power their spells.

It was surprisingly large and once Cerberus refreshed, we went back inside where I noticed on the side next to a huge sunken ceramic sink was a moon planting guide. Sorcery, it seems, had given these demons a calling of nature. I'd never have imagined vampires gardening, but if I had, then yes, under moonlight...

With Cerberus at my heels, I stood next to Aaron, who bent down. "Come here boy!" he said and swept Cerberus up into his arms. I laughed as he licked the Nephilim's face, Aaron scrunched his nose, moving it away from my dog's licks, then pulled the creature close.

"I'll carry him, Lucifer, whilst they do whatever it is."

I nodded. "Thanks." Looking at the vampires, I asked, "So, you believe yourself the King of Hell, do you? I wonder at that. I never saw you down there. Would you like me to address you as your highness, or your grace?" Wide eyed, I grinned at Aaron and shrugged. "I'm not sure these days which is the appropriate title."

The vampire shot me a smug grin. "It was a title bestowed on me, from Jack, or Lucifer, and the seventy-two demons of Hell. Paimon, the head demon in particular- I'm surprised he hadn't told you?"

"Paimon is deceitful and full of shit. I see he led you to believe that, well, you can keep the title. After Jack took my soul, I was rendered incapacitated, locked away, tortured. Things changed, though, once I had it back. It pleases me immensely that the bastard Bael is dead, though. How did he die, by your hand, I'm guessing?"

He looked worried for a second, avoiding my eye contact. His gaze darted around the room. I saw he swallowed hard. "Lucifer- or Jack to you- rescued two of my friends from Hell, then ordered them, mesmerized them, to bleed me dry. They did, and in that blood fuelled hunger, Jack compelled me to drain Bael, my father, which I did. I couldn't control it. Bael had said my soul was that of Asmodeus."

I smiled, my eyes half-closed. "How fitting. Good. So, you have the soul of Asmodeus? Demon of lust? I'll have to watch myself, ah, the coat, the tattoos." I raised my voice in a friendly taunting jibe. "Suits you, yes, I can see that. *Prince of lust*... But you must remember that Bael was untrustworthy, he came from a lesser deity originally." I spat, "A pagan one, so no surprise. I guess I should thank you, your grace?"

He busied himself in grimoires; he clicked his fingers and candles lit around the place, incense burned and the air thickened quickly with a spicy sweet scent.

"Asmodeus, eh? Figures, vamps don't wield power like you're doing now. In another time, another place, I'd kill you where you stand. Still, times change..."

He rolled his eyes. His friend shrugged.

I wondered out loud, "So, vampire lovers? Yes, Asmodeus. Your libido is the stuff of legends, so I hear."

The one in the leather coat now took it off and hung it up on a hook on the wall, strutted over, all tight jeans and T-shirt that showed off his defined body. Running his fingers through his wild black hair, he held out a hand. "Why Lucifer, would you like to find out? You'll find vampires, demons, we're very..." He eyed me over slowly. "Adaptable. I'm guessing you haven't been laid in some time? Shall we?" With his deadpan expression, he indicated to the steps, whilst I grinned, glancing at Aaron who knotted his brows smiling.

"Thank you, vampire." I touched my chest, smirking. "But you're just not my type."

"How would you know?"

I nodded, and said, "No, not because you're a vampire, because you're male. I'm not adaptable, not in anything. But I take it as a compliment."

He shrugged and scratched his forehead. "Well, I'd heard the devil was open to anything. What a shame."

"Indeed, it is my loss. Maybe another time, and I don't even know your name."

He stepped into me, his face almost in mine, "I am Anthony, this is Nathaniel. So, you're the real Lucifer? Suits you with your crimson wings and arrogance, you certainly live up to your name."

I looked at his hand that he held out beside me. Biting my lip, I admit I had wanted to kill him. Maybe I'd been wrong. I took his cold dead hand and shook it.

He shuddered as my energy pulsed through him. My upper lip curled. Yes, feel my power.

Nathaniel kept his distance, checking me over when he thought I wasn't looking.

"I'll need your blood if I'm to locate them, unless you have something else that links you to your brothers?" Anthony asked, standing tall and looking me in the eye.

My lips pierced together, I eyed him back.

"Blood it is, but I'm warning you..."

"Geez, do you ever shut up? No, I won't drink it. Yet!" He laughed and winked at Aaron, who rolled his eyes, shaking his head.

"Actually, I may need to drink it, tell me it won't kill me? The blood of angels-"

"Yes, you're right. The blood of angels can indeed be lethal to all immortals, and a good job, too. Otherwise, we'd have you lot fighting to bleed us dry in a never-ending battle. But you're not just a vampire, are you? You're half-demon, too, the soul of Asmodeus. As I live and breathe, still I will hand it to you Anthony, you are much improved in this new body. Your last incarnation as Asmodeus was a chaotic nightmare. So, to answer you, no, my blood won't kill. Probably."

His forehead puckered at my last word. He handed me a blade and a golden bowl with runes engraved on it; it sagged slightly in my hand as I took it, not expecting it to be so heavy. Solid gold, then...

The whole place was macabre but plush. Bottles with ghoulish body parts that seemed to move sporadically. Swirling metallic liquids, herbs, bones engraved with runes and possibly hundreds of books. Grimoires stacked around the extensive cellar on bookshelves, workbenches, the floor. Heavy with the musky scent of woody frankincense, the place was warm, dark wood bookcases against whitewashed stone walls. A few ancient weapons, swords, daggers and a spear hung from the sparse space on the walls. I wondered just what had gone on in this place, as my eye line followed another opening, an arched doorway. That room hidden in darkness but a glimmer in the distance revealed something of a more sinister nature.

Chains.

But who knew? Whether those were for pleasure or interrogation, I realised that these days, in this time, you just didn't know. And frankly, I wasn't sure I wanted to. Adaptable, huh? I'd seen that in Hell. And those who enjoyed it.

Realising they were all waiting on me in silence, I sliced my hand, my blood poured freely. A gleam of silver in it, I handed it back to him and Nathaniel handed me a piece of clean cloth to wrap around my hand.

Then they busied themselves whispering over a grimoire, looking to the centre of the pentacle.

"Where is this design from, the Key I guess?" I asked.

Now Nathaniel had obviously gained the courage to speak to me. "The Key of Solomon, yes."

"So, you're going to summon a demon to find my brothers then?" I threw him a half smile.

"No, not exactly. We use their energy to locate your brothers."

I nodded, frustrated this was taking so long, and grabbed out a wooden chair from the back of the room that grated loudly on the stone floor and sat alongside Aaron. "Vampires that don't kill, that wield magic and fight with angels. This is a strange time indeed."

He grinned widely, sitting back. "It won't be long now. Anthony, if you could see who's holding them, too, that would be mint, mate!"

His chest rose and fell, a heavy burden for such a low life, but I appreciated it, or would if it worked. I was contemplating killing them if they failed and I guessed it would annoy Aaron, but that would be his human side. His weak side.

They made me smile, though.

Vampires, like their demon cousins, are so fragile. They assume that they're the top of the food chain, that because they're faster and more vicious than humans, that it strengthens them somehow. But they've certainly evolved, I'll give them that. Two thousand years ago, most of them were just fangs in a body. Now, I glanced around. Now, the dead live better than the living. It was warm in this plush house, even in their cellar. I leaned into Aaron and whispered low in the language of our kin, "You ever think about taking their heads?"

He rolled his lips, his head bobbing back, answering, "Constantly, Lucifer. But I don't do it."

I nodded, good to know. But they were trying to help me, desperate that I don't smite them and all their kin, however much bravado they show...

Anthony, or the King as he said, stepped into the circle and started chanting in Latin.

"Impressive," I called. "You do not think Enochian more appropriate?"

Stopping, he eyed me fiercely. "You saying their captor speaks Enochian? From the research by our greatest occultist, that's a fake language, anyhow."

I held up my arms, smirking. "Ah, then your greatest occultist must be right. Couldn't be that he couldn't read Enochian?" I had to laugh. Though regularly I hated these creatures with a vengeance, these two were interesting.

"Would you like to come in here and perform this yourself, your unholiness, the devil?"

I laughed loudly. "Not a devil, The Devil! No, you are the experts. Please..." I indicated with my palms to continue, unable to wipe the grin off my face.

Anthony took off his boots and socks and then picked up the golden bowl that held my blood and smeared some on his face like a warrior readying for battle. I withheld a gasp as he drank some of my blood, part anger, part curiosity, wondering what effect it would take on him. Would it kill him?

The silver-red liquid swallowed, he chanted, his eyes now rolled into the back of his head. A strong wind brushed fiercely, almost sending Aaron and myself off of our chairs. Cerberus barked, then growled, Aaron whispered over him, pulling him tighter.

Gripping the edges of my seat, I felt a swaying in my stomach as nausea hit me. My mouth watered. I didn't get sick, but I felt it now. I clenched harder with my fingers, feeling the blood drain from my face, I strained against this ungodly magic.

Dark Gift

My fanged friends almost impressed me, almost because I didn't know if it would work but they were doing something, and I hoped they had not deceived Aaron as I was feeling the brunt of this spell.

A burning seared on my arm, hot like fire as the vampire chanted louder. A black haze thickened around him so that it almost hid him from view.

Gritting my teeth as my arm burned, smelling the familiar stench of burning flesh. Cerberus barked, and Aaron's face screwed up in horror. Getting up, I pulled off my leather coat but I couldn't see much in that dense fog and though I could certainly produce light; I didn't want to interfere with the magic.

Touching my arm, my skin was raised, blistering, and a sweat broke over the back of my neck.

Hard to swallow, my throat gravelly, an ominous weight seemed to push me down, my limbs like lead and my soul trapped in Hellfire.

The chanting, now oppressive, seemed to suck me in. Pounding in my head, assaulting and from what I could see, which wasn't much, the vampire had his head back, arms outstretched, and his feet raised just above the floor.

Convulsing suddenly, everything stopped, and he slumped down like a rock as gradually the air cleared.

Instantly my limbs, my soul felt lifted but not entirely. A hardness in the pit of my stomach remained, and as the room cleared, I glanced at my right arm.

Like a marionette, my mouth fell open, my belly flipped, I staggered up and shock made my wings burst open knocking and smashing objects near me.

Aaron and Nathaniel were attending Anthony as I stared in horror at my arm, sweat beading from my forehead.

Looking up, Aaron called, "What is it? What's that on your arm?"

I swallowed hard then cleared my throat. "I hope he found out where they are but now at least I know who has them!" My torment had only just begun. A savage fear gripped my heart, stilling my breathing.

"Who? What does that mean?"

"Cain, Aaron, Cain has them. This," I held out my arm, "This is his bloody mark! The Mark of Cain! A curse, an immortal curse of doom!"

I swayed as my head spun, rage building inside of me like a furnace, memories of indiscretions, of how I had been wronged. Hate now pumped in my veins, threatening to erupt out of me, violently.

My hands to my head as I fought against it, the anger, the Mark's rage, I forced myself to take deep, slow breaths.

Anthony came around smiling and dazed. He reached out towards me, growling I stepped back.

"Wow- your blood!" He chuckled, still high on it, I presumed.

"Is this your trick, bloodsucker? To drink my blood and inflict Cain's curse on me?" I lunged forwards, savage, violent, only to meet the brunt of Aaron's chest as he blocked me and gripped my wrists with force.

"Be still Lucifer, this is no trick. Anthony would not do that, he's not stupid! Look."

As I struggled to get free, growling, Aaron put his face before me. "It's the Mark, control it or it will consume you. Back down!" His voice boomed through me.

Bracing my impatience and temper, I asked, "Alright! Alright... But where are they? Tell me!"

"They're here, they're right here in Bath!"

"Where?"

"The abbey, I saw the abbey. Deep beneath it in the catacombs."

Nathaniel helped Anthony to his feet, the vampire swayed unsteadily. The rage that fuelled through me wasn't dulled by the fact that he'd drunk my blood. But logically I knew that he'd done it to find my brothers.

He continued, "They're cloaked in magic, powerful sorcery. When I looked, a silver-white light blinded me, I thought it was going to scorch my eyes out. The only time I've seen that kind of light is from Seraphs..."

"Cain..." I muttered angrily. "What the hell!"

"How do we fight him?" Anthony asked.

Spluttering a laugh, I shook my head trying to shake the crimson mist of violence that seemed to grip every muscle, every sinew of my body, "Thank you, you amaze me that you would help in my fight but vampire, you cannot. He would tear you limb from limb for even trying. He's protected by God, you see. I'm not even sure if I can, but I will try."

Aaron stood beside me. "Let's go then."

"No, and I thank you brother, but this I must do alone. Cain would slaughter all of you, and besides, I need you to look after this little fellow. Remember, Cain is a true immortal under God's protection. So, even if you took his head, he would heal. But if I don't return in twenty-four hours, maybe contact Azrael." I sighed, trying to get my breath back. "A last resort as my brother is likely to wipe out everyone and everything, but he will come. Now tell me, do you have any of my blood left?"

"Plenty. And how do we summon Azrael?"

I hesitated, knowing they'd hate the answer.

"With my blood, chanting his name in Enochian and a sacrifice, but ensure that sacrifice is not my dog or..."

Nathaniel raised his arm. "Don't fear. We only kill the evil."

Nodding, I braced back the rage that fired through my veins. "My brother comes to those in death so- I'll leave the details to you."

I went to step away, then paused looking at my dog.

"Just make sure it is Azrael. Do not, on any account, summon Metatron. He is the scribe to my father and out of all my brothers, he is the most... *unforgiving*."

Their faces went paler than usual and Aaron pulled Cerberus into his chest, resting his chin on Cerberus's head.

Aaron tilted his head. "How do we know we won't summon the wrong archangel?"

I didn't know really. Not having heard from them in so long. Shaking my head, I said, "Azrael is the Angel of Death, so a sacrifice with a spell in Enochian should get his attention." Then I glanced at him and the vampires. "Do not fear, it is unlikely to come to that. And," I shrugged, looking around at the strange jars of body parts and God-knows-what, "As you said, you can use someone evil as an offering."

I dropped my shoulders, after everything it came down to me. Looking at them one final time, I mumbled, "Thank you, I'm quite stunned at this world I've come back to. And... I," I briefly shook my head, "I don't know, maybe I was wrong about your kind? You two at least are honourable."

Taking a deep breath, I left the opulent house of the dead and sprinted back to the Abbey.

Pausing outside, I tried to feel if I could sense anything, my brothers, magic, Cain! Nothing, so I walked into the main entrance, sword in hand expecting a desolate church, but instead found Cain sat on the altar, his legs crossed, ankle on knee puffing on a cigar and bobbing his foot up and down.

"Geez, you're a slow bastard, I've been waiting for you for eons. Took your slow time, didn't ya? You're getting old Satan- just saying."

"What the hell are you doing? Where's Michael and Gabriel?"

"I have a special place for them, maybe I'll show you, maybe I won't. Still, I hear you got yourself a dog? Nice." He took a long drag on his cigar after that word and puffed it out slowly, watching the smoke before looking back at me. "I used to have a dog. Oh, way back when. Broke my heart when he died. Still, you're here now, so the show can begin, what do you say?"

Instantly my muscles tensed, my hand gripped my sword until my knuckles whitened. I went to draw it before gasping. My throat tightened suddenly. It felt like I was being strangled. Cain bobbed his foot, smirked through his cigar, and winked whilst I fought to swallow, to breathe, but some invisible force was gripping my throat. Unable to swallow, I shuddered as an icy chill trembled down my spine.

Cain raised his brows casually as he took another long, deep draw on his cigar and puffed his smoke towards me.

Unable to speak, to breathe, I felt my blood drain from my face, my free hand instinctively at my throat, but I couldn't feel anything corporal there, yet still it tightened.

My last-ditch attempt at this point, I flung myself towards him, sword drawn and outstretched but he didn't move and a few inches before him my sword hand opened against my will, a crash of metal on stone and the floor came flying fast at my face.

###

Mark of Cain

Hell is mainly old school when it comes to torture. Dante was close with his descriptions and until now, I never really believed people used iron maidens.

That was until I regained consciousness, driven out of it by the colossal agony that Cain hammered into me.

Still with a cigar in the corner of his mouth and puffing the smoke into my face, he acted so casually, as if we were just chatting around a fire.

He'd pulled the door of the torture device open and blood congealed around my wounds from the spikes that he had impaled into me. And if you don't know, lucky you, iron maiden, no, I'm not referring to the band. I had heard of them- the band, that is, when my soul was in Jack- he was a big fan.

An iron maiden is like a standing coffin that has spikes inside the door, so when it shuts, those spikes impale the victim- me.

It is true immortals are usually subject to more intense forms of torture since we cannot die, it's more barbaric perhaps that this was used in the past on humans. But just so you know, it was every bit of agonizing to me.

It was my own screaming that woke me from the magic induced coma. As I felt the spikes impale my flesh, icy fear seized my body, terror gripped my mind. Sharp, unbearable agony that even I could not escape. My mind blanked out until he opened the door.

Through a haze of frantic nausea as the spikes dragged out of my body, blurry vision and shock, that bastard stood there grinning, eyeing me over and puffing on his bloody cigar. I'd like to stick that lit cigar up his damned ass. Then take his head off.

We don't even use these in Hell- it would seem far too brutal.

I'd gone beyond pain at that point, blurred and my head slumped forward as I was only barely aware of him, hearing sounds from his mouth but unable to understand words.

I was torn, literally, shaking as I stood there as I felt him pull me slowly forwards, my legs staggered with him, piercing pain bolted and seized through me.

Then heat, which I later determined was hands over me and realised I was laying down.

Flickering flames in the darkness that bounced and bobbed made my mind think of candles as a cool chill brushed my face. I had been better off in Hell.

I tried to sit up, battling against the agony, ripped and broken. I tilted my head, fighting the pain and looked at my body. Mistake. Gaping wounds from the torture device that had pierced through my flesh. My mind froze, swam in a haze of shock as I felt unconsciousness wash over me. Only stopped by a clammy sweat that broke out on the back of my neck, my blood had mostly congealed around my wounds but still seeped in places. I bit down the urge to puke, too weak to do that as panic wrapped its icy fangs into my heart and my mind. Terror froze my brain as each breath became shorter and shorter, my legs useless. Cain was talking to me, but his words faded, echoed so that I could only hear every other word and my vision blurred. Nausea swished through me, I felt like I was swaying violently but he remained calm in front of me, so I don't know. As I fought to breathe, a dark circle started closing in around my vision, and all I could hear was a buzzing sound, then abruptly my pain ceased. My head fell back on the bed, or whatever he'd put me on. Peace seemed to kiss my limbs, my mind, my eyelids heavy as the urge to drift off overcame me.

Slower and slower my breathing eased, and before me I saw a passageway. Surrounded by an inky sky, a pinprick of silver light glowed bright in the distance and the voice of a familiar friend. Was that Dad? It called again; I let my eyes close, my body limp, surrendered until a sharp slap stung my face, forcing me to open my eyes.

Leaning over me, Cain grinned. "I'm sorry about that but you're a proud and obstinate bastard, so I knew, I just bloody knew, Luci, that I'd have to show you or rather demonstrate to you," he waved his cigar as he spoke, "the power that I wield. Now that you've had a taste, an aperitif as it were, I'm guessing you're more likely to cooperate? Am I right?" He nudged me, smirking.

Growling, I choked on my blood, swallowed hard, my head still spinning, the pain coming back with a vengeance, twisting and sharp in my gut. I mumbled, "Let my brothers go, Cain! What the hell..."

Casually he replied, walking around the dark room, "Well, maybe, but not yet. You of all people know what I want, and you and your brothers are the only ones who can help me. Possibly. So, you've got the Mark, eh? I admit I wasn't expecting that, a bonus to me. Now maybe I can lift this bloody curse. After all, your dad put the Mark on me, being the first human to kill and all, and we both know I can't die with it on my arm. But you... Huh, I did not see that coming, Lucifer Morningstar, no sir, I did not. So, technically, now I could die as I don't have God's curse of immortality. But here's the thing, do you want to know?"

He nudged me and I cried out in agony, sweat pouring from my face, my body.

"I'm still going ahead with my plan, more assurance to me that when it works, I won't be around any longer on this miserable, boring planet. Plus, it'll seriously, and I mean really, put a downer on your dad. I mean, this presents a whole new ball game. But, well, I don't want to divert too far from my original, and if I may add exquisite plan, I still want your power, and your brothers. Yes, the power of the three. I mean, I virtually have it anyway. You ok there? You look a bit... pasty."

Coughing through the saliva and blood in my mouth, I spat at him, groaning. "What? All this so you can die? Torture, cruelty? You're insane, God is now more likely to damn you, not release you, not set you free."

I spoke, but my mind was on what I had seen, or heard. The cliché, the light at the end of the tunnel, but it had been my father's voice I'd heard. I knew it. Why wasn't he here helping? Why wait for me to die? Why watch me be impaled? Where is my father?

But I can't die, can I? And now the Mark...

"Well, respect where it's due, the iron maiden, an antique you know and pretty effective. I had a little heads up it would work on you as it did on your brothers. Archangels, you're a pretentious lot, you always think you're above everyone, well not any more matey! Not anymore!"

"All this because you want to die? Ask me, I'm happy to oblige you!" I snarled.

"Well, that wouldn't have worked, would it? Hum, maybe now? But I have a better plan than merely my death, Luci, something far, far grander. And now I have all three of God's finest, I should have enough to at least get his attention. Three archangels, like the holy Trinity. So, you ready?"

Pain smarted through me, and my rage burned, craving release. Choking back on bile, I spat, "You honestly believe getting the three of us here and torturing us will get Dad's attention? Think again, dummy. I've been in Hell for two thousand years and nada, nil from Dad. So, no, you'll probably just end up starting a war with every archangel, every seraph on your trail." I panted, my mind fighting to outsmart the pain. "They'll torture you, you'll die and be reborn a thousand times but as for God, no, he probably won't raise an eyelid. You are Godforsaken, Cain, you imbecile, you've obviously forgotten that."

His smile slipped. "Well you got to try, though, haven't you, eh? Still, as you have the curse, the Mark, maybe I'd settle for redemption? An apology? I mean, I know killing your brother is a sin, but shit man, isn't everything? Abel," he spat on the floor. "Yea, he thought he was closer to God. I merely helped him along. And look at you? You only disagreed with your dad, and he sent Michael to cast you to Hell, I mean what the actual, Luci? Na, I think you should leave Mikey and Gabe to their own Hell, after all, they sure as shit didn't come running to help you, or did they?"

As my eyes flickered, battling to close and release me from the agony of the torture and Cain's mental torture of raving like a madman, he was leering right over me, puffing away, brows arched high, expecting an answer.

"Well, did they, Luci? I want an answer. Did they come to help you after you questioned your dad? And," he nudged me again, I screamed in pain, "I actually think you were justified in questioning your dad. Why shouldn't you succeed him? You should be proud, and humans, pah! As for vanity, well, he designed you to look good. A son should succeed his father, it's the natural order. No, screw your brothers. So tell me, when did they, Michael and Gabriel, come help you? An answer, Luci, or the iron maiden, your choice?"

Through clenched teeth I mumbled, "They didn't."

He bent down over me, the thick woody scent of his cigar a relief from my coppery blood. "Say again, I didn't quite catch that?"

Biting through the horror, I shouted, "They didn't come to help me, alright! They left me in Hell to rot. Left me in a place where men, women are flayed, burned alive for all eternity. Where they drown in their own excrement. It's all true, it's horrifying. And all I wanted, all I ever wanted, was to be seen again by my father. And he threw me there!" My body surrendered, I had nothing left. It was the truth as I saw it. I knew Cain was right, but I wanted, I would have my redemption if I rescued my brothers. And those who went against me would kneel. Or pay the price, the same as I had... in Hell.

With that, he walked away snickering and then paced back with my sword, beady eyed and wearing a sneer.

"I see, you want to save your brothers so that on rescuing them, all in Heaven will bow to you? They won't, they'll just throw you back in Hell as you well know, Lucifer. Geez, haven't you learned anything? They hate you, and well, me, too. We're a lot alike, outlaws of Heaven, of God... Shebang! But whatever, I still want your power, and those two do-gooder angels and I'd forfeit that, maybe for forgiveness from the big G, but the latter, Luci, ain't likely to happen. So, with Michael's sword, I'd been looking for that. Cheers Satan, may I call you that? Bit Christian perhaps..."

"How have you trapped us here? You're not powerful enough on your own. What malevolent magic did you conjure?"

He edged the tip of the sword to my chest with one hand, his lifeless eyes gazed over me, he trailed the blade down my chest. Obviously, it didn't harm me, it would him though.

"I can end your life if you release me and give me my sword, then you can meet... well, I can," I spat.

His chest rose and fell heavily. It was almost understandable that he'd gone mad, and I doubted his curse was meant to last this long as an eternal punishment. Probably and more likely dad had forgotten about him.

"Thanks Luci, I really appreciate that, I do, and you'd think I'd take you up on your kind offer and I may yet, who knows. But here I am, and you're there with my Mark, so I figure one archangel ain't enough to wipe little old me out but three of you... Phew, that'll be like a nuclear bomb to this doomed planet. That's the big plan Luci, nuke the place. Bet we get your dad's attention then, but hey, I'll be dead and that with blowing up his creation, you know, the world." He paused, eyeing the room. "And I have to tell you that gives me a deep sense of pleasure. Killing my brother was just a precursor, a trial run if you will."

He dropped his sword arm and held it beside his leg, leaning in slowly. "I thought reboot, start again, a new planet, hey? As for how I'm controlling you, well wouldn't you like to know, huh. It took me centuries of research, of study and then suddenly, in a heartbeat... *boom.* The answer came and oddly enough just outside this insignificant city in a little town which is even less important. So first I want to fire you boys up, then... abracadabra. The end of everything. I know what that look is Luci, I can see right through you."

I doubted he did, impaling him with my sword sprung to mind followed by decapitating his stupid big fat head and getting Cerberus and the other hounds of Hell to play fetch with it, but I frowned to look like I actually cared about the words that tumbled from his big mouth, looking intently at him. Plus, I was still reeling in agony, so there was little else I could do.

"Yes, you're wondering if God cares, will it- the annihilation of his three favourite sons, of his hairless apes, and this planet be enough to get him to raise his omnipotent head? I mean, I'm asking Luci, I really am because truth be told- I'm a little tetchy."

"What the hell is that? Tetchy?"

Smirking he replied, "Oh yeah, I forgot- how could I. Hell, not the best of places for current affairs or urban slang. Tetchy means pissed off, agitated."

"You're tetchy? Hello! So, because you're agitated, you're going to end the world? You're a top bastard, do you know that? A complete turd of an immortal."

I closed my eyes, bracing against the anguish that seared through my body, and the nausea that clawed in my stomach.

"Fine words coming from God's biggest failure, wouldn't you say? Anyway, it passes the time, you can get up now." He waved his hand dismissively. "You make the place look messy lying there."

Shooting pain blistered through my body, I grunted as I sat up, hands over my torso, jaw dropping in agony. A thought flashed through my mind to kill him, but I knew I couldn't, not in this state and not when he was protected by whatever the heck was protecting him. Anything but the iron maiden...

His voice echoed around the damp shadowy room. "I'm almost regretting having to kill you. You've been interesting to talk to, best conversation I've had for eons, unlike Michael or Gabriel. I assumed you'd be a pious git, but you're definitely different. Tell me, is that from being in Hell?"

"Look," I groaned, "The small talk is diverting, really, but I'm done. Free my brothers, killer!"

"Nope. Watch your tongue or back in there you go." He pointed with my sword to the torture device.

"So, what now then, we have tea or something?" As I spoke, blood splattered from my mouth.

"Now, now, I'm going to use this sword, God's sword on Michael and Gabriel, then I have to leave for a while. Power like this doesn't just create itself, you know. You're free to look around, you can visit them, they're through there. Ever seen Indiana Jones? No, I guess you haven't, well, this place is rigged with traps. So, if you try to escape, well, you'll wish you hadn't. Legs, arms, all fairly useful to have, wouldn't you agree? But by all means try, I won't stop you."

"A drink, I need a drink."

He chuntered and left the room, still clutching my sword. Relief slowly eased my muscles, knowing I wasn't going back into the iron maiden. I wiped my forehead with my sleeve, gritting my teeth to fight the pain that swayed through me.

Cain trudged back with a glass and bottle in his hand and passed them to me. "I'm only giving you a drink, Luci, because, well, I need you alive and as I said I enjoyed our little chat. You have no idea how lonely it is on this planet. Other immortals have always shunned me. I even tried a few times, back in the day, to have friendships with humans, but no... I usually ended up killing them when they annoyed me. I'm not the most patient. But you, yes, I liked our tête-à-tête. Still, won't be long and none of this will matter. So, maybe you can talk some sense into your brothers. I'd appreciate that, and, well, it would be easier for you, too."

Sneering silently as I watched him leave, leave with my bloody sword, I wished it had been cursed so that no non-archangel could wield it. Technically non-angels couldn't pick up the sword, but Cain, well yeah, Adam's offspring. Another of Dad's mistakes...

Putting the glass down, I unscrewed the bottle, poured some scotch straight down my throat before tipping some on this meat-suit of mine. That's the problem with Earth for me, I am a celestial being but my body is often vulnerable to things like impaling spikes through it and you know, torture. I can heal myself normally, but this place was wrapped tightly, cloaked in magic. It was sticky and heavy in the air, oppressive.

So, for now, I yelled as the spirit burned into my wounds. And I wondered to myself, why the shit is everyone drinking whiskey? Whatever happened to water?

Something else was off. Though I fought the urge to think about it in Cain's presence, a part of me felt empty. The Mark still seared and burned my flesh, the stench nauseating, but a hollowness gripped at my core. Slowly I got off the table I had been sat on, holding onto the sides, my legs like paper almost gave out. Panting, I doubled over in pain; I breathed deeply, trying to figure out what else was off, something hidden behind the agony.

As my mind raced through possibilities, the slow realisation, the horror that the torture had been a distraction. Cain had done that to get something else. I knew he wanted our energy, and using the power of supreme being whilst that being is in pain, fear, that is the most potent form of energy.

Fear is unlike any other feeling, its conductivity, its potency is dark, unwieldy and formidable. Sweat ran into my eyes, with one hand gripping the table, my other wiped my brow then reached for the bottle and took a glug. As I did, and the realisation began to settle, to make sense, my mind fog lifting. Cain had taken my celestial force. Though I had the Mark, so I was still immortal but without the celestial energy the lifeline to my kin, my family, to Heaven was gone.

My link to the divine had been weak, all that time in Hell had ensured that, but I had kept a sliver of heavenly power. And it wasn't pure like my brothers. My energy was corrupted, twisted. I had seen that for myself.

So Cain had lured me here to take my divine bond, and what am I left with? A shiver of cold sweat ran down my back. I knew that answer, but it was too terrible to contemplate. I had to push on. I had to find my brothers, though without my divine force I was terrified of seeing them...They would know and instantly.

Mustering my will, I stood away from the table, my eyes scouring the room for weapons.

I hadn't noticed in my tortures that on the walls hung the skulls of immortals, their faces echoing a sinister menace under the fluttering flames of the few candles lit around the room. Like sombre guardians, as I glanced around, one on each wall faced into the middle of the room a half-shifted werewolf, its hollow eyes seemingly staring into oblivion, the vampire with its fangs, the skull of a wendigo, and a contorted half human, half animal skull. Books were strewn across a few woodworm tables, some old chairs, their musty scent and thread worn fabric, but nothing else. I shivered as the sweat ran down my spine, an icy chill, but could see no weapons, not a dagger, not a thing, unless you count a bible, and I think I'm past that.

As I staggered out of that room, using the walls to support me, I wondered why Cain would leave me here to find my brothers? Another trap, something was off. I had to be careful.

But Cain had no idea I could wield magic, though it would be weaker now that I had no connection to Heaven.

Stopping for a moment, I breathed deeper and let the anger, the spite, rip through me. My jaw dropped open, I groaned loudly as hate fired through me. Maybe I could use the power of the Mark, its immortal curse, to aid me? I had to try, though I despised it, it was all I had. I had no choice now but to wield the force of death, of evil that the Mark symbolized by the grace of God. My eyes disappeared into their sockets, I realised I was screaming, head lunged back, arms open, then shaking violently I came to. Snarling instinctively, I felt a hunger, a burning, an obsession to lash out.

My fingers stiff, I lurched forwards, feeling the beast inside want to struggle out. Shit! Claws forced themselves from my fingers, my bones cracked. No! Anything but that. Not that...

I roared out the anger, battling down that thing, that monster that hid inside of me, but at least now I felt stronger. Swallowing hard, I looked about me, agitation and fury driving me. It was all I had, now I had to learn to master it. How ironic, I had left Hell with a temper unmatched by any other, then I had met Cerberus and I had to keep that in check.

Now, again, a harder lesson, being controlled, or trying to control the potency of this curse. Anger fuels the Mark. The Mark of Cain seeks it out and draws it in. Any rage I have? The Mark magnifies that, pushes the curse onwards. It would push me to lash out.

Just once it happened to me in Hell. I witnessed a horror so bad, so cruel that something happened to me, my ethereal power changed, mutated like a sickness from the torture, the never-ending savagery, the cruelty.

Corrupted I had changed, morphed into some form of monstrosity, the horned beast...

Swallowing hard, that was something I wanted to hide, to forget and the only demon who saw what I had transformed into down there in Hell was dead. At my clawed hands.

But I, I had mutated into the beast. And now it seemed, with the violence of the Mark, the beast that dwelt inside me wanted out. Again.

Cold sweat made me shiver at that memory.

Cain had written about it: the force of the Mark, how it sucked in evil, drove him to kill. It was by his sheer will alone that he had been able to control it for thousands of years. His writings had been destroyed but not before some Grigori had found them and copied them, hoping to use the Mark's force of evil against their enemies, pitting them against a greater, more savage horror. Keeping the underworlders, the demons, the vampires at bay. And I'd heard through whisperings in Hell that many in Heaven secretly opposed the curse of the Mark. That surely it was curse enough for Cain to be cast into immortality, day and night, year after year he lived in a torment of the guilt of killing his brother. But added to that, the Mark on his arm fed and thrived, absorbed all hatred, wrath and evil thought driving him to act these out.

That was why, without a doubt, Cain had gone mad, wanting to end all things.

Who could blame him? I guessed I would be next... And the beast? Part of me wanted to break down, fall to my knees and plead to my father, not that, not the beast, the creature within me...

The monster that all men feared, that lesser immortals cowered at. I had been created in an image of beauty, but inside me lurked a monstrosity. And now, with only the force of the Mark to aid me, and my divinity stolen, what did I have left?

I am the monster...

The Walls Have Eyes

I had to bottle my remorse. I'd spent thousands of years in pity, and that had got me nowhere.

The beast inside me shifted, settled, so clenching my jaw I pulled myself up, bit through the pain and strode forward into the tunnels that ran under this abbey. Shouting, my voice echoed through the empty chambers, bouncing back at me. Slimy stone walls revealed how abandoned the basement was, few lights dotted the corridors. The silence felt heavy as I walked on and on, though I felt slightly less apprehensive knowing I only had myself to fear... and Cain definitely didn't know that about me. No one did.

Focusing on finding my brothers, the tunnels seemed to run for miles, tiny arched wooden doors were strewn sparsely, opening each one only revealed thick cobwebs that caught in my hair, like dirty clouds and revealing only pitch-black darkness inside. Without my sword or angelic gifts, I could not cast light, so I had to be contented with feeling around in the shadows. Back in the corridors, covered in filth, my energy started to return, my arm stank as the Mark burned.

Ok, something's here.

"Hello? Michael, Gabriel?"

Nothing. Not a sound, not a whisper.

My strength almost restored, I could walk faster now. I kicked the doors open, stepping hard to keep my balance, I grabbed at anything, touched it, threw it out of my way... Screaming, "Michael? Gabriel? It is I, your brother! Where are you? Let me help you!"

"Hello? Help."

A woman's voice, faint, weak... I stormed out of the room. "Where are you? Keep talking, I'm on my way."

Silence. I spun around, wiping the cobwebs from my face. "Hello? Where are you?"

A faded echo of someone clearing their throat. "Here... we're here. We need help."

Musty damp air and a frigid chill whistled through the corridor, I stopped for a moment and called again, "Hello? I'm trying to find you."

Swallowing hard as I was greeted with silence, my stomach churned at the violence I had just endured. And who were these people down here? It made me feel like I'd never left Hell, but had in fact wandered right into another one. Dread pulsed through me, wondering what these victims had undergone.

At last a feeble cry, "We're down here!"

Striding on, I turned a corner and noticed only two old dim lights dotted the corridor. Suddenly distracted, I noticed something odd on the walls, something protruding, moving. Amid the dirty bricks' faces jutted out, my posture stiffened and a tingling sensation crawled on my skin. I inched closer; it looked like faces had been carved into the bricks. A heavy feeling in my stomach drew me away, turning, but as I did so a shrill voice barked at me.

"Malum satanas, redi ad inferos! Adolebitque, cremant, videmus tenebris tuam, quæ devoravit in medio tui ..."

It spat Latin at me:

Evil Satan, go back to Hell. Burn, burn, we see your darkness; it consumes you inside...

"We're here, please don't leave us!"

My shoulders dropped, the faces in the wall. It wasn't their voices I heard calling for help, though what sorcery this was I did not know.

I growled back to the wall, "Ire in gehennam!"

Go to Hell!

As I turned to find Cain's victims, the entire wall seemed to awake, more faces, now their voices reverberated throughout the tunnel, growing louder and louder, resonated all around me.

"Malum satanas, redi ad inferos! Adolebitque, cremant, videmus tenebris tuam, quæ devoravit in medio tui ..."

My arm scorched as the Mark seemed fuelled by this hate, I pushed forwards seeing only two doors in the distance. No lights seemed to be down this far. Coming to a door, I kicked it open, the nauseating stench of my burning flesh making my mouth water, fighting the urge to vomit.

A faint blue light glimmered in the darkness. "Hello? Is that your light?"

Relief in the answer. "Yes, yes. I can't keep it going much longer, I'm exhausted. Please, help her first!"

Making my way to the back of the room, I tripped over a chair hidden in the shadow, my knee smacked into it, I cussed as it clattered on the stone.

Outside the room, the faces in the walls still murmured. In here, I could just make out two figures.

Anger thrust through me as the events seem to build up, I was ready to burst, to lash out. Clenching my jaw, I felt the beast inside me move, shift.

Not now...

Before me two eyes shone out of the shadows, the woman, squinting I could see her hands were tied up high above her.

"What is your name? How long have you been here?" I whispered to her.

I had no blade, so as I stepped into her, set about trying to untie the rope that bound her. Oddly I trembled as I reached for the ropes, my hands shaking. Though she smelt of blood, of fear a hint of something warm, sweet radiated from her amongst the dirt.

Her voice was hoarse. "Eva. I don't know how long we've been here. Days I think." Her voice was dry, full of panic, and shook as she spoke. Holding in my anger at this diabolical situation, I ground my teeth trying to untie the insane knot that Cain had tied, unable to see anything, but running my fingers over it, feeling for the loops, squeezing my fingers inside them and pulling them apart.

Finally it released, I tugged on the rope hard, her arms dropped as did she, right into me.

As I caught her, a sensation wrapped around me, silken, my breath hitched. Heat from her spilled into me, my arm where the Mark was cooled, and a deep sense of calm filled my core.

"It's okay, I have you. Can you stand?"

I heard her swallow and slowly she seemed to regain her awareness. "Yes, maybe. What are those voices? I hate those voices!"

Without thinking, I wrapped my arm around her back, my free hand taking hers, and guided her to where I thought I'd tripped over the chair. As her hand gripped mine, a shot of desire spun through my veins, bolted around my body, speeding up my heart. I didn't know her, neither did she know me, but in that second, I remembered that I hadn't held another being, held a hand for over a thousand years. Not since...

Unfortunately, I had to let go of her hand. I felt around for the chair, stood it up, "Sit here for a moment, gather your strength. Let me help your friend, then I'll get us out of here."

"But who are you, you're not with him, are you? We knew you weren't with him; your energy is different. Conflicted!"

I cleared my throat. "No, I am not with Cain. It doesn't matter who I am, I was looking for my kin who Cain has taken. It appears they're not here."

I thought about scolding that damned vampire, but had I not come here, these two, and she was clearly human, well... I dreaded to think why Cain had them here.

Carefully I tread through the room to the back wall, following the sparse blue light which on closer inspection was runes tattooed and illuminating faintly.

"You okay? I have no weapons, Cain took mine. I'll just..."

He croaked, "I'm Austin. You're... you're not human, are you?"

I didn't answer, which in hindsight may had made the situation tenser. Again, I reached up over the captor. The knotted rope was damp, which made it stick together. Struggling, my arms started to burn.

"I found this." The woman held out something that caught the faint glow of this man's tattoos. "Careful, it's sharp."

My eyes had become slightly accustomed to that darkness. Reaching around I slowly took it, then holding my breath I pulled myself up high to reach the rope. Placing my left hand between the jagged piece of glass she had handed me, using my hand as a shield for the captor, I sliced the rope.

It cut the bondage fast, quickly moving the glass, my hand to the side as the guy fell forward into me, my other arm wrapped around him, steadying him.

"It's okay, I've got you," I muttered as his limp body fell onto mine.

"Austin, sit here." The woman helped me guide Austin to the chair. He panted, and I felt his clammy skin under my palms as I sat him down. He had no shirt on. The tattoos on his arms and chest faded. They were intriguing. I'd never seen glowing tattoos like that before. Some looked ancient, not unlike the Enochian symbols, I had a hunch that he hadn't gotten these etched on his skin.

The noise outside continued, the woman frustrated, angry, snapped, "What the hell are they saying? Why won't they shut the hell up?"

Austin went to speak, but his dry throat made him cough.

Drawn to touch her, to relive that immense calm I had felt when I held her, I reached for her arm and found her hand. She didn't pull away. My heart in my throat, I clasped it lightly.

"Be not afraid... I am Lucifer, though Cain has taken my divine power and now I'm not sure what I am. The voices, there are faces in the bricks, they are chanting for me to go back to Hell. I escaped to rescue my brothers, but my path so far has led me here. Cain has gone for now, I think, but not before torturing me. What about you? Has he hurt you, either of you? Can you walk?"

I felt her waver, but she didn't let go. She swallowed hard, her breathing loud. "Lucifer, the fallen angel? You were God's favourite son. I never understood why your father cast you to Hell, he made you. I'm sorry for that." She gripped tighter, and as she did, I found myself aching for her, her words, her energy pulsing through me like the light I've always searched for and never found until today. Except for Lilith, no other has seen me first as an angel, then the Devil. I shuddered.

Except now I was no angel, I was the horned beast... I bit back the deepest sadness.

"I'm Eva, a friend of Austin's. He's a mage, a true mage born to it. I'm human. I'm a veterinary medic who stumbled into witchcraft. I'm fairly good at magic thanks to Austin's teaching. Cain... yes, he brought us here and stole our magic. Then left us here to rot, as he so eloquently told us. Other than being in agony from being tied up like that, weak, cold, we're alright. Austin, can you walk?"

"Yes, I think so Eva. Lucifer... I knew I sensed an angel here but then that force vanished, blacked out."

Clearing my throat, intrigued I asked, "You treat animals? How did you become a witch?"

Austin managed a chuckle answering before she had the chance. "She found out her boss is a werewolf. So, that'll do it."

I heard him stand, stumble, and grab the chair. Letting go of Eva's hand, I rushed to him, wrapping my arm under and around his body. "Come, let me help you." Slowly we walked towards the door. "Eva, the corridor is narrow, but walk in front, will you? I can't see you if you walk behind, I may not have my heavenly powers, but I have something else. I will protect you, both of you, if I can."

She said nothing, but at the doorway I waited with Austin, who was weak as she stepped past us.

She recoiled at the moving faces. Their voices on seeing us grew louder, and I realised then there were hundreds of them protruding from the wall. All shapes, sizes, all male. Part of a face, eyes open, glancing with menace, noses, mouths, they looked like stone, but stone obviously doesn't speak.

"Maledictus murum!" Austin choked, his voice hoarse.

I nodded. "Yes, the cursed wall."

"What are they? There're hundreds of them." Eva flinched again as we walked slowly past the faces as they spat their insults at me. I thought in that moment I could probably stop them, if I let the evil of the Mark take me, let the beast out. And Hades! As much as I wanted them to stop, I couldn't do that. Not that!

Austin mumbled, "They are the enchanted keepers of the damned in the abbey. They are the stuff of legends, made by magic to oversee and guard all who enter catacombs or vaults under holy places. No one believed they really existed.

With all the malice from Cain, my guess is it activated their spell."

She gasped, walking gradually ahead, turning to squint at me. "Can you stop them?"

"No."

It was another form of torture. The same words repeated again and again in every brick on every wall, shouting for me to go to Hell. Mental onslaught, and that was the point. It would terrify any human, as Eva was. But as she apparently worked for a werewolf, she was obviously more seasoned than most mortals. How much more did she know? She didn't recoil from me, rather she had sympathy for me. That shocked me to my core. As for her energy... I felt an addiction to her unlike any other I had known.

Austin and Eva both shook slightly as they walked. She twitched at every noise. A strange yearning churned inside me to protect this mortal witch. The mage seemed scared but more capable, and I suspected he had experienced situations before. Mages, it goes with the job. Human witches though, not so much.

Silently I thanked my father for guiding me here, if indeed he had guided me here. In her presence the Mark ceased to have power over me, a tranquillity that I hadn't known since before my fall. And it seemed she had no idea. But my mind wasn't content with that, not trusting happiness, not after so long spent in pain. Could it be a trick? Were they really working for Cain, and when we got back to the room where Cain had left me, would he be waiting, cigar in mouth laughing, the door to the iron maiden open and ready for me? Would they laugh? Maybe she was just humouring me and actually hated the Devil?

If I turned into that beast, she would hate me. They all would, they will all turn their backs on me and damn me. My shoulders felt heavy, a thick knot churned and writhed in my stomach. I was no longer an angel. I was a thing, both immortal and monster. A foreboding clung to me like a wet coat, heavy, impending.

Eventually we left the corridors of talking faces and came to the room where I had such fond memories. Austin's face was a pale shade of green, Eva's drained of colour.

"There's nothing here, just an old bottle of whiskey which I fear won't do you any good. If you can, we need to go up, I think, to find a way out."

Weakly Austin unwrapped himself from my arm and pointed to a table. "Books, there're books. Could be spells?"

I strode over, followed by Eva as Austin staggered, wanting to stand on his own two feet.

"There, look, an old copy of 'The Dragon Rouge,' something there will help us." Austin leaned over to get it, his arm shaking, so I grabbed it and laid it on the table before him.

"Bloody hell, this place is creepy as shit! I thought I'd imagined those skulls, I'm guessing they're real? What the hell are they, I mean, I know the vampire one? But no, on second thought, maybe I don't want to know..." Eva strained, her eyes wide in horror.

Leaning on the table, I found myself lost in her eyes. "It is," I pointed, "Werewolf caught mid-change. The other is a Wendigo and honestly, the final one, I've no idea."

She spluttered a nervous laugh. "And maybe best not to know, huh?" Holding my gaze, it was I who felt enchanted. Shaking my head, I had to focus, I couldn't forget who I was, what I was. What she saw was a dream, a story, the fallen angel. Not a monster who had punished the wicked in Hell.

I concentrated on the grimoire. "What is the 'The Dragon Rouge'?"

Nodding as he poured over it, Austin looked at me. "It's a shorter version of the Grand Grimoire, or the Red Dragon, you've heard of that, surely?"

I grinned at him. "I should have, shouldn't I?"

Eva moved to stand next to me, her arm rested against mine as we three leaned over the book. "The Grand Grimoire, the Devil's book. Did you write it?"

I puckered my lips, scanning her face. "I should have. But no. I have practised magic though, I learned a fair bit in Hell."

Austin perked up, staring at me. "What magic did you practise?"

Hitching my breath, I answered, "Chaos magic."

He rolled his lips, nodding. "Blood or sex?"

"Excuse me?"

A cheeky grin on his face and a slight blush. "How did you release the power, make the spell work, with blood or sex?"

"Ah, blood. Not much selection for sex in Hell."

Smirking, Austin cast his eyes on the book, mumbling, "You can do that yourself you know. Geez..."

Sighing, I kept looking at the book, Austin piped up, "We could, you could use chaos magic now to help us get out, get our power or some energy back?"

"Ha, I'm not that good, and the Mark..." I decided they should see. They should know what I am. Pulling off my jacket, Austin's eyes narrowed, whilst Eva ran her fingers delicately around it sending a blaze of tingling sensations through me.

I gasped loudly as she did that, trembling.

"Sorry, does that hurt?"

Trying to maintain my control. "Quite the contrary, I assure you. When you touch me... I feel lighter, calmer."

Austin added, "Not just that, though, huh?" Then shooting me a weary smile. "I trained her myself."

"So, it's just magic, magic to control people?" My heart sank, even though it shouldn't feel, anyway.

"Uh, no. I mean I can normally do that, use magic to evoke feelings, both in a witchcraft sense and in a human, physical sense as anyone can. I'm not doing that now, I'm too bloody scared." She looked hurt.

"Oh."

Boom, boom, boom... shut up heart.

Yes, I like her. She and Austin were both shorter than me, Eva's tossed hair, though filthy was strewn about her shoulders. A faint shade of auburn curls contrasted with her dark brows. As for Austin his hair would normally be, I guessed a dark blond, but it was full of dirt, cobwebs, flecks of blood. He was lithe, young; she was older. I could tell by the lines on her face, she seemed twice his age. And age was something I hadn't thought about for a long time. She had a vitality about her, she seemed younger. Her eyes, though dark, tired seemed to penetrate right into me, soulful, yearning. Her touch... divine.

I stole my mind away from her and back to the present. "The Mark from Cain, it is a curse. It has its own power, making me want to lash out, to kill. You should know that. Eva, your touch seems to subdue it. If it's not witchcraft, then I don't know how. As for how I look, I didn't look like this when I entered Hell. My hair was short, though dark. The tattoos were scratched on me by demons who I befriended, though of those I could count on one hand. They helped me, aided my force, my power. Where I was once light, good, now... well, that's a grey area."

"Nah, man, all magic is grey. No such thing as purely good, well maybe for angels, but," Austin shrugged, "I've come across some Grigori, one of which I know. Asael, from what he says, well I'd say there's a fine line, and some of them overstep that. Some of them ain't good for sure, and they're angels! Maybe none of us can be one or the other, but we can certainly focus on what we want to be. Whatever you focus on, you get more of. Everyone knows that. I focused on getting out of here, and look." He pointed. "A spell to do just that. But as you said, the Dragon Rouge isn't a book of good magic. We need to call upon a demon?"

"Ok, stop right there. I will do the chaos magic, using blood to find a way out, or we could just keep searching?"

"No, we need magic, this place is soaking in it. Cain used magic to lure us here, drained our power and yours, we can't just walk out of the door," Austin argued, fatigued.

I leaned away from the table. "What if we try, you know, to just walk out?" Eva groaned.

"I wouldn't. It's not like something good will happen, and what actually is that? Is that what he did to you?" A sheen of sweat broke on Austin's forehead as he looked around him, seeing the iron maiden.

"Yes. Forget it, I do not want to talk about it. I'll-"

"Lucifer! Bloody hell!" Eva grabbed my arm.

I looked away from her, hiding my anger and my clenched jaw.

"Ah, that's when he stole your divine force, I see. Cain brought us all here to steal our power." Austin sighed, his face had a green sheen to it. I had to get them out, they looked weaker than me. His voice croaked, "Chaos magic, I know a little. For chaos magic to work, for any magic to work, you set an intention. You have to be one hundred percent sure of the outcome before you begin. For extra potency, and chaos, you use our own blood to paint sigils. The sigils that you see in your mind during the ritual. That's how I was taught."

I nodded. Eva touched my arm, I withheld a shudder, her cheeks reddened. "We'll help. We may not have any magic left, but both Austin and I know how to wield it. And look, we are three, the divinity: father, son, holy spirit in your beliefs, or in mine: maiden, mother, crone."

"Three, a small coven. Good thinking Eva, glad I taught you. Let's clear a space, geez, matches for the candles? I can't even spin fire. I'm impotent."

Eva giggled "So I'd heard. Come on Lucifer, you need some space."

Austin shot her a playful glare. Even in this torment, these two were a force. Indomitable, it seemed. I certainly hoped so.

I cleared a space. Although their spirits were improved, they were both weak, though fighting through it. Knowing that Cain could return at any time I didn't want to spend longer there, and tempting as it was for Austin to use a spell that had originated from the Grand Grimoire, with his lack of magic, and Eva's, and my lost celestial power that had the potential to go horribly wrong. Magic like that, well you paid a price, and you needed protection. So I sat on the floor with the intention of we three standing outside Aaron's house with Aaron answering the door.

Eva handed me the jagged piece of glass from earlier. I swallowed. It was all I had. I guessed it might work well with the Mark? A nagging in my stomach, I decided to change my intention, to see both Eva and Austin outside this place and not myself. As I was now wielding black magic, that had consequences that I didn't want them to become entangled with.

"I don't want either of you involved. This magic, despite what you say Austin, is tapping into malevolent forces, so it is just to be used to get you safely out of here. Any consequences will be mine and mine alone. Is that understood? And I need you both to promise because if I sense your involvement, I will stop. I am not joking. What I have seen, endured, done in Hell is worse than either of you can possibly imagine. That's it right there, that's the energy I have to link with. Whatever happens to me, whatever you see, get out. Now, do you both promise?"

"We won't leave, without you we'd be lost. That's my promise, Devil or no!" Austin replied.

"You will and you will promise. Neither of you have any power, any magic. There is darkness in me, it wants, it bays for blood. I'm telling you this, both of you, to save your lives. I cannot die, I have the Mark. As it stands, both of you can."

Ave Lucifer

As I settled myself, I realised just how fast, how much my life, solemn as it was, had changed. In the space of a few days I had changed. I'd never thought of another until I met Cerberus. It was painful to my core that I was learning this lesson now, now that the beast had awakened. It was too late for me and yet... I had to maintain a chasm, a distance to protect them from me.

Enough pity...

Closing my eyes, flashes of the torture came in full colour along with pangs of pain, my breathing became juddered. Concentrating, I held the jagged glass in my left hand, visualizing Eva and Austin outside this place, smiling. Seeing them safe. Breathing into that visualisation I had set the intention. Their safety.

But I felt nothing.

I tried again, seeing the sunlight on their faces, crowds of people around them, the noise, the smells of the city. Fumes and cologne, brightly adorned shop fronts. I could almost taste it.

And still I got nothing. I was doing it wrong.

What I needed was to channel anger. Channel the darkness inside of me.

Pulling off my jacket, my T-shirt, I tossed them aside, knelt down, my head tipped forward.

I thought about my life in Hell, the atrocities I'd seen, the pain I'd inflicted on those of an evil nature. Of how I was now, with no celestial connection or magic, a monster of nightmares with only hatred and evil to guide me.

I had tried to be good, to be the angel that I once was.

A pang in my belly as I had longed for that so badly it pulled on my heart.

But it was not to be so, it seemed. Everything pushed against me. The Mark, my stolen divinity, the beast inside me. Maybe the only way left for me was to embrace the darkness, the evil... maybe I could control it? Use it.

The scent of fatty meat choked in the back of my throat as my skin blistered. I thought of how my family had left me to rot, to become this foul shadow when my only crime had been to question my father, and my stomach clamped at that isolation. That sensation suffocated me, my breath hitching.

Slicing the jagged glass across my palms, my blood flowed freely. I placed one finger into my bleeding hand and shuffled backwards on my knees.

Breathing deeply, I started to draw using my blood, allowing whatever shapes to flood out from my finger and daubing these onto the floor. A spiral, its tail swiftly swirled up making a vertical line with a cross near the top. An arrow head at the end of the vertical line above the cross.

I drew it again, giving the symbol intense focus so that my vision blurred slightly, then a warming sensation bubbled throughout me, my limbs and my breathing now sinking into the magic. Every time I drew it the heat inside me intensified, my heart hotter and the vision of Eva, of Austin being safe was clearer.

Leaning back on my heels, my eyes adjusted at the sigils I'd painted. Now dozens of them. My eye lids heavy, lowering them I slowed my breathing, allowing the picture of the sigil to wash through my mind, over and over and over. Trance... Without realising what I had done, I tasted my blood, my tongue licking my bloody palm, the coppery scent rich in my mouth. Shivering, I had become aware that some time had passed, I swayed from dizziness. Now I needed to release this energy, to send out my intention, my focus into the universe.

With my head back, I started to roar, to bellow, the vibrations echoing throughout my limbs, the floor, reflecting back into me. I heard panting, heaving for breath, my chest heavy, jerking. It took me a moment to realise it was myself making that noise.

I was lost in heady, erotic iniquity.

As I focused on the icons before me, smeared on the ground, a crimson mist appeared before my eyes. Caught up in the enchantment, through the red fog, I sighed and was distracted. Staring at the wall in front of me, the candle light quivering, an ominous shadow of the beast, huge, muscular, long muzzled and massive curved horns, it taunted me.

My skin prickled ice cold as I heard its unearthly roar tremble right through my body. Its silhouette mocked me, bipedal animal legs, it revealed itself in the flickering light, leering forwards.

I was looking at myself.

My eyes disappeared in their sockets, my head thrust back. Consumed with an energy that twisted and clung to my core, my heart, the words spewed from my mouth, getting louder, echoing around me.

Lucifer malum, Lucifer malum, Lucifer malum.

Evil Lucifer.

Still chanting, I opened out my arms, writhing in the dark ecstasy of my shadow self.

The thick scent of blood and burning flesh, in that delirium so dark, so formidable l became obsessive, carnal, powerful.

Lucifer malum...

I felt myself lifted but just red blood before my eyes and my feet almost off the ground I panted, unaware of anything else except that toxic, alluring sensual energy. I surrendered to it, embraced it. I was no longer a fallen angel.

Now, now I was the darkness that lesser men feared. Now I was the beast.

It was so... *addictive.*

Salvete Lucifer.

Hail Lucifer.

A warm breeze travelled over me, soothing my skin when I found myself crouched over, arms splayed by my side, laying in my blood.

A glimmer of dread as I realised that they, Austin and Eva, must have seen the beast. Caught up in the delirium I had completely forgotten they had been there, now an icy shiver of sweat dripped down my back, but I realised her hand was on my shoulder, soothing me.

But nobody knew what was inside of me until now, and I braced to face their reaction. I didn't know them, only that she, Eva, seemed to calm the storm raging in my soul, and as I came around, with her flesh on my flesh a flash of benevolence came upon me.

I splattered a cheerless laugh of shame, remembering the whole ritual in every rich detail.

"Lucifer, Lucifer, are you alright? It worked, you broke the spell on this place." Her voice whispered urgently, so close to my ear I could taste her breath.

"Shit, Lucifer, you nearly brought the whole abbey down! Whoa, I never knew, the whole beast thing was real, I thought that was just fantasy. Wow, better than a werewolf, or even a dragon shifter. You were... magnificent!" Austin bellowed.

That wasn't the response I imagined getting. Staggering up, Eva gripped my arm to aid me. I had to fight the urge to shrug away, not that I didn't welcome her touch, but I didn't need her help and I was too proud to take it. Normally.

They were right. In the haze, I hadn't been aware of my surroundings. Rubble lay strewn around the room. A thick musty smell caught in the back of my throat as the dust hung heavy in the air like a grey fog. The walls remained, just loose bricks had fallen and some plaster from the ceiling. The bookcases had toppled, and books and the morbid skulls that had hung from the walls laid scattered about the place.

I pursed my lips together to withhold a smirk. The power that I'd wielded felt good. Intoxicating. I knew it was bad, dark, but also... addictive.

Beaming, Austin handed me my T-shirt and jacket, my eyes averted I frowned.

"It was no good thing what I did, Austin. Do not make light of it. I have... a terrible darkness, I have unleashed something atrocious. I doubt I can control it, though I will try."

Pulling on my jacket, I narrowed my eyes at both of them. Eva had fear in her eyes but also something else.

Wonder.

I cautioned them. "Say nothing about this to anyone. Not Aaron, especially not the Nephilim. What you saw, well, the last being who saw that is dead. By my own hands." I shrugged.

"Look, maybe I sound harsh, but..." I looked down at the symbols on the ground, "I never wanted that, any of it. I wanted to be... never mind. Never speak of it to anyone or to me."

I stared at the doorway and simply held out my arm, my palm facing so they could lead the way out whilst I contemplated how the hell I was going to manage the evil I had succumbed to.

I acted like I was ashamed, being something they had not expected. After all they had thought me a fallen angel. But I was not. For as long as I had lived I had wanted to be the angel once again, my father's favourite. Not only redeemed but welcomed. But now, after that ritual, that was a lie. And because I had been with little power for so long, this energy felt delicious.

I had welcomed the dark curse.

Frowning as I walked, I reasoned I would take steps to protect those I cared about, which until recently was only myself. And yet, within just a few days, that list had grown, which was ironic under the circumstances.

Cerberus, was I even safe to be around him, or Aaron now? Now that I knew I had unleashed it? But the beast had not broken through my body. If I could just hold it back long enough.

Austin led the way. Unlike me, he was animated. But he was a mage, so it was all just knowledge to him. A new experience for his grimoire.

Stepping carefully over the fallen bricks and pieces of ceiling along a dust hazed corridor, I shuddered at what I had done. Shuddered with pleasure.

I stopped abruptly amidst the chaos. "Eva, Austin, I haven't thanked you. You both could have run, you stayed. I... I-"

Her smile sent hope into me. "Lucifer, we promise we won't say anything. The Devil, the beast... well, Austin and I, we know werewolves, and met some both good and bad. You are not evil, you're still a fallen angel. Maybe without your celestial link. If you had not channelled the Mark's power, we'd still be stuck. You have to use what you've got. Play the cards you are dealt."

Austin grinned, narrowing his eyes. "I thought it was kind of erotic, if I'm honest, in a dark magic kind of way. I wouldn't sweat it, you should see some of the rituals I do. At least you kept your trousers on." He puckered his lips. "Well, this way your unholy majesty."

I liked him.

Their easy-going attitude still stunned me, but they were casual because they didn't understand the seriousness of this. No one could, only those who have lived, breathed the horror of Hell, who have heard the screaming, the constant torture that haunts the mind. And it never stops. I had unleashed my darkness into the world and they seemed to accept it. Fools. But kind fools at that.

With an ease Austin led us up the corridor. "These places follow the same layout. If you've been in one abbey, you know them all. Getting to the cloisters, usually not too hard. Cain drained our power but sealed this place up with something old, dead. My guess, he used a vampire grimoire, which is especially nasty as this is an abbey."

"A vampire grimoire?" I asked, watching my step.

"Sure, most supernatural species have them. Still, that's all I'm saying, now my turn, I'd ask you say nothing about that to anyone."

"And you know this how?" I queried him.

Eva twisted her neck to glance behind her at me. "Austin does some work for supes, I've helped him, though most are unaware a human is involved. It's mostly private, so we'd ask you to keep our secret. We'll keep yours."

I nodded, then replied, "Of course. And you know where these grimoires are kept?"

He shrugged as he trudged on. "No. But I'm guessing Cain has them."

"Why would he bother to go to all this trouble, no offense, to get your power?"

Austin stopped and spun around. "Because I am, or I was the most powerful mage, second only to... oh shit! Joash! I, we need to check he is alright." Austin glared at Eva, worry tugging at his features. Then looking to me, he said, "God only knows why he has your brothers, but he is amassing power, he's taken ours. Fortunately, he didn't take our secrets, phew. Otherwise," he pointed ahead, "When we walk out that door, well, there may not be much city left. Onwards, I need to contact Joash. He is the most powerful witch."

I withheld the information that Cain had told me about ending all things. For one, I didn't know if I could trust them yet, though my hunch said yes. Second, they had enough to contemplate, especially her.

"Austin, Eva, tell me then, what's the difference between a mage and a witch?"

Austin shot me a grin. "None really. Though back in the day, during the medieval times, the term witch meant someone who worked with demons. For me, I was born with this power, for Eva she wasn't. Joash actually identifies as a witch, not a mage. Warlock comes from the Scottish word deceiver or traitor." He glanced at Eva, who nodded. Then he continued stepping over the rubble, looking back at me at intervals. "Witches used the term warlock during the inquisition to describe anyone who, under torture, gave away names of coven members, but it was never gender specific. For that reason, we don't use it."

Warlock. A traitor...

As we trudged through the corridor, light poured in above us, the walkway opening up. Cool air lifted my spirits, Eva took the opportunity to ask me, "So Lucifer, *the* Lucifer, I always had a hunch you were nothing like what they write about you. I mean, it is said you're proud, vain, and that you believed that you should succeed your father, and..." she glanced back at me wide-eyed, "That you hated humans?"

I smirked. "Some of that is true. I didn't like your species. After my father created you, he discarded us angels, and as his favourite son, I didn't handle that very well. But, isn't it natural for a son to want to succeed his father? As for the arrogance and the pride, they were right. Spending an eternity in Hell, well it's hard to be proud in a place full of the wicked, and... well, never mind."

"And evil. You're so not that."

Austin chimed in, "Yeah Eva, but people say that about us, they say that those who practise magic are damned."

"Evil, that depends on your perspective. I wasn't all good in Hell, I punished sinners."

As she turned her head towards me, she frowned. "I won't ask."

"Good, because I won't tell you. In Hell, well hopefully you'll never know, but you cannot comprehend it unless you have spent time there. Punishment of evil doers was," I shrugged, "What I had to do."

"Do you regret it?"

I thought, pausing. "No. They were vile souls, heinous, cruel."

And thus began, perhaps, my real descent into darkness....

"Well I suppose sometimes, like the ritual you have to use what you've got, it's not like you were given a choice," she replied, still clinging to the hope that my soul could be saved.

After that ritual, my soul was beyond saving. It had already fallen too far from grace.

As we neared the cloister a bitter chill sent a shiver over me. An icy breeze blew fresh, cold for springtime. Not that I'd seen springtime in eons.

As we stepped out of the door, Eva and Austin cheered. Snow fell in heavy clumps, twinkling the light. Falling in an array of silver and white feathery clumps and had already settled outside the abbey. I knew about snow, my memory vague, but I had never actually seen it.

Their faces bright, full of laughter, Eva grabbed my hand. "Come on, snow fight!"

But before she could finish, Austin had skipped ahead, grabbed a handful and slung it at her, thudding on her back as she spoke to me.

A flash of anger in me was lost as she blurted out a laugh, scooped up a handful and threw at him. He dodged and it landed on a statue, splattering everywhere.

I bent down and felt the icy substance hard in my palms. Something trembled through me, the warm sensation like bubbling water, stirring in my belly, my heart, my limbs.

Laughter.

I threw it at Austin; it whacked him on the back as he strode off laughing.

Maybe I could handle the fire inside of me, maybe it was all about balance?

"I need to get to Aaron's house, what about you two?" I asked them.

Eva smiled at Austin, then at me, a handful of snow melting in her hand, "We'll come with you. Then we'll need to go to Joash's, if he'll see us." She rolled her eyes.

"See you?"

"He's quite a big deal. Come on, we'll tell you on the way. Aaron's home is a twenty-minute walk from here."

I eyed her hand; she stared at the snow, then at Austin, and we started walking.

Thud!

"Thanks, Eva!" I grinned. My first snowball. I shivered as the icy liquid melted down my neck, then my back.

Austin glanced back. "Hey, Lucifer! You don't look like what I imagined, I thought you'd have short hair, be kind of cherub looking? You're taller, though."

Yes!

I could hear Cerberus barking outside in Aaron's garden when we got there. Aaron was all smiles, red faced jumping around with the puppy who looked much better. As we walked in Cerberus ran to me, yapping and flicking his tail erratically. For a second I paused, I saw that Aaron noticed, his eyes narrowed, then I picked up the dog. In my hands it was a similar feeling to Eva's touch, a calmness spread through my body. The beast inside me settled.

"Hello! Yes, no thanks." I moved my head away as Cerberus tried to lick my face, spluttering. "I don't want your licks!" I looked to Aaron. "So, how has he been? He looks better."

"He's mint. So, no brothers? Austin, Eva, how come you're here, not that it isn't good to see you both."

Austin moaned. "Oh Aaron, would you make us some coffee please mate? Cain, the old bastard, kidnapped me and Eva. We are knackered, poor Eva. I was teaching her when he grabbed us, used my own magic against me, the wily sod. He stole our magic, and," he glanced at me, winking, "Lucifer's mojo. Lucifer here rescued us, Michael and Gabriel weren't there. I think, I think the only reason Cain had a beacon to alert Luci here to the abbey was so he could steal his angelic grace."

"Bloody hell!" Aaron traipsed in from the garden, the snow on his boots melting fast on the floor. Standing before me, his eyes narrowed. He was blurring his vision. We see differently than mortals, we see energy. By squinting he could read the energy signatures from me. These are usually as UV light. For me now, without my celestial connection, I couldn't see as much.

Realising the cold chill that whipped through the little room, Aaron turned and closed the door.

"Lucifer, are you alright? You look... different." His brows met. I knew he could sense the darkness, but he wouldn't say it, not here, not now.

Aaron swallowed hard, his eyes downcast for a moment. "Lucifer, sit." He took a deep breath. "Austin, Eva, sure, please sit down. Tell me everything. Biscuits?"

Austin laughed dramatically. "You're the best, Aaron." Austin leaned towards me. "Whenever I've been in some bleeding immortal scrapes, Aaron always knows how to help, whether it's patching me up or feeding me biscuits. I love him, I really do. He's the older brother I never had."

Aaron smiled, his cheeks slightly flushed then disappeared into the kitchen whilst we waited. Cerberus sniffed my dirt strewn clothes, his icy wet feet leaving patches on my jeans. I used my hand as a toy, Cerberus tried to catch it on my lap and in that moment it seemed surreal to me that I was a monster. Do monsters play with dogs?

Striding back with a purpose—and coffee and biscuits—Aaron placed them on the table, nudging Cerberus's head out of the way as the dog made a dive for the biscuits.

"No chance tummy boy. Look at you, hey. Getting a bit of pot belly already." Then Aaron's face looked slightly sterner towards me. "Don't let him eat them Lucifer, they'll give him an upset stomach. I have fed him. Come here, Cerby."

But he didn't. After grabbing and growling at my sleeve and me tickling his stomach, my dog crashed out on my lap. But he watched wide eyed with every biscuit that I picked up, dribbling onto my jeans.

Aaron sat next to me, coffee in hand. "Before you all spill the beans, Lucifer, something that's bugging me. I really need to know..."

I swallowed hard; he was about to say that he sensed an overwhelming evil in me, that darkness... They would fight me, take away Cerberus. I would be on my own. Again. Left alone to find my brothers, try to save them even though my soul was now beyond redemption and acceptance was now just a dream, I braced. Ready for another fall...

Aaron's voice strained, its pitch high. I waited as he sized me up.

"Lucifer, why do you hate vampires so much? I mean, what are they to you?"

The relief!

I sniggered, what a question- I mean, where do I begin? "I hated humans for the longest time. Weak, flawed, yet destructive creatures. But I came to see something of a spark in them, well some of them at least. No matter how flawed mortals are, their sense of mortality gives them an edge- unlike us, they possess an urgency of being, of living. And they create such beauty, such love that we don't fully comprehend. But vampires? What do they create? Death. They suck the life force out of a human and create more like themselves. They are soulless abominations, a perversion of life, of my father's creation. They create nothing except fear. And more death. Like parasites feasting on the vibrancy of life. Or perhaps I am mistaken?"

Aaron raised and lowered his brows whilst eating a biscuit, shrugged and added, "Oh, ok. I never liked them, either, the whole parasite thing, but a few I tolerate. Even like. Though, like is a strong word. I know many never choose that life, Anthony and Nathaniel amongst others."

I looked straight ahead then at him. "Then perhaps taking their own life would benefit humanity? Though you said they feed on only the evil- if that's true I see a benefit to their existence, perhaps?"

After the words marched from my mouth, I remembered who I was. Not the archangel now. Now I was like them, the bloodsuckers. Just evil. Wearing the mask of an angel.

Aaron glanced at me, then the mage who was chomping biscuits at a rate I couldn't keep up with.

"So, your brothers, Lucifer... Austin, will you scry for him?"

Austin, never one for formalities, spoke through a mouthful of crumbs, half covering his mouth with his hand, trying hard not to spit them everywhere, nodded. "I need to check if Joash is safe, but yes, we'll scry..." he swallowed, took a mouthful of coffee and continued, "We'll find them, Lucifer. Within the hour, I promise you that. If Eva will help?"

Eva was almost keeping up with him on the biscuit score and nodded sincerely.

"So Cain took the flaming sword, I see you don't have it?"

I nodded. Too weary to speak, Cain had taken everything. Cain... of all the immortals. No one saw it coming. But we should have.

I mumbled, "Yes. The sword, my brothers, my grace..."

"Alright. I have swords, let me find you one. You're sure you don't want me to help?"

The sugary biscuits and coffee helped a little, but my soul was weary. I know they needed rest, to eat, but I was still no closer to finding Michael or Gabriel. Anger welled inside me, an urge to fight, to spill blood. Cain's blood specifically. A restlessness that gnawed at my heart. Cerberus nuzzled into me. He helped, more than he could ever know.

Aaron got up, paced behind the sofa and pulled out that large box.

I picked up Cerberus, stood up and turned to Aaron. "No. I am done with swords, but thank you. Swords won't help me now. Cain took my sword using magic, so I will go without. I have another weapon, the Mark."

His smile dropped, looking down at the box then back up to me. "No weapon? Are you sure?"

"Yes, I am."

After all, I had something more potent, more powerful inside me now. I just had to unleash it.

Fire of God

The complete opposite of Aaron's home, and more like the vampire's home, Joash's house was a relic of the Georgian opulence found in excess in this city. In a crescent overlooking a manicured park surrounded by coppiced trees and edged with cast-iron railings, the honey stone houses looked down over the city. Ballasted roofs, pillared doors and imposing windows displayed decadence and uniformity. Power.

Austin in his eagerness had been quick to tell us that these houses sold for no less than five million pounds each.

Seemed it was profitable then, being a witch in this time.

Trying and failing to suppress his excitement, Austin gasped. "Ah, look, a white Ferrari, Joash's!"

"A what?"

"The car, the one with the horse logo?"

Something about that jolted a memory from long ago. A white car. A horse. An image of a white horse flashed through my mind but was lost again as Austin grabbed Eva's arm, his voice loud. "We're here... number thirteen. Of course!"

I smirked, what? Well, Austin had proved himself, so I guessed this influencer witch as he'd called him could be helpful. I needed them to find my brothers. I could do the rest.

Even the door knocker was witchy, coiled through an oval drop, a cast of a bronze snake was mounted on a square plate, Austin's face beaming as he pulled out his phone, blinding us all with his flash as he took a picture.

Whispering to Cerberus, who was tucked inside my jacket, I said, "This is going to be a long night. Now tell me if this witch is trustworthy..."

Cerberus responded by licking my chin, making me chuckle and twist my face away. I placed my hand over my pup's head, the other rested on my sword hilt.

Influencer. What the holy hell did that even mean?

Eva shot me a look, raising her brows, I grinned like a fool. Every time she did that, flames of passion rippled through my veins. I mirrored her actions, then rolled my eyes. Austin certainly seemed to have a dose of hero worship. Let's hope his icon lived up to his expectations.

The door opened, and before us stood Joash. Narrow, hooded eyes slowly surveyed us. His long blond lashes veiled ice-blue eyes, wide plump lips made his grin cat-like. Dark blond hair fell to his shoulders, outlining the high cheekbones in his elongated face. For a human he exuded a regal, quiet power.

His voice mirrored his cool calm demeanour, impassive but he gestured with his hands. "Ah, yes, the Devil, our father, of course... Do come in, make yourselves at... home." He swept behind the door, extending his arm out in one swift move. Austin gushed, I eyed the witch who held my stare and although he kept his face stoic, a light seemed to blaze from behind his eyes.

As he stepped behind me, closing the door, he brushed my arm. "Ah, a familiar. How interesting, I keep quite a collection myself."

The hallway was... huge. Elaborate monochrome floor tiles drew the eye towards the passageway, and glinting above silver orbs of light dappled the cream ceiling and walls, diffused from a delicate crystal chandelier. The place oozed affluence and elegance. Austin was right, the place even smelt of wealth.

Austin spluttered, "So you're alright? You haven't been harmed by Cain? He stole our magic, can you help us Joash, please?"

His lips curved slightly up, a small nod of his head. "Who, Cain? No, I am perfectly fine. Cain, as in..."

"Yes, the immortal," I muttered.

Widening his eyes, he eyed us all. "Cain. The first murderer. Killed his brother, punished by God. I always thought his curse was somewhat..." He averted his eyes past us for a moment, then settled his gaze on me. Inside, the monster moved, rumbled. "I always thought God was rather harsh on Cain. So..."

His voice was smooth, like a lazy sunset. Each word prolonged, exacting, and I waited as Joash closed the large wooden door. He turned around and stepped right up to me, his eyes scanning my face. His breath smelt of copper and coffee, and for a moment I was transfixed, drawn to a familiarity that I could not place. Stepping right into my space, Joash locked his eyes with mine, I breathed him in- it was like breathing myself in. His eyes, a recognition that I had seen him before, those eyes, but I couldn't place him.

His eyes followed the outline of my cheekbones, his lips pressed tight as his hand went to touch my face. I flinched, Cerberus yelped and nipped him, a trickle of blood, but Joash merely exaggerated a grin.

Thanks, Cerberus.

Instead of anger, which had been my first instinct from him, Joash's expression changed to a smile that wrapped his whole face. "Aw, he's so protective. That is almost... adorable. Please, follow me." Sweeping around, he beckoned me to follow him, his eyes still looking me over, a sadistic laugh on his lips.

A large drawing room with a vast ceiling where Austin was wide-eyed looking at a life-size quartz skull that sat on a coffee table, the table made of amethyst and both reflected twinkling purple and silver beads of light around the walls, under a host of candle lit iron sconces placed around three walls of the room.

Again, like the door knocker, the sconces had serpents on them. I unzipped my leather jacket, noticing in that flickering light a few paintings hung on the walls. Dark and sinister charcoal sketches of witches screaming, being burned. How ironic, so he was a fake?

Heavy velvet drapes hung from the windows and trailed onto the floor in a languid, sumptuous manner, oozing luxury. As if they'd just been thrown up there.

Rubbing the back of my neck as I was hit by the humidity, a roaring fire burned in the fireplace. I noticed Eva's horrified look as she stared at the wall behind the door which was laden with vivariums. This guy had a thing for the dramatic. And snakes it seemed...

Joash stood silently for a moment eyeing us all over, brushed his hair from his face, chin thrust up, chest puffed. He had a deliberate elegance, a regal presence, all eyes on him. Withholding a smile his cheeks drawn in, the light behind his eyes betrayed him. He loved the attention. Demanded it.

"Ah, welcome. My assistant will bring us some tea." He picked up a small brass bell from the window ledge, rang it, then set it down. Then surveyed us over in silence again, a slight curve on his lips.

"Do you mind if I let Cerberus down?"

Moving his head towards me he made the smallest gesture, blinking and a nod. Then with palm splayed, he showed me to the white sofas opposite the table. "Not at all... though keep him away from my familiars, lest they eat him."

I set my dog down, Cerberus immediately went about sniffing. "Cerberus, heel." Flashing a smile at Eva, Aaron's little spell had worked.

Joash, seizing on the moment, his manner changed in an instant, he exclaimed, "That's cheating isn't it, using witchcraft to get your familiar to obey. I'd heard you were the Devil, and I mean, Lucifer, the one and only?"

"What's with all the snakes, over-compensating much?" Eva laughed.

Austin shot her an angry look, his eyes small, frowning, Eva ignored him, wide-eyed, a mischievous smirk on her lips.

I knew what she meant. Snakes, sex, the Devil... And Joash it seemed had a thing about the three. Dotted in the corners of the room hung masks of the Devil, which I may add bore no true resemblance at all. Their empty eye sockets taunting, menacing in the low flickering candlelight. Interesting that he, according to Austin, presented himself to the world as a force for good, yet here in his home the energy seemed a little shady.

For a second Joash's face was frozen, then dramatically he locked his eyes with hers and laughed loudly. "No! Over-compensating! Ha, not at all, but Eva, I will make an exception for you and show you later. That is a promise."

No, you bloody won't.

"So," I cleared my throat, demanding his attention, "Austin tells me you may help me find my brothers, find Michael and Gabriel?" I watched as Joash's chest rose and fell. Dressed from head to toe in black, his svelte outline, hair, narrow eyes, again something stirred. A pining from the past.

Before he could answer, I continued, "I don't know what Austin told you about me. What I know about you, you have thousands of followers, you're the most powerful witch in the UK, maybe the world..." To which Joash smiled, nodding gracefully.

I stayed where I was, eyeing his movements. "And yes, you're right, I am Lucifer. Fallen angel I am. Cain has my brothers, he has tortured them and I mean to kill him."

Joash strode over to me, watching out for Cerberus who sat obediently at my feet. He wagged his finger. "Now, now, little dog, behave." I stood taller, we were the same height, his scent familiar, woody, a hint of something sweet, exotic. Leaning into me, he whispered as that light glimmered behind his eyes, "Ah, you have the Mark. I sensed it as soon as you arrived. That must be hard, battling with all that anger?"

You have no idea...

I frowned as he spoke, right into my face it seemed like he was leaning in to kiss me, I moved my body back, my legs still. But he pushed harder, his eyes staring into mine as if to find my soul and rip it out. Whispering as he scanned my face, "Luci... fer. How I've longed to meet you." Then in an instant he spun around and strode over to the vivariums, opening one and gently coaxing out a pure white snake.

"I can help you, I will find your brothers, of that you can be assured. Austin is correct, of course, I am the most powerful witch in the world, and I can prove it. But..." he paused as his assistant, a young woman of about twenty, came in submissively, face downwards and dressed as he, in black, placed a tray down on the table. She set about pouring the drink into four ornate cups, then set the teapot back on the tray. As she did this, I noticed Joash's face almost frozen in silence, a small empty smile as the sound of the liquid echoed around the heavy silence.

Narrowing my eyes, I noticed Eva who was sat opposite the low table broke the awkward moment.

"Would you like a hand with that?"

Joash watched his assistant in silence and she neither looked at us or looked up, nor answered Eva. After she left, Eva challenged him. I really, really like her...

"Oh my God, do you have servants? What the hell was that?" Eva chided.

Licking his lips as he held the snake, Joash gazed slowly over Eva. My blood boiled inside watching him flirting with her, but I was in no position at that moment to annoy him. I didn't have that luxury with my brother's lives on the line. So, I bottled it, glancing down at my pup who was looking up at me. I rolled my eyes and Cerberus moved closer to my leg. I think he could feel my emotions, too.

Animated, Austin tried but failed to contain his excitement. "Joash, your house is incredible! Where did you learn your magic? I've watched all your videos, your live calls, I just can't find your sources for the magic you practice."

For a second a smug smile tugged at Joash's lips, then he changed his mind. "Austin, your reputation is higher than you realise. It is I who am honoured to meet you. I simply just put myself out there. I would be happy to share my knowledge with you in private." Then he smiled at Eva, that fire burning behind his eyes. "Eva, I don't have servants. I do pay my assistant a lot of money not to talk to me unless absolutely necessary. You'd be surprised how much idle gossip and rubbish people speak unless you pay them to shut the hell up. Am I right, Austin?"

Austin, caught off guard as he studied the massive amethyst table, looked about him. "I hate small talk Joash. Yes."

"Please sit, Lucifer. Eva, you're not fond of serpents? There is nothing to be afraid of, I assure you. Why, even in the garden, did Adam and Eve fear the snake? No... see, he is quite harmless."

Eva leaned away, a gleam of sweat on her brow.

"Come Cerberus." I walked over to where she sat, glowering at Joash, who merely laughed, and held the snake before her as he glanced at me, then her.

"Joash, don't force her. She's clearly not comfortable, and I can assure you Eva is brave."

Austin was on Joash's other side, leaning over his shoulder, but Joash ignored his fan, still staring at Eva, then me. "Eva, if you are to work with me, and you will, then you need to embrace all of your fears. Indeed, you need to welcome them, it is your fears, your overcoming them that defines who you are. And who you can become. I can assure you that Nachash here, a white boa is perfectly harmless." He laughed, looking to me and glancing over at Austin. "Why, he spends most of his time sleeping. Here, touch it... embrace your fear."

"Clever!" My voice echoed around the room, brash and cold. "And incorrect. You named him after the serpent in Genesis, but it wasn't me who tempted Eve to eat the apple, I had little interest in Eve or Adam, for that fact."

A sudden change in Joash's face, anger as his eyes narrowed. "No, no, you didn't, did you. Lilith was more your style." Then, almost as if correcting himself, he smiled, his features softened as he leaned into Eva. "Or so I hear."

Eva reached her hand out slowly, shaking, Joash's voice silken, "That's right. Don't be afraid. We imagine, or rather we create our own fears. What the snake teaches us is to shed those feelings that we bottle up, a rebirth, a transformation. We are immortal if we only recognise and reach our full potential."

Joash flashed me a smile. His eyes grew wider as he watched as Eva's hand slowly stroked the snake.

I was not comfortable with that symbology at all. But I bit my tongue and let the drama unfold.

As Eva touched the serpent's body, Joash shuddered. A wry grin, his tongue brushed his top lip as a shadow touched her face. My anger welled up, but my canine friend nestled again at my feet. Instinctively, I reached down and scooped him up still watching Eva.

But then Eva recoiled, frowning. A flash of anger moved across Joash's face as his lips pressed together tightly, he got up and moved away, almost in one stroke.

He took Nachash away; I noticed he slipped a gentle kiss on the snake's head as he whispered to it, placing it carefully into the vivarium.

Then turning to us, he beckoned me. "Please, have some tea."

Moving swiftly across the room, he placed himself next to Eva, flashing me a smile as he poured milk into the teacups before handing them on their fragile saucers to us. I sat opposite him and Eva with Austin alongside me.

Bobbing flames from the candles cast shadows and from the corner of my eye it looked like a figure crept across the room, but on looking there was nothing. A quick glance at Cerberus revealed he was enraptured by something I certainly could not see.

Wetting his lips, Joash leaned against Eva. "Your boyfriend here doesn't trust me, and that is good. You see, I don't trust him, for who would be fool enough to trust the Devil? But I will help, I am happy to. And in fact, I'm honoured you asked me. So, tell me what you already know, and we four shall hatch some magic this very night, but first I would speak to Lucifer in private, if you consent?" His face questioned me.

Without looking at Eva and Austin I nodded, handing Cerberus to Eva who immediately made a fuss of him.

Joash signalled, cocking his head, his catlike smile on his lips. I followed him out of the room, intrigued by what this witch wanted to say to me in private.

We walked into another room, the library, all dark wood and gold embossed books that were stacked on bookcases from floor to ceiling.

A huge teak desk sat at one end, another fire blazed under the mantelpiece. At the far end sat two upholstered chairs, a small oak table with a decanter.

Extending his arm he said, "Please sit. I don't think what I see is fit for their ears..."

He leaned back in the chair, his fingers locked, resting his index fingers on his chin as he cast his eyes over me.

I tipped my head to the side, waiting for the usual questions I always got in Hell.

Did I have a tail, am I evil, do I hate God? To the latter, no. He is my dad. Obviously I'm not happy with him, but I'd never hate him. The tail could be right, but Joash wouldn't know.

His voice like creamy velvet, he almost purred, "You like the power. I can feel it, sinful, smooth, addictive. Dark..."

Clenching my jaw, I eyed him saying nothing and sat opposite him.

He grinned slightly. "We take power where we can. It's survival, Lucifer, and you wield it so naturally, but," he indicated with his palm, "I suppose you would, being what you are. Magic that dark, and yet I see no malice from you towards those you hold close. That takes real command. Respect. I doubt many could do that."

"And what would you know about my magic, about Hell, the Mark? I can assure you that anything you've read in a book is nothing compared to the reality."

He nodded, still wearing his catlike grin. "I believe you and between us we'll rescue your brothers. Punish Cain."

"Why did you want to speak to me in private, Joash, and why would you want to help? Ah, for the glory, the recognition?"

Joash dropped his hands and leaned towards me, whispering, "Yes for the recognition- the chance to rescue two archangels. Just like you, Lucifer. That's why you're doing it, isn't it? To be redeemed, to be welcomed back to the golden city of Heaven?"

"You know nothing about me," I muttered, not breaking eye contact.

I flinched as he moved closer still. "Ah, but I do, Lucifer. I do..." He moved to the edge of his seat, an excitement, a force radiated from him.

"How?" My forehead creased.

"Well, all this," he splayed his palms, "I mean I don't just magic it up out of thin air. I have to do my research, hence all these books. And Hell, I may know more than you realise."

He shifted in his seat, adding quickly, "Many demons seem to find their way out of there."

I nodded, sitting back. "Well, don't trust a demon. I've never met a sincere one, and I've been trapped there longer than most. I am grateful for your help, Joash. You are quite... different from what I expected, but I have little experience in this world. And you have followers?"

He nodded but was distracted, glancing away then holding my eye contact. "They don't realise the potency of your power, or that it is so incredibly malevolent. But Lucifer, I feel it, even now sitting here with you, it is raw, unyielding, dangerous." His chest rose and fell heavily, his forehead gleamed slightly. "I would like to show you something, something private." Leaping up in one move he was beside his desk. He waved his hand over the drawer and a lock clicked. Pulling the door open he grabbed an object and brought it over to me, his hand outstretched holding the mysterious object with reverence.

"I can see inside Hell itself."

Gasping, he held what looked like a faceted clear crystal where inside swirled black soot. Casting his free hand over it, the smoke, or soot cleared and indeed revealed a glimpse into Hell. Lava river travelled sluggishly, a demon leapt over it and around I saw the horrifying images of people being flayed. Pinching my nose, I leaned back. "I've seen enough! Where did you get that? Here, hand it over!"

Frowning, his manner turned sullen. "All right then." As the crystal touched my hand the scene disappeared. "What the..."

Almost spitting, "It's not the rock that holds the magic Lucifer. It's my magic! You know nothing, have learned nothing."

"You found a way to spy on Hell? Joash, be careful, if-"

"Thank you for your concern. I see, you are worried that it could bring me trouble, do not fear, it will not."

He was wrong. "Joash, why would you want to see in Hell?"

He sat back down, his face now impassive. "I can see most places if I choose. I was just demonstrating my ability. So now you know."

"And you'll be able to find my brothers using this?" I knew that hope spilled into my words.

He shook his head. "I will cast a ritual for that, Lucifer. They are no doubt shielded by magic, Hell, like many places has cracks in it. Cracks that I can break. Now, I have a favour to ask."

Reluctantly, I handed him the crystal. "Of course."

"Would you mind if I saw it, the Mark? Not out of morbid fascination, but as a witch, a spell caster, I am intrigued."

I noticed he strained, biting back his fervour and in his close proximity to me, again his scent seemed familiar. I had never met him, of that I was sure, but he seemed somehow known to me.

I stood up abruptly; he darted back in his seat as I casually took off my jacket and sat back down with my right arm towards him.

A slight hiss escaped his lips as he was instantly transfixed, almost hypnotized by the ridged scar tissue in the shape of the Mark on my arm. He grimaced as he saw how red my flesh was around it. It burned almost constantly, like a living nightmare. I watched him, my lashes lowered, his fingers reached out to touch it. He looked at me. "May I, can I touch it?"

I thrust my chin up. "Why?"

"It's power, it is... immense!"

"I don't think that's a good idea. It is strong, obviously it was made by God, my father. But it is turbulent, wrathful. I know you're attracted to the macabre Joash, the strange, but don't fall too far." I leaned into him, my face almost touching his. "Lest you fall beyond redemption and be damned.

You're young, have a care. However tempting the darkness is, believe me, once it's touched your soul, it is hard to regain the light, if not impossible."

A shadow fell across his face, tightening his lips as he looked past me. The fire in his eyes dimmed, almost glazed. Then he caught a breath, smiling widely.

Then strangely, he blurted out the words, "I have seen inside Heaven. Using the crystal, do you want to see?"

Caught off guard, I blinked and swallowed hard.

"Who are you? How is it that you, a mortal is able to access such things?"

Joash reigned in his composure. "I told you. You don't believe me?"

Thumping hard, my heart beat, breath caught. Heaven... *home*.

He sucked in his cheeks waiting for my answer. "Of course."

His mouth curved up, holding out the crystal in his right hand, he used his left hand to utter some spell, so quietly I couldn't decipher it.

Again the crystal, its flat pyramid sides revealed a smoke inside that was dense, dark then like fog, lifted and cleared. A sharp intake of breath as I saw for the first time in over two thousand years, the golden city... Skilfully made structures soared into the sky. Towers that defied gravity. Slender and far reaching, peppered with arched windows and ledges of pristine marble, luminescent from the gilded buildings around them. Some perching, some sitting on these overhangs, legs swinging, dangling over the ledges, angels sat with furled wings and animated faces as they took in the scent of Heaven. The scent I nostalgically recalled, lilacs and rain! And that memory reminded me of Eva...when I first met her, she'd had a distinct sweet smell amongst the musty catacombs. The scent of lilacs, sweet and delicate. She reminded me of home.

Spires from towers that reached beyond the eyeline, their walls gleaming and shimmering. The golden buildings where my kin sat and talked, their wings ice white, and the metallic scarlets, blues and silvers that edged their feathers. As warmth wrapped my heart, in an instant it felt gripped. Tight, unable to breathe as I realised that I could no longer go home. Not now. I didn't belong... A lump in my throat, my heart thudding dully. My smile faded and my eyes looked Heavenwards...

Distracted by the ceiling, confused for a moment by the huge painting of a fallen angel above me, something stirred deep inside.

Joash's smooth voice, almost caressing, said, "Ah, I had that commissioned. It is the painting by the artist Alexandre Cabanel. Fallen Angel. It's meant to be you, though I see you don't have red hair?"

"Me?"

"God's favourite, cast out from Heaven. A stunning painting, don't you agree?"

It was exquisite. Wild auburn hair, angry reddened eyes with a tear, the depiction of me, sitting naked complete with grey wings, the art work moved me, stole my breath. For a few moments I could not look away, swallowing hard as my chest shuddered.

I looked back at Joash. "That is how you see me, outcast?"

"It's the truth, is it not? Damned by your father, and why? A son should always look to succeed his father, do more, be more powerful, don't you agree?"

I shuffled in the chair, sitting up. "It doesn't matter what I think. Perhaps yes, for mortals. Put the crystal away, I have seen enough."

"You don't like it? I thought it would make you happy?"

Withholding a sneer, I answered, "And why, Joash, is it so important to you to make me happy? Me, the Devil? It does not. It only reminds me of what I have lost."

He rubbed his forehead, his face wrinkled. "I don't care about making you happy. I was being polite, I thought."

"You thought wrong. Do Austin and Eva know about the crystal?"

"No!"

"Good. Keep it hidden. If you value your life. There are those that would kill to have that."

He stood up, his face going back to the stoic impression. "You can have it, the crystal, if you want it."

I knew he *was* trying to impress me, God knows why. I was angry, no, heartbroken that the only link I had to home was through a crystal and even then, I could not enter. Not now.

"A face, Lucifer, look."

I stood as he walked back and stared into the crystal.

We watched as the image changed to a view of angels talking. It was outside the building of the High Angelic Order. A building where angels are taken that require healing from the Seraphim. Seraphiel, the Prince and highest of the Seraphim was talking to my brother, Metatron, and Seraphiel's helper, Jehoel.

Unable to breathe as I watched, I noticed my jaw slackened. My heart thundered. My brothers... A pang of sadness and happiness fought in my heart, entranced I couldn't look away at the scene. They looked divine, the reflections of golden light sparkled on their wings. Pristine, celestial... I felt... worthless.

"Uh! Close your hand, close it!"

It was too late, my heart almost smashed through my ribs as Metatron turned around and stared right at me, then Joash... how had he known? Had he actually seen us? Joash closed his hand around the crystal but a warm bronze light radiated through it. He was smirking, then puckered his lips and with small eyes, looked into mine. "Don't panic Lucifer. So you don't fit in? You're hardly the black sheep, are you? More the wolf."

I sat back down as my heart raced, gripping the edges of the chair. After swallowing hard, I watched him as he strode back to the desk, locking away the crystal. "You don't understand, Joash. The only thing I had in my favour was that Heaven didn't know I had escaped. Their power, compared to you, they'd wipe you out with a flick of their wrist."

Joash busied himself at his desk, pouring drinks. He handed me one and sat opposite me. "Don't underestimate yourself, Lucifer." Swigging the water, and thankfully not whiskey, he said through gritted teeth, "Do not underestimate me. This place..." His eyes looked up, "Warded from, well everything. Demons, angels, vampires...You are safe here, with me."

I hoped he was right.

Running his finger over the rim of his glass, his brows furrowed. "They were wearing jeans. Except, Metatron, is it? He was wearing gilded armour. Why, why was he dressed so differently?"

Putting the glass down on the small table, I leaned forward. "They were wearing jeans because they leave Heaven. The place they were standing outside, it's where they go when injury succumbs them. They leave Heaven occasionally to fight evil. Metatron never leaves Heaven." I paused, still seeing my brother's angry eyes that stole right into my soul. "If Metatron ever leaves Heaven, well, you'd better watch out."

He settled before me in the chair, his elbow resting on the arm, his fingers casually twisting his long hair. "So, that went well. Anyway, I have that should we need it."

"And I suppose you won't tell me how you managed to spy on Heaven and Hell?"

His hand dropped to his lap, his gaze fixated on me. "Well, I could but, you wouldn't understand the magic. Anyway, have you seen the internet?"

My attention was distracted, compelled to look again at the desk where he'd put the crystal before returning to look at him. "I have seen the internet, though I know little about it. We don't have it in Hell."

He smiled. "Well, I imagine it's hard to get a signal down there." Pulling out his phone, he typed for a few minutes until I heard some dramatic music, then he handed it to me.

He was on there, on a show of sorts called Fire of God. "Ah, yes, your name, that's what Joash means. Well researched." I glanced at him.

On the screen, Joash introduced himself. As he did so, I saw comments from viewers at the side of the screen. Many of them showering him in adoration, asking questions. My eyes narrowed. "You offer them... hope?"

He looked smug. "Yes, but much more. I help those who are pushed to the side-lines by society. The underdogs, the outcasts, male witches particularly, they're not always welcomed by female witches. And I teach them simple magic, encourage them to harness their power, their free will, their freedom. It's mainly how I bought all this, that and-"

Nodding, I answered for him, "And a pinch of magic. So, you are a modern-day saviour?"

His grin wrapped his whole face. "I wouldn't say saviour. But leader of men, yes."

I watched in fascination as this witch used his ethereal charms on the viewers, telling them how to harness their power, to allow the chaos of freedom to embrace their souls. Then on the screen he read out testimonials from fans who he'd helped, seeming miracles, helping them obtain their dream relationships, money, health. And all using ancient witchcraft. The comments flooded in. As I watched, transfixed, he leaned over me. "I also use this, it's called IG. I do live videos here, too, see."

A few seconds later I watched him as he spoke to his followers close to his home, teaching them about astronomy and the signs in the stars, of how they should not trust orthodox religions, which after all were written by men, and as he pointed out, flawed men at that.

Breathing deeply, I handed it back. He reminded me of someone, but like a block I couldn't think who. Maybe someone I met before I fell.

"And you're not concerned with using your magic, your energy for human's petty desires?"

I frowned.

"Petty to you, Lucifer, the Devil. Not to them. Or to me. If I can help those whose society has brandished outcasts, then," he touched his chest, a slight tilt of his head, "is it not my duty to help others? I, too, am shunned, not one of the neighbour's here will even look at me—unless I command it."

I shrugged. "That's because you make a point not to fit in, your door knocker for example, the way you dress? They are probably quite simple people, few have the capacity for diverse thinking, creative minds. But what do I know, I've been in Hell for eons."

He nodded. "I never imagined you to be a thinker."

I laughed. "That's because I am not. I just had a lot of time to do very little, and what I did do, well, that's best left unsaid. So, your followers adore you?"

He took a deep breath. "I wouldn't say adore." Then standing, he gestured dramatically with his arm. "But I help them and they appreciate that. So many people these days, I just help them to be seen, Lucifer. Everyone wants to be seen. To have a voice, to count. That's where I come in. Surely you of all people understand that?"

"A leader of men..." I mused, "Where's your white horse?"

His eyes darted to the floor before taking a long breath, then looking over me. "Lucifer... come, no one has horses anymore. I know you saw the white Ferrari. Surely that's good enough?"

I nodded as I went to walk back to Eva and Austin, he stopped me, his hand lightly reaching out and settled on my chest.

"You are the Devil, why don't you embrace that?"

I scanned him. "You have a choice, you can be whatever you want. I never asked to be this... Devil. I was an archangel, my birthright. Now I am... For me, well, that choice has gone now."

Still resting his hand on my chest, my jaw tightened as he whispered, "I have an idea how we can find your brothers. And I need to help Eva and Austin. You're not at all what I expected, Lucifer."

I didn't know what to make of him; he seemed human, but there was something off, though I couldn't place my finger on it. But then I'd been in Hell surrounded by demons, so I wasn't the best judge. He would help, and now I needed that, and he seemed sincere in his plight to help the downtrodden and that had paid him handsomely judging by his home and the luxury he surrounded himself in.

Back in the drawing room, Eva and Austin were playing with Cerberus, Joash whispered to me, "So how come the Devil has a dog?"

Distracted, I smiled at Eva, a lightness in my heart seeing her and Cerberus and the Mark... the Mark seemed to cool.

I gestured to Joash. "Oh, Cerberus was the first creature I saw after leaving Hell. Someone had abandoned him. That tiny thing could not survive on his own. So..."

His voice cracked, "So you adopted him, a dog? The Devil and his dog."

"Aaron believes my dad put him there."

His face wrinkled slightly. "Whatever for?"

"To curb my anger, of course. To teach me. My dad loves his lessons. It's a nice thought."

He nodded and answered before I finished, "You actually believe that? Why would he care?"

Shaking my head, my eyes half closed. "I understand, Joash, why indeed would my father, my creator, care after all this time? I was his first creation, and I was his favourite. He is omnipresent, well maybe not in Hell. Dogs were his favourite creature, but regardless," I shrugged. "I shall do my best by the tiny creature. It would be reassuring if my dad did do that. I'm not a fool, I doubt he did. Coincidence is all that was, finding Cerberus."

I turned around to face his vivariums. "And you, why snakes, and why so many?"

Clearing his throat, he eyed me. "I rescued these snakes, all of them." He held out his arm and continued speaking, "Snakes have an interesting meaning in spirituality, but maybe because they are so different to people's perceptions. Humans believe snakes to be cold, non-thinking creatures, but each one has its own traits, its own personality. None are what they seem."

I nodded as we walked back to Austin and Eva.

"So, how will you help to restore their power?"

"Come see."

"Austin, Eva, you ready? I will not promise I can restore all the magic Cain stole from you, especially you, Austin, but I can open the channel to it so you can invite it in for yourselves."

Laughing, Austin beamed. "Thanks Joash. Much appreciated."

I crouched down. "Cerberus, come here." He bounded over, tail wagging, his shrill barking bouncing off the walls.

"Good boy, come on."

Picking him up, I looked at Joash, his posture stiff, a slight rise of his eyebrows, lips curled. Sometimes he reminded me of myself. Biting down his emotions.

I carried Cerberus, and we followed Joash up the grand staircase, scent of teak hung in the air. Polished to a sheen, the bannister was smooth to touch, whilst orbs of light caught Cerberus's attention as they bobbed around the walls above us, reflected from large crystal chandeliers that hung. The sun blazed through the huge Georgian windows, warming my skin. If I'm honest, I felt pretty scruffy in this elegant and immaculate house. If I stayed here, if I remained earthbound, I, too, would need a place. But if there was the slightest chance I could get back home, I'd take Cerberus with me. The angels would love him.

We trudged up two flights of stairs, before coming to a door that Joash opened and stood aside for us to enter. His lashes lowered as he grinned.

A sweet scent of incense hung in the air and wisps of smoke like long ghostly fingers stood waist high.

Lining one side of the room, bronze statues stood sentry, hoods covering their faces. As I looked closer, their faces were carved metallic skulls. In their hands, they held ornate pentagrams. The statues towered to the roof, and these rooms were at least twelve feet tall. Their presence gave a foreboding, chilling presence, like watchers.

An intricate pentagram with runes inscribed in gold lay in the centre of the wooden floor, an ebony desk and book cases edged the room. The rest of the room was sparse, but the bookcase and desk were piled with arcane books and tools. Wooden wands with intricate gold leafing, engraved skulls and jars with various herbs and plants.

I walked around the edge of the room after a dark glint of an object caught my eye. I found myself drawn to an obsidian dagger; it looked authentic. From a few demons I'd met in Hell, and only a handful of them had these, I knew the dagger originated from the Aztecs.

"Fascinating, isn't it? It's original. The Tecpatl knife was used in human sacrifice, grisly I know but potent energy."

Joash handed it to me. As I took it, the Mark burned, a force from the dagger pumped through my veins. Turning slightly to face me, Joash surprised me. "You can borrow it if you like? On your quest to kill Cain, I would let no other touch it."

"Touch what?" Austin blurted out as he wandered over.

Cerberus whimpered in my arm, feeling the energy, the heat. So carefully I placed it back down. "Thank you, Joash, I appreciate that."

His face brightened. "Austin, don't touch it, especially not yet. It's a-"

But in his eagerness, Austin cut him off. "A Tecpatl. Ew, grisly Joash. I hope you don't go around sacrificing things."

Frowning, Joash answered, "Certainly not, though maybe a mage's blood would be worth it."

Austin rolled his eyes as Eva joined us. "So, what spell will you use Joash, any we might know?"

"To help you, Eva, I think a bite of Sumerian witchcraft. It amplifies its power in its lineage, ancestral magic and they predate Babylonian, Egyptian, all really. You and Austin should sit in the circle," he pointed, "I'll light the candles and start." Joash turned to me and smiled at Cerberus. "You two can stay here, there's a chair beside the desk." With his palms facing me, he said, "Please, be comfortable." A slight twitch in his eye sent a chill through me.

Cerberus sat on my lap as we watched Joash snap his fingers and the candles' light with flame. An easy trick for a witch or mage, one I'd like to learn. Then Joash chanted in Sumerian. Swaying slightly in front of Eva, who sat cross-legged within the circle, a dark crimson light glowed from his heart, travelling through his arm and onto the top of her head.

Trembling, she gasped as the light radiated through her, thrumming rhythmically as it travelled through her core, then into her legs. All the gold runes around the circle and pentagram beamed red. Licking his lips, Joash stepped away and repeated the simple spell on Austin. Except this time the verse he muttered was different, and the illumination was brilliant blue. With his eyes closed, Austin made no sound but sat bolt upright, his lips pressed firmly together.

The light wobbled, changing colour to arctic white and seemed to waver from Joash through to Austin. I noticed the smallest shiver in Austin, as he did I felt a cool breeze. Where Eva's energy was warm, Austin's was cool. I'd never realised magic could hold a temperature. Cerberus barked, I rubbed his chest and noticed it, too, what my dog was looking at. Tiny fragments of sparks flew and whipped around the room, the power of the enchantment only seen on a different wavelength of colour. I sunk back into the wooden chair, relieved that I at least could still see these.

Tilting his head to the side, Joash took a breath and strode over to a cabinet. Pulling out four crystal glasses, he poured sparkling water in, then handed us one each, rolling his eyes to me. "I know, but if I get Maddie to do this, my assistant, we'll die of thirst before she gets here. It's the best and will aid in cleansing before we start the ritual, but... Cerberus?"

I put the glass down on the desk and felt his eyes burn into me as I did so. "I need to take him outside and get him water." Not waiting for an answer, I strode away with my dog in my arms and stepped quickly down the many flights of stairs, looking for the backdoor.

I ran around the back garden with Cerberus, found a stick and threw it for him. Like the vampire's place, this garden was extensive, walled and immaculate. The fresh air revived me and my dog, and only then I noticed how tense I'd been inside the witch's house. With Cerberus refreshed, I found the kitchen and a bowl, gave him some water and was conscious that I needed to feed him soon.

"One more hour, then we'll get you back to Aaron's, and get you some chicken."

I scooped him up. As I made my way to the stairs, I noticed Joash's assistant. Head down, she bustled quietly about and disappeared into another room.

Upstairs Eva and Austin, wide eyed, still sat in the circle, drinking their water, chatting as Joash crouched alongside them.

"Ah, you're back, good. I have an idea to find the archangels, please... oh, Cerberus. I think it may be best to tie him to the chair. Does he have a lead?"

"No, do you? In fact," I splayed my palm, "Please, don't answer that. Cerberus will sit on the chair, I don't believe in chaining animals."

His eyes narrowed, a slight nod, and I placed my dog on the chair, whispering, "Stay there. Good boy. Lucifer loves you." And discreetly rested my chin on his head for a brief second.

Returning to the circle, I caught Eva's eye. She lowered her lids, her long lashes sweeping down, then eyed me over.

Racing, my heart thumped, my stomach fluttered and I glanced away feeling my face burn but clenched my jaw hearing Austin chuckle.

"Lucifer, sit next to me?" Her voice brushed over me. I don't know, between her and my dog, the beast inside of me was calmed but without them?

I knew it would hit with a vengeance.

Joash startled me by stripping off his clothes. No one seemed shocked but me. He kept taking off layers. His jacket, his shirt, a T-shirt...then his boots, socks and trousers. I wondered if he was going to do a pagan style ritual, and held my breath as thoughts of him chanting wildly, naked right before me filled me with horror.

Ah, a warming eased through my limbs when he at least kept his shorts on. I'm no prude but I don't need to see that, either. A smattering of tattoos on his lean torso seemed much like Austin's, to be glowing a crimson light, I recognised the patterns. Sumerian spells, some of the oldest magic known.

"Before I start, I need a strand of hair from each of you, I will bind it with my own." Joash passed Eva a tiny pair of ornate scissors. I eyed him, but as she and Austin had no trouble giving him a lock of their hair, I did the same. I wasn't happy about it, though. A witch having some of your hair... I cut a few small strands, handing them to Eva, who reverently gathered our hair together, and gave it to Joash. Then he did the same. He glided over to the desk, putting the scissors there and brought our hair, placing it in the centre of the circle.

Then he signalled a flick of his wrist. The incense thickened in the air, more candles burned and a flicker of light beside me. Turning to see, the sculptures of the hooded skeletons burned flames in their hollow eyes, taunting menacingly, and I thought I should have asked about the magic he would use. Time to buckle up, I doubted much would shock me after Hell.

I doubted wrongly, of course.

Striding back to the desk, he picked up the obsidian blade and with chin up, entered the circle, a scarlet flame in his eyes.

Then kneeling on the point of the pentagram, he dragged the blade across his chest, head thrust back, lips parted.

Letting out a loud sigh as he did this, he quivered, then lunged forwards as blood gushed from his chest and pooled before him, placing the dagger in the middle of the circle and his hands on the ground as his blood collected around his fingers, his palms.

His voice deep, it shook and reverberated around us. The power had shifted, I could feel it like a thick, powerful web, "Mother... Lilith... Open my eyes to see. Show me where the archangels Michael and Gabriel are hidden. Show me Cain!"

For a moment stillness hung around us, then rasping his eyes bulged, teeth bared, he twitched. His eyes frozen open, curling his lips as he twisted up onto his knees, lashes now fluttering, mouth twisted, his lower lip quivered, he paled.

The pooled blood seemed to bubble and froth, and spewing from it, tiny snakes slithered across the floor.

Cerberus barked wildly, I turned to calm him, as I did so Joash uttered Enochian of all the damned things, his eyes disappeared into his head...

"Mapsama ol mother, queen c demons Lilith, darsar i a immortal Cain, darsar gnay tia hide archangel Michael od Gabriel, ol ooanoan, zarman ol."

As he spewed my language, I translated, muttering the meaning aloud.

"Tell me mother, queen of demons Lilith, where is the immortal Cain, where does he hide archangel Michael and Gabriel? Open my eyes, show me..."

Joash sunk back on his heels.

Now words spewed from him, I shivered. These were not his words, but a message being relayed through him. His voice had an icy edge, unfamiliar to him. One that sent a shiver down my spine.

"G a tabges darsar witches faonts, a elo murderer, arp a spear daziz tia killed Abel g od crip oi trian stop tia... Hail Lilith!"

"In the caves where witches dwell, the first murderer, take the spear head he killed Abel with and only this will stop him..."

Slowly the incense cleared.

Cerberus barked, interrupting him, I jumped up and went over to him, rubbing his back.

Joash lunged forward again, his hands in his blood, rasping he shivered. Glancing around, I grabbed his jacket and quietly placed it on his back. As I did this, his head turned to me, muttering, "Thank you... thank you f-" but his voice trailed off as his breath caught.

Eva was by his side having scooped up a blanket from somewhere and we replaced the jacket with it. I strode over getting Joash a glass of water as Austin, who looked as pale as Eva, slowly got up and went over to Cerberus. He eyed my dog with a forced smile, obviously quite affected by the intense magic that clung to us all in there.

His hand shaking, Joash took the water and downed it. Then he sat back without consequence of his legs and feet covered in his blood. I noted the wound on his chest had already began to knit together. I was indeed indebted to him. When he'd said he would look for my brothers, I expected him to see, use a vessel to look into. He had gone above and beyond.

Clearing my throat, I picked up my dog. "Joash, Lilith? You worship her?"

"Ah, the mother of magic, yes. Many under-estimate her power. Of course, and because I encourage male witches, you may well ask why I draw upon the mother, but," he glanced away, a slight curve to his lips, "As I said she is the mother. And I, as we," he indicated to Austin and Eva, "Are her children. She wasn't always thought of as demonic. That curse was brought about by your father, Lucifer, I believe? When Lilith refused to lie underneath Adam, being independent and free spirited, and both traits I highly encourage. And she is known as the goddess of family of course, in Sumerian lore, she was always the goddess of family, sexuality and love."

I bit my lip. Were we talking about the same woman? I think not. Certainly, she was no submissive, the opposite, but she was so full of vengeance- the latter hardly surprising after what my dad put her through for disobeying him. But she was sometimes cruel. Though, for all that I had searched for her in Hell for eons and was punished for it. This mortal had seemed to have a romantic ideal of the demon queen. Still, I wasn't about to tell all on my ex.

"Well, thank you. That was a most... interesting ritual. And we can find my brothers in the caves where witches dwell?"

Austin who looked like he was going to burst, said, "It's Wookey Hole, Wookey Hole caves. In Cheddar, Somerset-oh, I don't know, maybe twenty miles from here. The witches, it's called the Witch of Wookey Hole. There's a petrified witch inside the caves, it's famous man."

Joash smiled, nodding.

Eva grinned at me. "It's said that back in the seventeenth century during the later witch trials many witches were hung inside the caves after the villagers discovered a coven in there. Austin is correct," Eva added.

Austin beamed.

Eva continued, "The witch of Wookey Hole is famous, although she doesn't really look real since she was fossilized in stone and over the centuries water formed and cast over it. I think if I remember rightly, though. she predates from much, much earlier. It definitely is a place of power, not in a good way. But the caves are vast, so Cain I'd guess would be well hidden."

"Indeed." Joash turned to face me. "It is also said that deep within the caverns lies a secret passageway, a gateway to Hell. So, I will," he gestured his hand on his heart, "If you'll permit, help. I am eager to meet this Cain."

"Well, thank you, all of you, but I don't think it's wise you join me. Cain is a true immortal, in the fullest sense, and he's holding and torturing my brothers, archangels. And with only his Mark I doubt I will be able to protect you."

"But we insist, and now we're prepared, or will be. You'll have a coven of three at your back. And... well Lucifer, we are the best, if I say so myself," Austin added.

Cerberus licked my face, wriggling in my arms. "So Eva, Austin, how do you both feel now?"

"Better thanks to Joash." She glanced at Austin, who beamed. "I'm ready, look..." Holding out his arm, his tattoos glowed their brilliant bright blue.

"Well then, if you want to guide the way, but I'm going to take Cerberus to Aaron's home. I don't expect him to dog sit but-"

"Oh, no need. You can take him to mine, my house mate has a dog. They'll get along fine," Eva smiled and came over to pet my dog.

"Will you accept the dagger?" Joash asked me.

I withheld a grin. "You are very benevolent Joash. You have done so much already. I accept it."

He nodded, grabbed up his clothes and strode towards the door. Then he paused turning to us, looking at me. "I know, the ritual looked... extreme. It was, if you want something powerful-"

I interrupted him. "But your wound, it's healed, aren't you human?"

An abrupt laugh, he grinned. "Yes. It's only magic, Lucifer. Magic runs thick in my blood, I am not like you, but I heal fast."

"And you've imbued your magic into Austin and Eva, they'll heal fast, too?"

"Yes."

"So, before Cain took my divine power, I infused some of it into Cerberus. Will someone put a protection spell on him for me? I couldn't live with it if something happened to him, because of me."

Joash lowered his lashes slightly, his eyes following Eva.

She was rubbing my dog's head. "I will, but Austin or Joash would be stronger."

"Me, I'd be happy to, Lucifer." Austin scrunched his eyes and scratched his head, "Um, a simple elemental spell should suffice."

Wetting his lips he stepped forward, Eva moved to the side as Austin bent his head to match Cerberus, who responded by licking the mage.

"Ugh, thanks Cerby! Right..." Putting his right hand on my dog's head, Austin breathed deeply, slowly as arctic blue light shimmered down his arm and into Cerberus's head. Cerberus responded with a soft whimper as the illumination travelled through his black and white hair, his body, then he barked sharply. I felt him tremble against me, felt the power grow inside of him. Then Austin muttered, "Factum est!" and stepped away.

It is done.

Cerberus nestled down. "Thank you, Austin, really appreciated."

"You're welcome," he winked, nodding with a big grin.

Placing my chin on Cerberus's head I said, "Good boy. Now let's meet Eva's friend."

"She's real nice, another witch," Austin replied.

"Please, make yourselves at home downstairs," Joash indicated with his arm.

Plodding down the stairs everyone fell silent. My shoulders aching, even Cerberus rested on my chest. The ritual's after effects seemed heavy.

As I passed the library, I couldn't help but glance in where he had put the crystal, a shudder down my spine. This house was warded Joash had said, but the door to Heaven had been opened. Now they knew I was out of Hell. Though, why they hadn't helped my brothers, that worried me more.

Once Joash had washed and changed, we walked to Eva's, though Austin could technically transport us there, I wasn't keen on having Cerberus go through that and Eva lived just outside the city.

A bitter chill hit us as the northern wind bit and nipped at our skin. The snow had settled, and I let Cerberus down to walk and play. Not the type of weather I'd imagine for spring. But then again, England had no weather rules, other than rain.

Dark clouds rolled in, tiny flakes falling, and my dog barked and yapped in the cold snow, Eva running alongside him, laughing.

Daytime was fading, I watched Eva and could see that she was tired. Bloodshot eyes and dark lines, her energy was sinking, we would need to rest. We had been up nearly two days. For me, I also needed to sleep. On Earth I lived by its rules, the circadian cycle, as do most immortals. And I wondered what their beds must be like if their chairs were so sublime. Eva and Austin laughed a little way ahead of me throwing snowballs for Cerberus to chase, their movements sluggish.

Joash strode over to me. "Lucifer, you forgot this, here."

Handing me hilt first, it was the obsidian dagger, the Tecpatl.

My nose wrinkled, staring at it. As my finger wrapped around it, the Mark scorched on my arm. Inside me the monster seemed unsettled. For a second, I saw my shadow cast before me, its silhouette like the beast on the snow before me.

My breath caught as a chill made the hairs on my arm stand on end and I could only hear the sound of the breeze. As if I was totally alone in an icy abyss that clawed at my soul.

Jolting abruptly, I came back to the present as Joash had touched my arm. "Lucifer? Are you alright? You drifted off just then."

I swallowed hard, my tongue stuck to my mouth, clearing my throat. "I'm fine. Thank you, are you sure?"

He nodded abruptly and rushed to catch up with the others.

Cerberus bounced happy enough, I called to them, "I need to feed Cerberus, where can I get him some food? And we need to rest, all of us."

"Oh, that is a glorious idea. I need my bed..." Eva groaned as if my mentioning it suddenly made her aware of how sleep deprived she was.

"Lucifer, let me or Joash just transport us all home. Where will you stay?"

I watched as my dog padded through the snow like shimmering diamonds, the last of the sun's amber rays casting wisps of warm light in places. My chest rising and falling, I hardly realised Joash was talking. "Lucifer? I said you can stay with me. And Cerberus, though, we'd have to get him some food, I only have snake food."

Austin snickered. "Joash, what, you eat only snake food?" His eyes as wide as saucers, laughing.

"Thank you, Austin Fay. No, I meant my familiars, pet food. So, Lucifer?"

I looked from Austin to Joash. "Yes, thank you Joash. Eva, I'd like to make sure she is protected."

"Simple. Joash, can you text me some of the warding you used?" Austin asked.

"No, I'll go with Eva and ward her house. Only I know the spells, since I wrote them. Then I'll transport you to your home, Austin, and do the same, no..." Joash shook his head, his shoulders dropped. "Look, why don't you all just stay at my house? Look at it, it's bloody big enough. Why are we out here in the freezing snow? I'll get Maddie to get some dog food. I've plenty of bedrooms, Maddie can buy some more food. Good, that's settled then."

"I can't, but thank you. I have to work tomorrow and I'm knackered now." Eva leaned on Austin, who wrapped his arm around her.

"Yes, and she can't annoy her boss." Austin groaned leaning into her, then his voice booming, "Or she'll eat her alive."

I put my hands in my pockets to stop the biting cold. "Joash, thank you. But we shouldn't send Maddie out, that's hardly fair. It's freezing. I'll go now, but I have no money."

He eyed me, his lips curved up slightly. "Then allow me. You should borrow some clothes really. Eva, stay tonight, shower, eat, rest and I'll transport you to your home in the morning, then to work." He turned suddenly on his heels. "If that's alright with you, Lucifer?"

I caught her eye. She looked exhausted. I raised my brows in question to her, and with a relaxed reluctance she turned around to face Joash's home, "No thanks Joash- I appreciate your offer but I really need my own bed. And Lucifer- thanks, but to be honest, if Cain does want to kidnap me again- and why would he- I'm too dead tired to care. I have to sleep."

She held my gaze and my stomach fluttered. What I would do to have her sleep in my arms. My chest tightened before I took a long inhale.

Then I noticed I stank, I hadn't washed since rescuing them.

And the fact that I'm no longer an angel.

It wasn't Cain I was worried about- it was Heaven but then again, they hadn't seen her or Austin. I kicked some snow, my mind on her as the sunset cast an amber hue across the park and wondered what it could be like to wake up next to her...

"Cerberus, here... boy." I threw him a snowball.

A pounding on the wind caught my attention, gazing sky-wards great wings beating fast, flying towards us, sword out-stretched, Demogorgon came hurtling down.

"You need to get back to Hell, Morningstar, or die here," he roared.

Barking wildly, Cerberus leapt before me, growling.

"Eva, Austin, get out of here. Take Cerberus, I'll find you later. Go!"

Eva grabbed up my dog, Austin stood defiant, so I narrowed my eyes at him, "You cannot fight him, he is a Hell demon, leave!"

Only Joash stood silently to one side, his lips curved slightly as he surveyed Demogorgon.

The demon bared his fangs, fetid breath making me cringe he landed before me, his feet thumping on the ground. I pulled the obsidian dagger from the scabbard, my chin raised, locking eyes with him.

The Mark burned, the stink of my searing flesh in the air as anger gripped my heart and fired through me like an explosion. I roared into his face, "How dare you threaten me, demon! I am the guardian of Hell! Kneel or be damned!" My voice echoed around the buildings, the park. I was grateful that the common was empty.

"You belong in Hell, and I have been charged with returning you!" Demogorgon spat.

"You and no other in Hell have any authority over me! I am still an archangel!" I lied. Again. "I will save my brothers. Whether that's over your slain body is your choice."

For his size he moved swiftly, his sword at my neck. Using the dagger, I pushed his sword aside, facing him. "Go back to Hell." This time I didn't yell, even though anger coursed through me. He was stupid, like an automaton, following his orders. And he couldn't kill me. True, he could injure me, but even without my divine power, I had the Mark.

His head lunging forward, eyes narrowed. "You have been cursed, you smell different. No longer angel, now damned."

Laughing, he roared, "My sword was forged in Hell, you'll die. It's killed angels before."

In one step he lunged forward with his sword, using the dagger's hilt I locked it with his blade and with all my anger shoved it out of his hands.

A thud as it landed. Beneath the sword the snow melted. Hot as Hell.

But before he knew it, the obsidian blade had slunk through his leathery skin. Again his stinking breath engulfed me. My eyes were drawn to his right hand which was grappling for his dagger, I shoved the blade in deeper, his inky blood spilling onto my wrist, he bellowed.

Leaping away, sweat ran down my back, Demogorgon snatched my wrist, beating his great wings, I unfurled mine as he lifted me with him, fast above the park. Almost reaching the cloud line, his eyes blinked fast, head tipping back and held his free hand out muttering.

I held fast, my palm sweaty against the obsidian hilt, then wrenched the magic infused dagger out of his body, lunging away. A whistle on the breeze distracted me. His sword came hurtling from the ground to his hand, then his hulking coal mass bulleted up and away.

I caught my breath, gripping the athame tightly in my bloody hand. Obviously Joash's magic hadn't been enough to stop him, but as I had said to Austin, this demon was forged in Hell, with all its horror and enchantments.

Hovering on the wing, I scoured the surrounding sky. It was clear, so I ascended, relieved that Eva and Austin had listened and had gotten away safely, when suddenly I was winded, my breath shoved out of me. I remembered my hand wanting to loosen, but something automatically told my brain to keep gripping the dagger and in slow motion the world before me became hazy, like ghostly fog clouding my eyes. As I looked down, I saw the reason for my disorientation.

Demogorgon rested his head on the back of my shoulder, his laughter in my ears like a muffled alarm, and sticking out of my chest was his sword.

Spluttering a laugh in shock, my body tingled with fire, I swayed then fell forward, the sensation of metal grating against bone as my body's weight pulled me downwards, sliding off the blade and hurtling towards the ground, unable or unwilling to organise my thoughts.

Incoherent images, sensations wrapped around me, my limbs numb and a shouting that I couldn't distinguish. A hollow thud as my body hit the tarmac. A vague vision of Joash peering over me, then I looked up, small eyes. He was pointing his finger, but the dark cloud descended faster towards him, landing with a crash.

It was too late. The lumbering mass of muscle and anger sped towards Joash, whose face paled to ashen. Even casting his spells, it seemed the witch was no match for a Hell demon. Battling past my pain, I could feel my skin fusing, knotting together. A quick look at Joash, whose mouth was like an 'O' in shock, I got to my knees, and gritting my teeth, pushed myself up.

He screwed up his face, eyes scrunched shut with his left hand out, lips muttering, and his body shivered and a whirl of luminescent blue-green light surrounded him.

Transparent at first, something motioned to his hand, a long sliver of blue light that radiated from the witch. Demogorgon was almost upon us, I turned to face him, the dagger handle slippery in my hand.

"Lucifer!" Joash called as he tried to maintain a barrier of light between us and Demogorgon. It was a nice gesture. It didn't work.

Staggering with one hand over my wound, I recklessly stepped forward into Demogorgon, grunting as the Mark seared my skin. The onslaught was savage, hate fired from his eyes. This demon had some kind of personal vendetta against me, I did not know why. Unless because I was archangel by design, him not so much.

He shoved me back, I stumbled, losing my balance and falling back, struggling past agony, regained my feet and beat my wings. I was keen to take this fight away from Joash, away from mortals. Groaning, mustering all my strength, I ploughed high above the clouds, spied the abbey tower and headed towards it. With each flap of my wings, each laboured breath my body ached, the pain gripping my heart from the sword wound, but thanks to Cain's curse; the skin was fusing together. But with it seemed to bring a new level of fury that smouldered through my veins, a red mist before my eyes blurring my vision.

Demogorgon landed behind me, charging forward. Spinning around, I held my dagger steady; he swept in at the side, his weapon low, aiming for my leg. I jumped, grunting and aimed for his colossal head. Both of us missed.

An angel and a demon fighting on top of an abbey, how cliché.

Demogorgon roared, so I flew up into the air, then dived down fast, shoving the blade between his shoulder blades but this demon is another realm of brutality, thrusting his sword backwards, which sliced my side, he acted as if my dagger just tickled him.

Tugging hard to dislodge my blade from his back, he took his chance. A great mass, he spun around, his roar echoed around the rooftops. The abbey spire silhouetted against the inky sky, the crimson fog before my eyes, bent double with one hand over my side where his sword had carved my skin, his foot smashed into my ribs sending me on my back. As the mist cleared, his face blocked out everything. Everything except his sword that came hurtling down towards my heart...

Angel Blood

Heaven was bleeding. Showers cascaded down, and wiping the rain from my face it felt sticky and thick. As my eyes opened, squinting against the onslaught, I saw a splattering of brilliant white illuminations pouring from the sky, each leaving a trail of sparkling lights.

Angels were falling to Earth.

Beneath me, the ground shook, I jolted as a loud clap of thunder echoed in the distance, and I realised I was frozen to the roof with the demon's sword pierced right through me. My mind like a dense fog, the falling angels looked like a mass of shooting stars. Numbness seized my limbs, only able to move my head, I panted.

A massive thud on the roof seemed to jolt my body into waking, shaking painfully I twisted my neck and saw the crumpled wings of an angel. His body splayed on the rooftop beside me. Heavy footsteps, rasping as Demogorgon leered over me, fire in his black eyes, he pointed upwards, "The apocalypse, the prophecy is upon us." Lowering his hand, he bent over, reached for his sword hilt, the bloody rain glistened on his coal black skin. I yelled as the metal scratched my ribs, winding me and sending my mind in another world of pain and confusion. Yet he continued, his voice gravelly, deep, "Out there the Antichrist walks amongst us. Now!"

In my weakened state, Demogorgon grabbed me by the scruff of my neck, hauling me up. Struggling, I turned my head, wanting to see the angel. Did I know him? Was he dead?

"They're all dying Lucifer, Heaven is dying. You'll never return home, Hell is your home now. Now and forever, eternal punishment. You deserve nothing less."

My jaw popped, my body wretched, but the Mark glowed and my wound knitted together, agonising. This was what Cain had been through.

The angels kept falling, my anger burned, I struggled against him but my limbs were too weak, all my energy thrust into healing, as I felt my feet lift as the demon beat his wings taking us off the roof, higher and higher and away from the city.

Muted in the wind, the screams of my kin, glimpses of their faces ashen, screaming wide-eyed in terror as they crashed out of Heaven, hurtling towards the earth. What had the power to do that? Darkness closed in on me, pressing, demanding answers... Why was this happening, was Cain this powerful, how?

The demon chanted above a clearing, his black eyes merging red and I writhed in his grip to struggle free so he clenched his fingers tighter, and before us a hole opened in the ground, the earth spewing out, ground rumbling.

A faint stink of sulphur and metal caught on the wind. A mad flurry of rage fired through me. I had no weapon; I had dropped the dagger; I punched him in the kidneys. He laughed. His skin was so thick, and part armoured and I was still reeling. I screamed as he flew over the hole into Hell and let go.

Unable to open my wings as the cavity into Hell was too narrow, I sped down towards a stream of lava far, far beneath me. My heart leapt into my mouth, breathing hitched as adrenaline and a frenzy of terror clawed at my gut, at me.

In seconds he was almost on top of me, sword pointed down, aiming for my head and a cackle and roar of demons below me howled as I fell into Hell. About to open my wings, metal touched the back of my neck, an intense blaze of red illuminated before me.

Frozen Souls

Rasping hard, I could not feel my limbs, my body. My breath trapped in my chest and from my neck down I was in a body of ice, a frozen lake. Desperation clawed at my throat, a sour taste in my mouth.

He'd left me... here? Abandoned me? Hell was one thing, but this...

As my vision cleared and my eyes adjusted to the infernal gloom, I saw a shape before me. Squinting, it looked like an arm, fingers splayed, reaching out, desperate, stretching out for help.

Arctic cold pierced my core, my heart, bone-chilling, cutting deep into my soul. I saw shapes of skulls protruding through the ice, bodies spilling out of it, contorted, twisted that had tried to struggle free of this frigid purgatory and died, frozen to death where they'd tried. This was my fate? Except I am immortal, and now before me an eternity of isolation, loss and trapped, unable to even move limb or body...

I gulped, choking as my mind went numb. The shimmer of the icy lagoon that seemed endless, its murky green surface looked rippled like old leather. Except it did not move. Ridges were frozen, only a glimmer of illumination spilled through a gateway from somewhere in the distance, giving the illusion of movement.

My stomach rolled with loss, defeat. Was I damned? Maybe, my mind raced over possibilities that my father had forsaken me. For good.

A distant cacophony of shrill screams echoed through this vast cavern, as dread loomed like an eager embrace. I could not move...

My heart struggled, hammering sporadically. As my consciousness cleared, I shivered violently but could not break free.

This lagoon, one of the pits in Hell, was located in a vast cavern. Ironically designed for Cain, Adam and Eve's firstborn. And now I remembered from long, long ago that I had been told by a demon who found it grossly amusing that they also constructed the frozen lake to hold Satan. I'd never believed that since I'd spent an eternity in Hell and never even seen the lake, and many lies were told about me. But here I was...

Well, shit.

They reserved this area for those who caused treachery against their own blood. Lacus Proditione. Lake of Betrayal...They're big on Latin in Hell. It's an old language and let's face it, everything sounds grander in Latin. Well, call it what you will, it was no picnic.

Seconds seemed like hours, heavy, raw and my hope faded, everything weighed on me. My life or lack of it, the waste of my existence, but the Mark burned hotter.

Fear braced me, my stomach twisted as my mind tried to make sense of this, why? I couldn't comprehend that they'd tossed me here for all infinity when I'd fought for them, suffered for them, been tortured for them- that they would actually throw me in Hell and in the frozen lake.

Unable to move more than my neck across the gloominess, my eyes focused on those contorted and screaming faces. The lake's victims, frozen, captured in time as they'd realized their fate. They were, I knew, semi-conscious existing in this icy purgatory in Hell.

Despair ripped at my soul, clawed at it, and you cannot imagine the torments of my mind as it replayed every act, every feeling, every loss before me, magnified in my mind, relived in full colour, sounds, scents, sensations. Until it stole my hope. That's what Hell does. It replays your every nightmare larger than life until it destroys your soul. Sucks the life from you. Then you are sent onto the next phase of punishment.

Again, I scanned the place, searching for something, anything, but there was nothing before me. The only thing that surrounded me was slow death.

Clenching my jaw as my mind whirled and wrought about my predicament, my despair started shifting... The Mark burned and so did my anger.

A low guttural growl, my skin seared as the Mark grew fiercer along with my fury and I noticed I could feel the surrounding ice around my arm, trickle, melt slowly.

I would get out, I had to, this couldn't be my end, my fate.

Only a faint light shimmered off the lake before me, and the frozen sea of dead souls dotted my view, contorted and perverse amid the icy landscape as their soulless eyes stared lifelessly into the abyss.

The distant din of wailing torment filled my ears made me more determined.

The beating of wings distracted my thoughts, large as they flapped above, a slight breeze over my already frozen head and hair.

"A fitting end!"

Demogorgon hovered above me, all muscle and mass, his huge sword in his hand thrust down towards my head. A wry smile on his lips.

Trying to swallow, I said, "I've never seen you smile Demogorgon, I'm glad I helped."

The troll has arrived. I would have been relieved if he could actually kill me and I didn't have the energy to argue with him, I simply closed my eyes. If he tried to kill me, so be it. I guessed there could be the slightest chance he could, being born of fire and brimstone, though I never heard of it.

"I want to fight you, here in Hell, on my ground."

Clearing my throat, I gritted out, "Well you put me here, didn't think that through very well did you, unless you'd like to join me. The water's a bit cold though."

"No, they commanded me to drop you into Hell. I obeyed, that is what I do, but I didn't know he would put you here, and this..." His eyes darted over the vast lake, "This is too easy a place for you, Lucifer. Not enough pain."

Swallowing hard, I sighed out, "Really? I'm frozen solid, I can't feel my limbs and I'm surrounded by people caught in between life and death living out their nightmares endlessly. Are you mad? And who commanded you? I am the guardian of Hell and I don't remember telling you to put me here."

The demon looked confused. Maybe I'd used too many words. But he could be my way out if I could think around the situation.

Small eyes burned into my soul. He landed lightly and for a beast of his size, that's no easy feat. As his weight bore down upon the lake's frozen surface, a crack appeared under his feet but he didn't flinch.

"I wanted to kill you Lucifer, I have always hated you and now this?"

Unable to withhold it, I splattered a laugh, shocked at his absurd response. I pinned him with my eyes, especially as I couldn't move. "I am deeply sorry, Demogorgon, that I find myself in the Lake of Betrayal. I would get out and allow you to try to kill me, but..." my eyes gazed around us, "Some turd of a demon dumped me here."

His expression cold and piercing, Demogorgon snarled, his lips down-turned eyeing me over, leering forward. He peered around me trying to see my body under the black ice. At times he seemed uncomfortable in his own skin, moving like a puppet, disjointed. As if he was wearing an armoured costume that was too big. Demons like him are a perverse creation.

Wincing, I moved my head back futilely as rancid breath heated my face.

"If you're going to kill me, then just bloody do it, or do you lack the bravery of your conviction?"

I opened my eyes in the nick of time to see his huge muscular leg lift then stamp down, cracking the ice underneath him and, as if fortune had smiled on me, it shattered around my body.

Scrabbling to grab at the surrounding ice, my hands could not grip it and I slipped back, falling backwards, the currents trying to drag me under it. Unexpectedly hovering above me, his mighty wings beating, the demon offered me his hand.

Gulping, I took it, shock written on my face as I gasped in air. He flew off gripping my hand in his until he landed us safely on the shore.

I staggered, my legs still in a state of inertia from the frozen lake, my body chilled to the core, I bent over, hands on my thighs trying to regain some semblance of normality, heat. Breathing deeply, I stood up, seeing his left hand held up behind him, his sword raised, narrow eyes cut through me. "I hate you, Lucifer. You have no idea, do you?"

"Demon, you're tedious. You should know you can't kill me, you're too lowly for that but," I lifted my chin up, "Thank you for getting me out of there. You are welcome to try to kill me." I held out my arms, mocking him to try with his sword.

His eyes went wide and colour drained from his coal red skin, mouth open I noticed beaded sweat on his forehead. If he could kill me, so be it. I was ready...

Instead, he lowered his sword, his arm falling to his side, shoulders dropped.

"You do not remember, do you? No, I was too lowly then as apparently I am now." His chest heaved, his head low, he suddenly screamed, "I followed you!" His voice echoed in the vast chamber, "I followed you in the rebellion! No, I was no archangel, I was, as you would say, a lesser angel. My name was Xaphan, then. You never even noticed me, you didn't care, yet I believed in you, stood with you and for over two millennia, I have been cast in this shit pit to fire the flames of Hell. I was once a celestial being, touched by the grace of God, your father! And now I am this... thing, a monstrosity.

And you treat me like excrement! Two thousand years of torture and hate have created this monster you see before you, this atrocity, and still..."

He fell to his knees. My body broke out in a sweat. Was he lying? His words, the emotion from him smacked me in the gut, winding me, breathless, he couldn't be. I'd created this monster, chastised him, belittled him, and loathed him with every hair of his being. And I, Lucifer, had abandoned him. Just as my family, as Heaven had abandoned me.

My throat tightened as guilt consumed me, wincing inside I stared at the creature who was once an angel, a celestial being who had believed in me, followed me to the very depths of Hell and I, in my arrogance, hadn't even known. Or cared. How many more suffered here because of me? Did Gabriel know this? Was that why my fate was disregarded, as I had done that to, perhaps, countless others?

Unable to speak, wracked with remorse, shame, I went to speak but my breath shook, choking on my guilt. My rage at myself.

He had followed me, been condemned and then I, the one who'd led him to his torture, my very fault had shattered his soul.

I remembered the fall when we were cast down and abandoned. Now I thought back, and I recalled all those who fell with me, I hadn't cared about any of them then at all. I had been too angry, too arrogant in my own defeat to give a thought to lesser angels. I was, had been God's favourite son, I had surpassed my father and as punishment they had thrust me into Hell under lock and key. And it had filled me, brimming with rage. But I was conceited, I'd only thought of myself, of the audacity, the humiliation and the rejection of my father casting me aside. I'd never cared for another, not Demogorgon, not anyone else. Just me and how my father and brother Michael had wronged me.

Anger and remorse at my impropriety. Forcing my limbs to work, I stomped forwards, legs and feet laden with frozen water. The massive, ugly demonic beast before me stirred my soul.

Demogorgon rasped on his knees, his suffering consumed him, his soul so twisted, so evil and I placed my hand on his head and willed what divine grace I had left to flow into him, which would be surely nothing after Cain, but I had to try... Maybe I could muster something?

Closing my eyes I breathed deeply, trying to feel, to sense the celestial power that once bound me together, but after minutes with my body shivering in that huge dark soul sucking place I stopped.

His sword was by his side, I crouched beside him; he did not move. Picking it up I dragged the blade across my palm, Cain be damned, I was still an angel by design. I may have a soul of a cursed man, of a monster. But my father, the creator, made me by his own blood. My blood was still that of angel's blood.

The crimson liquid flecked with silver poured from my stiff hand, glistened slightly in the darkness. Rising up I placed my bloody hand on his face, whispering, "Drink my blood. My angelic force is gone, stolen, but my blood is from our father, from God."

He wobbled slightly, looking into my eyes, as if trying to steal into my soul, then his gaze fixed on my bleeding palm, so I cupped it over his rough lips. Closing his eyes he took it, drank the blood of the devil, I did not know what would happen, but I hoped... hoped something good. It was all I had.

My throat dried, tongue stuck to the top of my mouth as my gut contorted. Shit! And how many more of the fallen lay in Hell by my doing?

My palm grew hot. He didn't move except for his lips as he drank the metallic red blood. As it travelled down his throat, a soft white-gold light spun out of him, illuminating him, glowing through his body, his veins, his skin.

Then an intense heat from my blood, this small amount of celestial energy overwhelmed us both, I lifted my hand and Demogorgon held out his hand now for me to help him up; he staggered.

Illuminating golden light, his eyes closed and before me I saw the hate, the ravages of anger, of evil melt away like a tide washing back out to sea.

It was like looking into a mirror...

I withheld a gasp as rotten flesh fell from him, his skin underneath pale with a bronze hue and like the glow of embers, tattoos etched on his skin, whirls of gold sigils. Dark piercing eyes fluttered, replaced by caramel coloured eyes glinting and the tangled mess of hair, thin and matted, grew white and thick before my eyes.

Shifters, werewolves, I'd seen these transitions at a distance, but now I was seeing, I didn't know. Even his wings, like ink on paper, turned from dirty dark to pale grey, leather transforming to feathers so soft, a golden sheen glowed from their edges.

His face soft, wide pallid lips, straight nose, angular, yes now I saw the angel, now I was looking at Xaphan. Fallen but with grace, with hope, maybe even redemption.

Biting my bottom lip too hard as my body braced watching the transformation before me, my stomach flipped and I vowed I would do right by him, whatever the cost. He had saved my life, maybe I could help absolve his?

Swallowing hard, I fought back a tear, ashamed that I, righteous and arrogant, had bestowed such a cruel and treacherous fate on this angel. And I hadn't even known such was my conceited and condescending nature.

Xaphan stopped trembling, looked down at his body, his wings, soft smoky wings like storm clouds. He took in a deep breath, jaw slack. A smile tugged at his lips. He backed away, awe in his face. His eyes locked with mine as he said, "I wanted to kill you. For a thousand years, I had wanted to give the anger, the revenge that you gave me. But... I could not. In the end," he looked about him, at the lake, at the bodies jutting out from it, at the death. "In the end I had to save you, even though it went against every fibre of my demonic being. I had to save you, you Lucifer Morningstar, who I stood with in the rebellion thousands of years ago. And now I am this..."

The words spewed from my mouth, "I couldn't help you before, Xaphan. I was locked away. But you are right, I didn't care, wrapped up in my own vain wrath, in my selfishness. I cannot undo my wrongs, I can only try to make amends now. I am truly sorry, but I am not stupid enough to think that redeems me, or that you can accept my apology."

He eyed me, then glanced back down to his transformed self, touching his arms and flapping his mighty wings with a lightness that stole my breath.

Little did I know, way back then when we rebelled, that I was totally and utterly Godforsaken.

My father, who made me and surely instilled these traits in me, if not to succeed him, then why?

Rejected, unloved, defied. Every day had been a torture, as rage tightened in my gut, around my throat and it had been never ending. Even my wings, once ice-white, were altered, red and battered. Occasionally a sliver of light had shone into my cell as a demon came to leer at me, that light would, for a second lift my spirits, I was to be set free, forgiven, liberated by my father?

Then it would fade back into the putrid darkness in the bowels of Hell, and it would replace my hope with despair. An eternity of punishment, of hate and isolation.

My father was far from all-forgiving, at least to me and Xaphan, it seemed.

I paused, swayed by the memories from my life, if life was what you can call it. Xaphan stared at me, his eyes small as he assessed me.

"Come, we need to get out of here. My brother's lives hang in the balance with the bastard Cain. If I am to save them, I can't do that here. But I must ask, were there others like you, angels that fell that are now... demonic?"

He nodded, went to speak, and uncertainty fell upon him.

"M... mo...st of the others are unaware of the fate that befell them. I was alone in my knowledge of that fateful day,

I have been for two thousand years, trapped in Hell, my mi... nd consumed with chaos, anger, abhorrence. But I don't want to be alone again. I don't know what you've done to me. I am not the beast I once was, yet I am not divine, either, but... I am grateful. I will now fight by your side, I..."

His face scrunched up, so I finished his sentence, "I know, I know. Loneliness, I, too, was trapped here, locked away in isolation for eons. Until Bael stole my soul and somehow trapped it in a vampire who then took on my powers. I hadn't seen the world above. I'd heard only whispers, mutterings and was too rage fuelled, too exasperated to think of little else except my own damnation. Come, brother, let me atone for my crimes." I held out my arm, looking down as Xaphan strode slowly towards me. He sheathed his sword then his pale eyes bore into my soul.

"I am still angry, but..." he breathed deeply, "I am this, more like myself."

Still bracing back my reaction, the difference was shocking. Soft features, flowing white hair and his skin as mine. More human than demon, it was a complete transformation.

A moment of tension as Xaphan stood before me, I noticed the tremble on his limbs, his eyes bore into mine. Isolation, wrath, abandonment. I, too, shook a little, I took a step forward, then another, never looking away from his gaze. I opened my arms and pulled him close, holding him. He made no sound. But angels, though not made to have emotion, want affection. We are not created to be forsaken, forgotten.

Pulling away, my breathing eased, "Well Xaphan, let us find Cain, I have something to return to him."

"The Mark! How will you do that? I don't think it can be done."

"I know, but I have to try. There must be a way and I need to find it, before it annihilates me."

Sacrifice

My body felt lighter than I'd ever known, being able to help the creature gave me an unexpected energy. Something strange stirred inside of me as I glanced at Xaphan. Maybe it was hope. I had felt this... emotion when I had rescued Cerberus. I thought of him now. A surge of relief rushed through my heart knowing he wasn't here but would be safe alongside Eva at her home.

Eva... When I was with her, the Mark lost its hold on me and the monster within was silent. And desires stirred that I hadn't felt for a thousand years since I'd found Lilith, then lost her. I had wanted to return to her and searched for her over this damned place, only to find they forbid me to see her. Hell is not to be a place where you find any comfort, any companionship. Unlike Lilith, Eva's heart was warm, open, not scorned by betrayal and loss. I would search for Eva and Cerberus once Michael and Gabriel were free.

Would I find my redemption from Heaven?

The frozen lake was bigger than I realised. After helping Xaphan, we ran around one side of it; the land surrounding it was rocky, hot and barren. Slowly my body was recovering from the trial of the lake, even though I'd given him my blood, my limbs, my body had warmed and a feeling of faith slowly grew stronger. I only had to remove the Mark. Well, that and stay out of the shadow of Heaven.

A faint gleam of light shone as it caught the water's iced surface, but I couldn't see the horizon.

"Let's get out of here... But I have one question, Xaphan, why did you rescue me?"

A wry smile sat uncomfortably on his now soft features. "I was going to punish you, impale you over and over. I knew it wouldn't kill you, but I wanted you to suffer, to inflict pain so you would know, or at least have a glimpse of the agony I suffered. But... I just couldn't. I knew I probably could kill you, Lucifer, the Devil... but although I'd lost all hope, without you, I would have nothing. Be nothing." He turned his head away, breaking any chance of eye contact...

Nodding, I continued to sprint. "Understood."

He shook his head. "Do you have any ideas of how you will remove the Mark?"

I thought about Cain's punishment as I scoured the lake, my eyes falling on the trapped souls frozen there, their faces contorted in agonized screams, horrifying. Hundreds of them, but they were not dead, not quite...

"I do, as a matter of fact, but I doubt I can find what I need here. We need to leave, now. And we need to find another way out, the last time..."

He sniggered, I could feel his energy almost like it was my own. A surge of cold trickled down my back. It happens when we share energy, my divine blood into him, I couldn't read his thoughts, but emotions, definitely.

It was a nervous laugh, probably because he hadn't laughed in over two thousand years, but now his bright eyes gleamed. "Yes, I remember the last time you broke out of Hell. There are many ways out of here. Come, follow me."

Like him, I had been full of wrath. Both of us, victims of our own desire to be free of judgement, to be free to choose our destiny and ironically losing everything to be trapped here.

Xaphan knew the tunnels and corridors of Hell. Last time I'd broken out I'd totally winged it, but now we sprinted lightly down a rocky path with walls that towered so high they seemed endless reaching up beyond my eyeline. In no time, demons approached, I had no sword to fight, so like a mortal had to use fists, kicks- it wasn't elegant.

I would need to find Joash's dagger... God knows who would find Tecpatl on the abbey roof.

Two approached us, like Xaphan had been, they were muscular with coal red skin, armour plating over their arms, chest and lower legs.

Grunting as soon as they saw us, they charged in unison, swords glinting under the flashes of volcanic flames that erupted violently far away, furiously lighting up Hell's sky.

Xaphan fought with the grace of an angel and the fire of Hell. His sword fast, he twisted around them, leaping and striking, killing one of them before it had the chance to start.

He leered at the other; it charged me; I stood still as stone until the last second, then crouched down fast, but not fast enough.

But Xaphan was there, grabbed the beast by the scruff of its neck, stepped back and slew off its head before it could blink.

I stood up, blood poured from my back, it itched and burned as I felt the skin, the sinew knot together, healing.

Picking up a sword from one of the dead demons, it felt good to have a weapon in my hand. Not my own, but at least something to defend myself with.

My sharp wit probably wouldn't be enough to defend me here.

"Thank you," I said.

He stopped abruptly, his eyes lost as he thought for a moment, then walked on slowly, whispering, "When I fell, I looked like this, but my wings were golden. They took me to a pit of other fallen angels. We had our wings clipped and were thrown in on top of each other. I was literally buried alive, almost crushed under the bodies of my kin, all of us in a state of horror, hardly able to move but not dead.

"Eventually, they pulled me out, tortured me, infected me with some kind of hellish blood and inflicted agonies on me. I don't know how long this lasted. If I had to guess now that I've been up there, on Earth, I'd say centuries, longer... Over time my flesh darkened, rotted as did my mind. My kin, most of them died in the torture chamber, others forgot all semblance of who they'd been before the fall. Many died, they tortured many, Lucifer, in your name."

Seeing the Mark blazed on my arm, Xaphan looked at it, then at me.

"I did not know, my father..." I mumbled.

"Your father, our father, is the creator. We defied him, imagine if he hadn't punished us. As sick as it makes me feel, we were wrong. Without him we wouldn't exist, none of this would, so who were we to question him? I followed you, I blamed you, I still do. His eldest son, the most beautiful, surpassing all others. For the longest time before the fall, I worshipped you, wanted to be you." He let out a breath. "They sent you to Hell on the command of your father, God who charged Michael with plunging you here. Because they don't believe you can ever change. Can you, Lucifer, can you change?"

Swallowing hard, shit. I thought I had changed. Now this angel questioned that. And I knew the answer, didn't I? Not wanting to lie, and feeling the beast inside me stir, I looked away. Avoided his eye.

"No Xaphan, it was wrong. He, my father, should have only punished me, I led you, all of you in my righteous indignation." And I wondered then if I'd ever be able to live with the guilt. Sure, he was here now, Xaphan, but forgiveness, I doubted I'd ever be able to forgive myself, let alone my father. Like stones churning in my stomach, my core was heavy, my shoulders weighed down.

"And I fled Hell to rescue my brothers, even though Michael fought me when my father cast me off, it was Dad's orders to my brother to send me to Hell."

We walked on in silence, the Mark scorching my arm as anger seethed inside of me, my lips down-turned at the thought of Gabriel and Michael under Cain's hand.

The place was eerily quiet and deserted. "Isn't it strange that no more demons have come this way?" I muttered.

"Not at all, this leads to the causeway across the Pit Malum, that's why there are no demons here. I take it you know of it?"

Unable to suppress a shudder I nodded, whispering, "The evil pits, the worst place in Hell. Shit, Xaphan, really? You thought, hey, things can't get much worse, but, well, I don't know, let's make it worse. The Pit Malum, really? So, if we're unlucky we'll end up being hung upside down and being burned alive by Hellfire... for all eternity?"

He glanced at me, a lopsided smile. "Exactly, one of the most feared areas, so yes, it's guarded by demons but not as many since the souls of the damned cannot escape."

"You think! Great. And it's guarded by the thirteen demons, and they make your last incarnation look weak."

"I am fully aware, Lucifer, but just so you know, they also have Hell hounds here, too. At the back of the ditch there is a slight opening in the rock face, and there onwards a tunnel that leads out of Hell. Few know of it, I have travelled through it before but as Demogorgon, I had to squeeze through it as its narrow. Alongside the great ditches there are tracks we can pass but we must be stealthy, otherwise we'll face an eternity of far worse than anything we've ever known. You have never been this far?"

I shook my head, I'd been imprisoned, but I'd heard the tales. I wasn't looking forward to this. Hell hounds, the worst demons in Hell and a pit, one of many reserved especially for those who they, the demons deem too angry. And here I am with Cain's bloody Mark and only a matter of minutes away. I especially don't like the idea of being hung upside down and engulfed in Hellfire, you know. And it's only Tuesday... I sighed, wondering if I'd ever get out of this rancid, boiling shit hole.

"Wait, we have to pass through the viper pit first, the Serpens Mala."

The Serpens Mala. Hell is so vast, I'd never seen it. I'd heard tales of it, though. But nothing prepared me for the reality. Creeping through a narrow winding tunnel, a flicker of torchlight seeped through the passageway. At the end, in the vast cavern, a colossal head of a snake, carved from stone, its mouth open with fangs that hung down the size of a man. A split tongue spilled onto the ground, a walkway into the head, and the scales on this carved sculpture were gilded in gold radiated under the firelight. Two massive ruby eyes seemed alive as they caught the light of flames that spat and licked the wood in golden vessels that sat alongside the walls.

The faint sound of hissing reverberated around the cavern, mixed with the crunching on gravel from our footsteps. Maybe it was instinct, but I caught a whiff of lilacs and found myself walking up the granite tongue of this serpent and into its mouth where I found slouched against the mouth wall, Eva!

My blood curdled, I shivered as a frigid chill whipped through me, crouching before her. Her skin was icy, lifeless.

"Who is she?" Xaphan whispered behind me, and bent over her beside me.

"A friend." Her eyes moved rapidly under their lids. She was breathing so gently I shook her, edging back as her eyes shot open, her mouth opened and she gagged violently.

Coming out from her lips, a thin black viper slid out, causing Eva, my Eva, to choke, heaving fear in her eyes. She clutched her throat, wide eyes full of terror as it slithered out of her, away, fast on the floor as she convulsed, coughing violently, I pulled her into me, willing her well.

Her cold body shook into mine, her face clammy with sweat. Wiping it with my hand, I whispered, "It's alright, you're alright. I am here. I will let nothing hurt you." Cold sweat dripped down my back. What fresh hell was that?

Sucking in air, her body calmed. I thanked whoever that I'd walked inside the head of this weird sculpture. In all my time, I had never seen this part of Hell before. Had I not found her... was unthinkable.

Rasping she muttered, "What happened to me, where are we? Lucifer?"

With my name on her lips, I pulled her tighter. My heart was on fire. Who had done this to her? I would have his head, I guessed it was Cain. Again.

Xaphan whispered, "Come, let us guide you out of this place." He shivered. "Serpens Mala is sinister even by Hell's standards."

Carefully I stood up holding Eva, who trembled in my arms. Tears stained her cheeks, and I wiped her face with my hand, brushing her skin. "I'm so sorry, dear Eva, you have been cast into a net of evil. I will have Cain's head for this."

A slight sparkle in her eyes, but she wasn't ready to let go of me. Who could blame her, she was mortal thrown into Hell and after being in Cain's clutches once before? Immortals never bothered humans usually, so Cain's motives confused me. He had stolen her power, so why he wanted to continue tormenting her made little sense. And even being a witch, this was too much for a mortal to bear.

Wrapping my arm around her, I stood by her side, gently encouraging her that we needed to leave. Her legs gave out, I caught her, pulling her into me. Maybe I should carry her? But as soon as that thought came, she pulled herself up, breathing heavily. A slight nod. She leaned into me and we left.

Her presence though, it was as if the Mark on my arm didn't exist. As if all the anger, the millennia of hate had washed away and even in this predicament, a quiet power, a serenity held over me. Realising that Xaphan was staring, his mouth hanging open, I looked at him.

"Xaphan, may I introduce Eva. A victim of Cain alongside a mage who I found in the vaults of the abbey. Eva, this is Xaphan. An angel."

She tried to smile, but fear had too strong a hold over her. Xaphan took her hand, staring into her eyes. For a moment she seemed light headed, I realised he was trying to use the angelic gift of calm on her; it worked a little. Had he not been brutalised into a demon, it would have worked well.

Eva possessed a strength and kindness that was rare. Strong mortals had a tendency to be snide, pushy, as I'd seen through Jack's eyes. Kind mortals, a tendency for weakness, but Eva... Everything was balanced. I guessed that was why Austin had chosen her to learn from him.

We walked slowly out of the serpent's mouth. Below us a host of black snakes, their whip-like bodies writhed along the ground. Where they'd come from, I didn't know, but I had a hunch.

Eva shuddered, so I asked Xaphan, "Can you cut off one of their heads? I don't believe they're real."

In a flash, Xaphan unsheathed his sword, pulled up a snake and struck off its head. The whole thing burst into a cloud of black soot that sparkled in the light like obsidian stars.

"Demons! The snakes were never real, just a projection of your fear." I gripped her arm tighter. "Not that it didn't seem real, Hell does that. It takes hold of your deepest fears then turns them into a living nightmare, but bigger, scarier."

She breathed deeper, looking at the snakes on the ground and following the flecks of black soot that still caught the light of the flames. "Thank you, I..."

My arm slipped from her shoulder as my hand found hers, and my gaze found her lips. Her lips the colour of ripe cherries held sway over my heart. Finally, I looked her in the eye. "There is no need to thank me, I am only glad you're safe. Now, let's get you the hell out of here."

She gripped my hand tighter, my heart pounded, and even in this stinking place of doom, a glow of warmth, I needed her like I needed to breathe.

Swallowing hard, I pressed on, shooting her a glance behind the veil of my hair and my heart boomed when she caught me, my face burning.

Grinning, she caught my stare and held it. In the darkest place on Earth, the most evil and terrible hole, Eva lit up my soul, my heart was on fire...

"Come on lovebirds, we'll never get out of here with you two!" Xaphan teased.

"Where next, Xaphan, The Fields?"

"Aye, The Fields. Eva, is it? You'll want to cover your nose, the smell is enough to, well you'll want to cover it. And look straight ahead, better yet, look at your feet. Do not under any circumstances look up, or beside you. I will walk behind you, Lucifer, before you. I have known them to drive a demon to insanity, but we have no choice but to cross them."

I ripped some of my T-shirt and passed it to her. "He's right. I have been through The Fields before, I..." I glanced away. An urge to shelter her from the horrors, the sounds, swelled strong, but there was no safer way out, and we still had further to go. We still had to pass through all the pits. I looked at Xaphan. "Who commanded to bring me to Hell, you never told me?"

He blinked, his soft eyes, long lashes, then a flush of pink to his cheeks. "It was King Paimon, obviously. I had always answered to him, though..."

"Yes, the highest Prince of Hell. But was it, I think it's more likely Cain had somehow bewitched you? I know Paimon, not well, but he always answered to me. With me out of the way, with my grace Cain is free to do as he wishes with Michael and Gabriel."

I turned to face Eva. "I cannot prepare you for what's next, and neither can Xaphan, our powers are lost. I would rather you walk by my side and bury your head in my chest. If you falter and look around you, madness may consume your mind. And... I cannot undo it."

Her lips curved up a little. "Thanks Lucifer, but I'll walk between you and your friend. I've seen horrors, but I promise I'll try not to look."

His voice harder. "Just remember, the souls, the people in The Fields have committed the worst crimes, crimes awful by Hell's standards."

She nodded, we pressed on until we came to a huge, blood splattered wooden gate, and the cries of the damned filled our ears.

The Fields

A mixture of rotten flesh, human waste and blood hung like a lead chain around my throat, imposing and oppressive. The moans and screams carried on the air, only a soft breeze swept my hair away but unfortunately carried the stench with it.

Hell. It's no picnic.

Xaphan's idea, just before opening the gate, had been to give Eva a strip of cloth, not just for her nose to cover the stench, but also to cover her eyes, a blindfold. And whilst she argued, I, too, insisted that he was right.

Strong she certainly was, I had to argue passionately with her that I never doubted her ability to overcome adversity, to adapt. I loved her for that, though, I obviously wouldn't tell her.

But I and Xaphan were right when we'd known lesser demons to lose their sanity having seen this place. Hardly none dared to walk through it, and so it had no guards, no demon overseers. They deemed it too cruel to set the demonic under lords the task of guarding this place. Only the damned came here to live out eternity in abject suffering. Eva argued that she'd seen a movie where they were blindfolded, and that imagining the horror would be worse.

But she was wrong. Very definitely wrong.

As it was, I also insisted after surveying The Fields that she walk by my side. The ground was craggy, uneven, and the path through was set on the verge of a hill. With Eva on the inside of me, Xaphan walked behind, we both had our swords drawn. I had torn a second piece of cloth from my T-shirt and ensured it was secure, the first covering her nose.

A dirty smog knee high hung across the plain before us. The wailing from those souls there seeped into the mind until it became like white noise. But not to her. I'd spent so long in Hell I was almost immune to the cries, but Eva, though putting up a brave front, shook and clung to my side tightly.

It tore my heart in two seeing her here. I knew what she was going through. When I'd first arrived in Hell, I spent the longest time dumbfounded by the horror. And the screams, they never leave your mind even though you can blank them out. Nightmares plagued my every moment, smells repulsing me, sending my stomach into a spasm constantly and the perverse pleasure the demons took in the cruelty.

It changes you, darkens your soul, and that change cannot be undone. Though I believe vehemently that they should punish the evil, I also wish that Hell did not exist.

My left arm wrapped around her body, I whispered, guiding her through whilst Xaphan kept silent. Some horrors are best left to the imagination.

A growl in the distance had the hairs on my arm on end, I pulled myself up, ready to fly at any time but aside from the people here, in between life and death no vegetation grows and we could see nothing moving on the horizon.

"Do you know how you came to be in Hell?" I asked her. It was no doubt Cain playing, toying with her, but I wanted Eva to concentrate on something other than the current circumstance.

"I was running with Austin, with Cerberus when I felt a ... a bolt of lightning shot through me. And then nothing until you woke me up." Her fingers gripped tighter. "Austin, Cerberus, could they be here?" Sweat poured down my back, thinking I may have left the mage and my dog behind.

Xaphan spoke quietly, "I doubt it. Does Cain know your feelings towards Eva?"

Heat again on my face, her fingers digging harder. "I don't know what that bastard knows. You think he did that to her to get at me? I think he's toying with her. What happened when he captured you and Austin, Eva?" I almost growled but withheld my anger at the thought of Cain punishing someone I cared about. I'd only just met her. What could he possibly know?

"When Austin and I were under his capture, Cain told us he scryed. So I suspect he knows a lot about everyone," she mumbled.

"Well, I'm not letting you out of my sight Eva, not until he's dead, a true death."

"But you cannot kill him, can you? Surely you have to get the Mark back to him, retake your celestial power, then lock him away in purgatory, preferably the lake where Paimon put you, it's named after Cain." Even though Xaphan spoke softly his voice carried on the breeze. I tensed, uneasy in this morbid landscape. Trying to repress a shudder, not wanting to alarm her, I braced my limbs, clenched my jaw.

To the side of her, rubble fell down the slight incline, gathering before us. I stopped, pulling her in close. "Xaphan we should fly, now!"

His voice hurried, "But if we do, they'll detect us. All manner of-"

But he never finished. In a flash, winged demons, much like Xaphan's last incarnation, flew directly at us. Roughly, I pushed Eva to the ground. "Stay down, do not get up, whatever you do. Xaphan!" I yelled.

"I know," he said.

We were lucky; I guess. Only three demons. They charged at us, their blades glinting in the gloom, their roars making Eva shake badly as she crouched over her knees. I stood in front of her, my knees slightly bent, sword at the ready, side on, waiting for the attack. Panting, Eva rocked slowly, Xaphan bent over her. "Here, take this." She was confused, dazed and no wonder, so he lightly pulled her blindfold off and handed her a long-handled dagger. His eyes narrowed, I muttered, "Eva, listen. Stay behind us, you will be alright. Be strong."

Dread gnawed at her face, and her body shook from shock. I whispered, "I know, this place... hold on Eva. We will get you out of here. Just a bit longer."

She nodded, her eyes blank as her mortal side battled with her emotions, the horror of Hell. I knew the wails would forever haunt her; the screams locked in her mind that echo throughout the underworld.

Xaphan turned around, his poise like mine ready to battle. They would not harm her. Over my dead body...

Landing with a thud before me, two demons sneered. The chink of steel on steel, I growled sweeping my weapon low, ducking fast then stepping forwards to drive two of the beast's back. A fast glance over my shoulder, Xaphan stepped swiftly backwards, just avoiding the blade. The two in front of me stalked me, then both attacked at once, the burning in my arm, the Mark fuelling my need for blood, their blood on my sword. For a moment my body almost spasmed. The beast wanted out. Bracing, clenching my teeth I held it back, instead unleashing the frenzy that whipped through my veins, I roared back at them, the acid in my arm burning as my sword arm blocked one on my right, then the other on my left, fast, again, again. Rapidly I crouched, sweeping my sword low which sliced one of the demon's shins. He wailed, stumbling back. This drove the other demon on my left harder. A slice on my left arm stung like hell, blood seeping fast down to my wrist.

Eva made a noise, I couldn't look to see as the demon tried to drive me back, his sword thrusting at rapid speed. Shivering as the cold sweat down my back merged with the heat from my muscles, my mind twisted into a battle fury.

I edged forwards, my blade pushing his to the side, brute force as the tip met his body. Thrusting his chin up, he locked eyes with me, and launched forward onto the blade, bellowing hot putrid breath, an act of defiance.

Eva screamed, this demon it seemed was unstoppable. Thinking fast, I dragged the sword out of him as he raised his right arm; I spun fast to the left, sword high, my blade lodged in his neck. It sliced halfway through. Not pleasant. A final act of defiance from him, he swept his sword towards me as I tried to take his head, but was met with a block. Eva stood there, legs bent and apart, face scrunched as his sword fought hard to bite past her long-handled dagger, caught on the dagger's hilt, his strength against hers. She stepped towards him, her jaw clenched. It was enough. My blade stuck on his neck, his gnarly spine, I gripped with two hands, my knuckles white and grunted, pushing my strength to take his head. My sword bit into his bone and his head rolled to the ground, a bloody, hacked mess.

The other demon limped towards me, anger in his eyes a hint of red in the blackness. My chest rose and fell, I glanced back and flashed a smile at Eva. My Eva.

She stood a little behind me; her face ghost white. It would be easier now with her by my side, I picked up the beheaded demon's sword and smirked at the beast before me. I liked to even the odds, and I like killing demons even more.

Snarling, he staggered on his wounded leg, but to be sure he was still powerful. Laughing I stepped forward, moving my left hand, but that was a trick, as he blocked it my right sword arm thrashed towards his neck, he blocked it fast. Eva went to move alongside me. I growled to her. "Stay back..."

Now he let his anger fuel him. His blade swished so quickly it was all I could do to parry him, using the two swords to block his one. Swinging them in front of me, he struggled forwards, lunging steel whacking on steel, clashing a frenzy of hate. My left arm felt numb from the lost blood, but I had something worthwhile to fight for.

The sound became louder, metal clanking, his grunts louder as we fought harder, but he did not relent and I leant back, narrowly missing his blade from my throat.

But the Mark had taken hold. I continued in a frenzy, lashing at his crumpling body, grunting. Sweat poured from every pore as I thrashed before his sword dropped from his hand and I felt her touch on my back, her voice calling my name as a red mist of hate started to clear, slowly.

I turned my stance, driving him down the slight incline; he lunged back just enough, there I buried my sword tip in his throat, pushing it in.

Collapsing like a bag of rocks he tumbled down, my arm too weary even to wipe the sweat from my face I turned to find Eva staring and Xaphan sat down next to his dead demon, grinning. "Bit slow, aren't you, Lucifer? I've been waiting ages!" He laughed, got up and strolled over, blood splattered but hardly a hair out of place.

Gritting my teeth, I said, "And you didn't think to help me?"

He wrapped an arm around Eva. "Suits you, a weapon in your hand." Then he looked me over. "No, I thought you could do with the practise. Seems I was right. Come on then, Hell waits for no man."

"Oh god, that woman!" Eva paled, gagging. "She's crucified?" The shock of her surroundings now hit her. Hard. She stumbled. Catching my breath, I wrapped my arm around her, but though horrified, she could not look away. Rasping, "She's still alive?"

"Do not feel remorse for that woman. She burned a child alive and when the child screamed and cried to be saved, that abomination of a woman merely rolled her eyes as if it were a minor inconvenience. She deserves her fate. And she deserves to be alive whilst crucified." I frowned. "That is the point of the punishment. If she were dead, she would not suffer. This is Hell, Eva, where the evillest pay for their sins. Eternally."

"But... but how do you know?"

"There is a pool where we can see the crimes of your species- the worst ones."

I explained to her as we walked. "The Fields, an endless landscape filled with the most abhorrent of mankind, on and on they go. There are only a few who dare to look into the pool of sin. Most, even those demons we just killed, would go mad if they stared into it for too long. They say this place is one of the hardest to cross, not because of guards, there are hardly any, but because of the presence of evil. Come though, you fought, survived Hell. And only a human, I've never met such a strong mortal."

"You had never met any mortals, Lucifer, but you hated them all the same, remember?" Xaphan cut in.

I laughed. "Yes, yes, I did." I shrugged. "I'm realising I was wrong."

"Hum, maybe... still, we have a long way to go to get out of here. Damn Paimon, damn Cain."

The hairs on my arms tingled, I had the odd sensation that we were being watched, as if our journey out of Hell was a game to some overseer. Maybe Cain, but how he could have gained so much power was beyond my comprehension. I squeezed Eva's shoulders as we walked, my arm wrapped around her. She mesmerized me.

Pointing with his sword, Xaphan murmured, "Up ahead there's a causeway. We'll need to move fast. Eva, you have the dagger, I suggest you lose the sword, no offence. But it will weigh you down and that could cost us our lives." She dropped the sword, but clung to the dagger.

Bracing myself, not just for the horrors but also for the smell, we walked lightly around a corner where we found ourselves exposed on a huge stone ledge leading to the bridge.

Xaphan nodded to me and Eva, so following him we sprinted across this vast open rock face until we came to a cliff edge, fortunately one of few not consumed with lava.

"Eva, now watch where he places his footing. The way ahead is full of horror, and the path treacherous. Walk in front of me, but not too fast, so if you slip, I will grab you." She sighed, resigned to the fact we were not leaving this place fast enough, and I knew that feeling. Except for Xaphan, I knew that feeling more than anyone else.

Watching as I put each foot in front of the other, I made my way down, stopping only quickly to notice first where he had placed his feet. As we circled around a corner, the drop beneath us took my breath away. Of course, we could fly and I could take Eva, but to do that here we'd have another battle on our hands, and where I escaped last time was miles away and I'd had the element of surprise. Here, with hordes of armed demons flying at you, no chance.

The hairs on my arms stood up, I shivered at the screams and wails as whips broke flesh, the demons here beat the damned, forever, and ever and ever.

Knowing this and being up close to it are two different things entirely. I'd seen a lot of torture in Hell, but never in this section, and I swallowed back the bile that retched in my throat. This area, it only got worse.

The sinners, as they're called here, are lashed until their skin is raw. Then it heals. Then they're lashed again. And on and on it goes. As soon as I saw it, I was transfixed in utter horror, seeing that terror in the eyes of mortals condemned to Hell, and knowing they would endure this for eternity. Sweat trickled down my back, I reached out to Eva who glanced back, her face white with shock.

"Come," Xaphan whispered.

Shutting my eyes tightly for a second, the stench of flesh, of dread, my breath caught as a hollow emptiness gripped me, and the icy fingers of fear tingled down my spine.

We followed him down slowly across the craggy rock face, aware that not much cover stood between us and the pit of the shameless. Flogged repeatedly for pushing their deviant behaviour on others, I gulped, knowing that this pit, this atrocity was one of the least bad. I worried for Eva, she would be forever changed and I vowed that when I got my grace back, I would use it to heal her. No mortal should see this. But then I believed most of them did not deserve to be here. And now we had many more pits to travel through, if my geography was right, but the next one I dreaded most of all.

Unnoticed, our saving grace as boulders, juts in the rock face and crevices hid us as we tread fast from boulder, to peaks of rocky crags, then hiding in fissures in the rock face, before carefully leaning out to find the next place to run behind.

The demons below never thought to look up, for who in Hell would willingly come here? Their demented faces, curved horns and lithe bodies bent and twisted in form from an eternity of lashing sinners, huge fanged mouths fixated in malevolent grins with wide unnatural eyes, pale like Xaphan's, a trait of Hell.

Earth bound demons have black eyes. Me, mine went red. No clue why. Maybe I'm special? I'd like to think so...

We made it through, oh joy, to the second ditch. As expected, we smelt it before I saw it. Eva lurched forwards, her hand to her mouth, trying to stop herself from gagging. I nudged her, signalling with my hand to pull up the cloth wrap she'd used before to cover her nose. Tentatively she handed me the dagger and pulled the mask over her nose, bracing, without breathing. It wouldn't help really, more psychological than anything. But you use what you've got. I shot her a small smile, my eyes cast to the ground. She would see me differently now, I realised. For this is where I'd spent thousands of years. And who could love that? I gave her back the dagger, her hand shaking. She almost dropped it. Xaphan turned around, touching her arm, rolled his lips and nodded.

Here, the offenders live in a lake so deep it's said to have no bottom, but unlike the lake I was in, frozen and black water, this is black for another reason. A lake of filth, yes, you heard me right, I mean, what the actual hell! Who designed this torment of Hell? Not my dad, that's for sure. As the wicked manipulated others on Earth with their false flattery, I glanced as I saw the damned continually sinking into the shit. Literally. Neither of us breathed much, I could tell Xaphan was doing the same as I, bracing his breath, but the stench drenched us, seeped into our clothes, our hair.

Maybe it's Hell's sewers, which poses questions really. Toilets. In Hell. Hell isn't like Earth, though my body is part physical. Down here I wanted water but food, not so much. Still, my random thoughts kept my mind from screaming obscenities from the actual horror of our current situation, or actually just going into shock, then realising our plight wasn't as bad as those constantly drowning. As I sprinted, I slipped, I held my breath. Xaphan threw himself to the ground, then twisted his neck to stare at me and Eva, his wide eyes imploring us, along with a nod to do the same.

Shit, I must concentrate. I wished I was back at Aaron's, sat in his comfortable chair drinking coffee. I laid on the rocky ground, willing no demon to see us, especially not here, in the shit pit.

After far too long, Xaphan edged up a little, and we all ran crouched as low as we could until we scooted around the back of the rock face to enter the next ditch in the bloody pits of Hell. But at least the shit was behind us.

Ah, to be hung upside down with Hellfire. Burning you for all eternity.

The scent, and I use the term scent lightly, isn't any better than sewage, I realised. It got stuck in the back of my throat, my instinct to gag violently but we had to stay quiet. Eva, for her due, was aware enough not to look into this pit as we passed it. And on the plus, we were only passing by.

The Mark glowed as my anger seethed. There must be a quicker way out, bloody hell! Xaphan, however, sprinting carefully across the rock ledge, we were too close for comfort. With each pit we entered we were getting perilously close to the bottom, still dodging the eyes of demons, they seemed content with feeding the Hellfire's; the screams echoed through the valley, causing some rocks above us to tumble down. Covering my head with my arms and still crouching as I ran, I caught up to him, taking a breather behind a boulder. Rancid, vile place, here they punish those filled with wrath. The criminals in life are fuelled by fire, and so, ironically, they are in death.

My arm burned, my only solace was that the air was dense with the stink of burning flesh, my arm was undetected.

Nodding, Xaphan tore forwards, and my heart missed a beat. Possibly the weirdest, most disturbing pit, the pit full of magicians or false prophets.

Austin's and Joash's pit...

A mass of mortals, their heads on *backwards*, bodies contorted as punishment for looking into the future and thus now, to be forever looking backwards. Dante had more clarity than humans realised. He had actually been to Hell, not that mortals believed that! Well, until they came here, that is. I glanced, not looking where I was going as a low moaning sound, haunting, bellowed across the pit walls. Their distorted bodies reflecting their twisted sins, well in the eyes of Hell. Shuddering, it was a sight I'd never forget, a nightmare beyond belief. Eva froze in sheer horror, unable to move at the sight below her, Xaphan quickly noticing, grabbed her hand and pulled her to safety.

"Look, Lucifer!" A roar echoed across the huge cavern.

Shit!

I froze mid run caught in the open as Xaphan and Eva stayed hidden. Too late, if I ran now, I'd doom us all. The mortal was standing about twenty-feet away from me, his backwards head, eyes boring into me, and abnormal limbs a contortion of horrifying proportions.

I decided to wing it. I had no other choice. And I owed Xaphan and Eva every chance of freedom. Pulling myself up, I extended my arms out to the side, opened my wings, throwing my head back, allowing my pride full-reign. Superior, arrogant, commanding. "Yes, it is I," I bellowed, my voice echoing over the pit. All of them stopped. The mortals turned around backwards, watching, and for the moment, demons stopped flogging them, their whips silent as dozens of eyes bore into me. I swallowed. "The Devil, I come to see the fine work of my demons in all their glory. I am making my way through every pit in Hell, to survey its glory! Hell's demons!"

Shifting from foot to foot, a demon's eyes narrowed, one of them, a burly beast with twisted horns, plate armour and a mouth so full of teeth, it surprised me he could talk. "We thought you'd escaped. You're our prisoner. Get him!"

There's always one.

Holding my arm out in front, palm facing, I shouted, "You are right, I was a prisoner, and I escaped. But I brought back Cain and see, I have the Mark. I have been chosen to preside over Hell and all her demonic creatures, I cannot be killed. You'll find Cain in the frozen lake, go, see for yourself!"

I know, but they're not likely to look right now.

They stopped and turned to the huge demon. Another demon by his side looked at me unsure, I knew that slight fear in his eyes.

I wore a smug grin, and impatiently the creature called across the mass of disfigured mortals, who disturbingly were all still turned to face me, their backs to me, watching me.

Think about that...

"He is the Devil, he can roam and wander where he will. But who is that angel and woman with you, we must know, we know all the souls here?"

Lying, it wasn't something I liked, but I surprised myself as the lies tumbled out so easily and so fast, maybe because they were partially true and I was desperate.

"Why, that was Demogorgon, he was cursed above by a witch. Made angel from demon, preposterous!" I blared out the last word. All the sinners gasped in alarm. "And the woman, why, she is the witch that cast that spell!"

A rumble of growls bellowed around the pit.

"I am now taking them to the last pit, to the pit of... Liars!" I was really winging this because I almost forgot its bloody name. "See, he is now a false demon, and she, she changed him, so..." I echoed loudly, "I myself, the devil, your devil will deliver them to their fate of torture!"

Eyes from the demons bore at me, their grins grew bigger. "Let us take you! We know an easier way!"

Shit. No thanks.

"One is all I need for a guide, for I wish to have the pleasure of delivering these... these things myself."

Kudos to Xaphan and Eva, they wandered slowly forward, heads bent. I knew Xaphan was fake shaking. This wouldn't scare him. Eva though...

"I will guide you, my Lord Satan!" The massive demon bawled across the obscene pit. His heavy body thudded as he jumped and landed from the ledge he'd been standing on, striding across the pit towards me, he pushed, with ferocity, the sinners out of the way, sending them hurtling into each other, screaming.

I vowed then that if I lived, I would find and burn this place to the ground.

"Come Satan, I will lead you and..." He hissed and lunged at Xaphan and Eva. "This way through the remaining pits."

I nodded and ushered him along by flicking my hand. To be honest, it surprised me no one had died from his rancid stench. His breath alone could wipe out a small city. Maybe Bath?

He bounded heavily along the lower edge of the pit face, the wall's curvature made it awkward to walk, rocks slid down from his every step. Taking a deep breath, it relieved me to leave behind those tortured souls. But I instantly regretted the foul stink that I breathed in.

"Ah!" he boomed, "Here is where we torture corrupt politicians and bankers. I think you'll enjoy this."

I feigned a smiled.

A sea of bodies struggled to escape the scorching pitch, every time they tried to get out, wicked demons along the ledges jabbed violently at them with spears.

Broken and bloodied, the sinners fell back in, their screams had almost now become white noise, the smell... I'd never get used to it, but anything was preferable to the sea of excrement. We didn't stop, sweat poured from me in buckets. With my head thrust back, I pulled out my most arrogant demeanour; I am after all the *Devil*.

"Here we house the thieves. See how the snakes bite them. Look, one there."

Great, more snakes. Joash would love it.

We stopped to observe as a snake leapt up at a man; he covered his face with his arms, but the serpent was faster. He yelled in agony as the snake sunk its massive fangs into his cheek, then fell away sliding off quickly looking for another victim.

On his knees, wailing, the man burst into flames. I stepped back in disbelief. In seconds a pile of ash was all that was left where he had knelt. I turned but the demon beside me smiled, a nasty smile and he dared to touch my arm, then pulled back seeing my wide-eyed disgust. He nodded excitedly. "My Lord, wait! It is not finished, see..." He pointed to the pile of ash, which as I watched, it morphed back into the man, the demon sniggering. "And so it begins again. He will die a million times in Hell and on and on it goes."

"Why? Why this torture?" I snapped.

"Well, a thief takes from others, so down here we take from him and inflict pain."

I could only nod. It made sense in a sick sort of way. A longing to be up on Earth tugged at my heart, mortals... if they only knew their fate. And restraining my thoughts, as at that moment I felt protective of the fragile, mortal species.

Eva gasped, trembling. The demon turned around to her, laughing, then looked at me. I laughed back, nodding. And as he turned away, Xaphan pulled her into him. I nodded slightly to Xaphan. I had to act like it was funny. I had a plan for the demon, though; I mean, it wasn't likely he'd just let us walk out of here.

Oh, the glory of Hell!

My feet were sore from walking on a gradient for hours on rubble and rock. I knew we were coming to the end; my chest rose and fell heavily at the thought.

To breathe clean, fresh air.

We passed through the next pit, now the screams and wails that pierced and echoed around became fiercer as sinners were covered in shrouds and over and over burnt with Hellfire, they would die then be reborn to repeat their torture. I didn't ask. My stomach twisted like vipers, nausea compounding my every step, and keeping myself from vomiting all over the place was a constant battle of my wits. Eva tried her hardest not to look. Her pallid face glistened with a sheen of sweat, and I noticed Xaphan gripped hold of her hand. I wasn't angry at that; I was glad. She needed strength right now, he could give it.

But our demon consort glanced at the scene, stopped for a moment with a huge smirk on his coal red face. The demon nodded, greedy for more brutality.

I just hoped that my hunch about him was right.

Disembowelled sinners dragged their torn and ripped bodies. Dead eyes of despair followed us as we walked. I already saw that some were in the process of healing, no doubt to relive the slashing and mutilation all over again. I had no will to ask of their so-called sins. Nothing justified anything that I'd seen here, so I pressed on, my gaze now firmly fixed on the path ahead.

The thick stench of rotten meat greeted us in the final pit, I tried to abstain from looking, but macabre fascination had the better of me, disease ravished victims, their moaning like some twisted chanting echoed around the pit.

Xaphan shuddered and pulled Eva into him, her face buried in his chest. I knew that if we were not here, I'd be angry as, well as Hell, but with this big oaf of a demon I had to play my part. I'd noticed that following the demon Xaphan had rarely looked into the pits that we passed through, but instead kept his focus straight ahead.

Smart move, but then he'd seen it before, when he himself was a tortured soul trapped inside a demon's body.

Abruptly, the demon turned and paced heavily back to me. "What say you, my Lord Satan, is this all befitting enough, or should you wish us to use more extreme methods?"

Extreme? What the actual hell! No, I wish to release them all from this evil nightmare.

"It is... effective."

I glanced at Xaphan who stood subserviently behind the demon and I narrowed my eyes. He widened his, the slightest nod of his head.

"I do not even know your name, demon? Come, kneel before me, tell me?" I commanded.

His enormous feet tromped over, kneeling uneasily before me he glanced up. "My name is Sagos, Lord Satan."

"I am pleased with you Sagos, you are a fine example of everything evil and corrupt that a demon should be. I shall, because of that, bestow a gift, open your mouth."

He twitched, unsure. So I put my hand out to Eva, casting her my most evil grin. She gasped. Then nodded and handed me her dagger. Slicing my palm, I placed my hand firmly over his mouth, and as soon as my blood touched his crusted lips, he could not move, his body became rigid.

Was he a fallen angel? I didn't know, but to fight him would cause too much noise and honestly, if he had been an angel like Xaphan, another life would fall on my conscience. Heavily. So, I'd at least try.

Xaphan went to speak, his eyes wide and bore into mine, but I clenched my jaw and shook my head.

Sagos gulped harshly. Now Xaphan stepped forward, his mouth like a marionette, his face pale, eyes like saucers. "He is not one of the fallen," he gasped.

Blinking, I didn't move. Celestial blood pulsated fiercely through Sagos.

"No? Um, ok." As I finished speaking, Sago's convulsed, frothy spittle coughed out of his mouth, damn... I leapt back, not wanting his vomit on me. Then I strode fast to Xaphan, whispering, "Where's the exit?"

He winced as the demon's skin split, grabbed Eva and me by the arm. "Run!"

An explosion of demon flesh splattered over us before we could reach a nook in the vast rocky walled pit. It seared my skin, but we kept running.

The gradient now sloped up, we had to run bent over, the nook through the pit walls was only slightly wider than our shoulders and in total darkness we continued on up. I hoped Xaphan wasn't misleading me.

A heavy stench of sulphur assaulted me, Xaphan covered his nose with a hand, I did the same but it was thick all around us, the heat oppressive.

Eerie silence surrounded us, but that was preferable to the wailing and screaming, but still an overbearing energy seemed to zap me of my energy, my senses. Like lead, my legs struggled. Xaphan was slowing down, too. Panting, he turned, his arms out to meet me in the darkness, "We... we have to keep going. It wasn't like this last time, maybe because I was different."

He turned back. As we sprinted, one foot in front of the other, the walls narrowed further still and I realized something thick and slimy was brushing my arms, my shoulders.

Finally, the slightest breeze caught my attention and my adrenaline kicked in, I must get out of here.

With freedom before us, I puffed out my cheeks and bolted with Xaphan and Eva before me, up, up and out!

Staggering in the fresh air, I went to keel over, but the angel grabbed at my arm, his nails digging in.

"Look, we have to keep going. By now they'll have found Sagos. Our only luck is that they probably don't know of this passage and most of them couldn't fit through it, anyway. When I explored it as Demogorgon, I had to walk sideways for most of it, and it was the sheer desperation that drove me to it. Come, we need to get away."

Nodding, I picked up the pace, we'd exited Hell in a little woodland grove. Odd, still I would not wait to be taken back, so I ran, and as the trees cleared, I wrapped my arm around Eva, smiling and opened my wings and soared high, free from that nightmare.

Coven

A flash of darkness embraced us. We found ourselves in a room. I widened my stance to stop Eva and myself from falling over. Dizzy, blinking rapidly only to find a grinning Austin and Anthony surrounded us. Joash, as ever, his lips curved up slightly, a restrained smile. They eyed us like we were test subjects.

"It worked!" Austin yelled, bounding over and alongside him, his barking piercing my ears, Cerberus. Wagging his tail frantically, I scooped him up, and he licked my face. "Hello boy! You don't want to lick that muck, it's demon and will make you sick!"

Relief melted through my muscles. "Austin, you're safe!"

He went to hug me, and succeeded, then Eva. "It wasn't just you, after that demon was fighting you, Eva and Joash disappeared before my eyes. I sought Anthony's help, we scryed, though..." laughing, "We didn't do a ceremony like Joash."

Joash narrowed his eyes, a wry grin and placed his hand on his chest. "Well you wouldn't pull that off, Austin."

Austin's face was animated. "It was tricky getting Joash out, but we managed it. He had to use his magic, too. Then we set up finding you, wow, we saw the whole thing...Xaphan! And Eva! Anyway, it took us some time, and I am exhausted." He puffed his fringe out of the way, red-faced. "But we managed it, a coven of three male witches. You're welcome." Austin did a mock bow, so I returned the favour. "Thank you."

We were back in the vampire's basement, and now he guided us to some chairs. His friend Nathaniel handed us hot drinks as Joash, composed, stood forwards. "We know where Cain is, but to defeat him we will, I will summon more magic, more power." He eyed us individually. "Just to be sure."

A panting had me twist around to see Eva falling, Joash quickly grabbed her as Austin reacted fast pulling over a chair. Anthony disappeared up the stairs in a flash. I scanned her face, her lips had a blueish tinge, her breathing was rapid, along with her pulse.

Shock.

Anthony reappeared with a glass of water and some pills, and a damp cloth which he placed on her forehead.

I placed Cerberus on the floor, the pup fussed around her. "Eva?" I turned to the others. "Maybe she should lie down, she's been—"

"To Hell and back, yes, exactly." Anthony's voice was breathy.

Her eyes fluttered, coming around she started to sit up. Everyone moved back except me and Joash, Anthony handing me the water. "No, you offer it, my hands," I muttered. Splaying my palms, they were flecked with dried blood, he nodded.

"What? What happened?" Her voice strained.

Crouching before her, I softly put my hand on her leg. "You are in shock, you passed out. Here, Anthony has some water and some...?"

"Herbal sedatives, they're not strong. Just valerian, some CBD oil infused. They'll help."

I frowned at him. He rolled his eyes wearing a smirk. "No Lucifer, they're not for me. I do know a few humans. I just keep a supply of herbal medicines."

She sounded croaky when she said, "Thank you," and took them downing the pills with all the water.

Austin reappeared, I hadn't realised he'd gone, and he brought us... ah, coffee.

"Cream and sugar, there you go. Though it's not dairy, the cream."

Standing up, I scooped up my pup with one hand and took the coffee with the other. "Thanks Austin, life saver."

He grinned, licking his lips, then bent over Eva, handing her coffee.

I glugged the drink, still clinging to my dog. I think my heart beat as fast as his, though I caught Eva glancing at me and my face grew hot. The weight of her stare warmed my heart. I smiled back. Now my heart skipped a beat as her pupils dilated. She returned the smile.

How I can dream...

"Austin, thank you for looking after Cerberus, he looks well." I rested my chin on my dog's head.

His eyes widened. "He's mint mate. He's been fed and watered and I took him out for a play in between rescuing you and Joash. He has a large supernatural family now to watch over him. And Eva, I called Ali. She said to take as long as you need. Rez might pop by later to check you're ok."

She caught her breath, a smile on her lips. "Thanks Austin, you're a star. I didn't think she'd sack me, but I'm glad she knows. Rez, I haven't seen him for ages. Look guys,

I need to speak to my boss and I definitely need some rest, though I'm so flipping freaked out I'm not sure I'll sleep."

"Eva, would you allow one of us to stay? I'd feel a lot better knowing you had someone watching over you."

"I can do that... Oh right, I'm guessing you want that job, eh, Lucifer?" Austin beamed.

Rolling my lips I felt the heat on my face as everyone's eyes burned into me. Swallowing hard, I answered, "I just want to make sure she's safe."

Xaphan, who had been looking at the books on Anthony's shelves turned around. "It's up to Eva really. But, Lucifer, if you want to find your brothers, may I suggest you leave this mortal behind?" He flashed a smile at her that made my blood boil. Wide eyes, he rolled his bottom lip. Subtle as a brick. Then again he hadn't had much practise.

Joash's voice oozed, "Let Eva choose, Lucifer. I'm guessing Austin can take care of himself? Eva, your boss is, as Austin said, a werewolf?"

He tilted his head as his eyes drank her in.

Now her face burned scarlet. She glanced to the floor before locking eyes with him. What the hell! I just had to wait for Anthony to make a play for her, too, huh?

Slightly wetting her lips with her tongue, she stared back at Joash, I noticed her breathing was heavier. "Yes, Ali, my boss, is a werewolf, it's how I came into the supernatural world. And..." her eyes surveyed all of us, "I don't want anyone watching over me. I'll speak to Ali and Rez. They're like family. No offence, I need some down time, but Lucifer..."

I had been staring at Cerberus trying to avoid the on-slaught of Joash and Xaphan wanting her attention. Or more.

Before I could speak, Austin blurted out, a smirk on his lips, "Oh, bit of competition, eh Lucifer? Eva, I told you. You're a knockout." He shrugged. "She never believed me, guys. Sorry, carry on, Lucifer."

Sucking in my cheeks, I rolled my eyes.

She glared at Austin then shot me a smile that sent a flush of heat through me. "Lucifer, I will help you rescue your brothers. You look tired, too, you should stay with Joash. I'll speak to Ali and Rez, they may have some ideas?"

I held her gaze, my lips parted and a shudder tingled down my spine. "Thank you, Eva. Take care."

I wanted to hold her, to touch her as she got up getting ready to go but that was a bloody stupid idea. She was a human, I am the Devil, part man, part beast. And Xaphan, Joash were obviously vying for her attention, Joash at least was much better qualified in dating. With being human. He could protect her, even though he was somewhat odd and dramatic.

I smiled, tucking Cerberus's head under my chin. The tiny, sickly pup was now shining, strong and wriggled constantly in my arms. I only wished I had time at the moment with him. I didn't know these supernaturals, as they called themselves, but I was grateful. I needed to thank Aaron, too.

But I had to stay in the present. "Thank you for your help, Joash. I am eager to find Cain now, I don't want to rest, wash or what-not. So," putting my cup on the floor, I gestured with my hand for him to proceed. "Please, show us your magic, what you intend."

Joash moved his head, a smile tugged at his lips. His voice soft, he strode over to me, his stare piercing. "No... You will rest up, Lucifer. We all will. Come."

"Xaphan, please, you are more than welcome to stay here with us," Anthony piped up.

"Na Anthony, he'll stay with me. I'd love to find out about your life, Xaphan, if that's ok?" Austin insisted.

Anthony rolled his lips, shrugging. "Well then, that's settled." He pulled his phone out of his pocket, tapping away. "I'm hungry, so I'll bid you lot good night."

"You getting a take out, at this hour?" Austin asked. "Ah, no... you're ordering blood? Which reminds me, can you spare some?"

"Who, what?" my voice stung in the room. My nose wrinkled, "You're ordering blood on your phone, and you, a mage, drink his blood?"

Anthony pulled himself up. "It's the twenty-first century, Lucifer. We can, if we want to order..." His eyes darted around the room, "Out. A blood delivery service. You can order anything these days. You may be shocked to know the amount of evil people in this city." He held his phone up. "This lists them all. *Dial a Bite.* For a fee, a subscription, we can have an evil doer brought here, though we normally have their blood delivered in a bottle, fresh. We don't like to kill in our home. As for Austin, sure. It keeps him going. Hunting is fine, but who can be bothered to do that every day? Especially when it's raining! Remember Marcus? The fallen Nephilim?"

"No, I do not."

Anthony shifted uneasily. "He is a Nephilim who changed the species. He drank the blood of a vampire. He's a good friend of ours. Still, I'm not offering. Only to Austin. Eva, you ready? I'll take you home myself."

Anger and shock bolted through my veins. Made worse by the vampire escorting her home. But I was in no position to demand anything. As much as I wanted to protect her, she was her own woman. She was strong, independent, I had to remember that's why I liked her. Still, I had no intention of dragging her or Austin, or anyone into this further.

An uneasy quiet fell on us after that, without another word Joash sized everyone up. A bite of disdain in his narrowed eyes, he turned on his heels. Carrying my dog I followed him out.

Outside was warmer, thick clouds embraced the air like a large blanket insulating us from the sky above.

Our footsteps crunched on the snow, it glistened like a thousand amber jewels under the orange streetlights, the stillness of the evening embraced us. It seemed only we three existed in this nocturnal white city, no people, no vehicles, that all the world slept as we crept quietly in this tranquil and enchanted city. With the splendour of the tall, neo-classical buildings, cobbled paths and antiquated lighting, archways and pillars it was like stepping back in a bygone time. Taking long strides Joash remained quiet, and I was grateful for the respite, for a moment to lose my thoughts, and drink in the city. Cerberus sniffed and investigated as we walked but stayed close to me. I stopped at times letting my dog explore and play, finding new scents and Joash, without speaking waited patiently. My dog was the balm my heart needed, soothing and made me realise the beauty in the mundane.

After twenty minutes of walking up through the city, we came to his home, taking his hand from his pocket, Joash waved his hand in front of the locks. A series of clicking sounds, the door opened, I stepped in as he held the door open for me.

"Lucifer, up the first flight of stairs turn left and follow the landing to the last door on the right. You'll find the bathroom there. A guest bedroom is the door proceeding it, but you'll join me for a light supper before sleeping?"

"Yes."

Taking my boots off, his house mirrored the outside world. Quiet, calming and I wondered if his staff lived here. That was answered next.

He held out his arm, palm splayed towards the stairs. "I don't have any dog food, but I hear Cerberus likes chicken? I have that. I can put some on now, it'll be ready in about forty minutes. Please, shower, freshen up."

I left immediately and went up to the bathroom with Cerberus. Inside there was a separate shower and freestanding white marble bathtub with matching hand basins. The monochrome ceramic tiles were warm underfoot. A smaller crystal chandelier hung from the high ceiling reflecting on the mirrored walls. I breathed in the scent of citrus and cinnamon as I picked up a towel from a stack on a shelf.

I wasn't prepared for the pressure of the water, it was heavenly. My dog found a spot on one of the plush thick rugs and settled down, dozing in the steaming room.

After washing the filth of Hell from me I dried off and found a robe of sorts on a door hook. Looking at the clothes Aaron had given me, now more like soiled rags, I couldn't face wearing them right now. They stank.

As I opened the door, I hesitated catching a scent in the air, as a feeling wrapped around me. Fire whipped through my body, not fierce like anger, more like a hearth fire, warm and soothing. Sensual. I shuddered as desire gripped me. Taking a deep breath I scooped up Cerberus and carried him downstairs.

Feeling clean and with my dog I felt almost normal. For me.

"Leave your clothes. I'll have Maddie sort you some fresh garments tomorrow. I whipped together this." He splayed his palm towards a door where I caught a whiff of fish and something else. Wine.

Almost puckering his lips, the rest of his face neutral he waited until I entered the room then in his swift graceful manner he was beside me. "Please sit. Eat. The wine is a delicate one and not strong. It should fortify us."

I sniggered, "I expected a pasty."

His lips immediately pressed tightly together, he stiffened. "A what? I'm not sure I know what you mean, Lucifer, but if lobster isn't good enough, well then that's all I have! I'd send Maddie-"

"No, no I meant that is what I ate at... this is a feast, Joash."

He shrugged. The lobster had been prepared for us so there was no breaking into it. Along with herbs and leaves and fresh bread with olive oil.

I sat down placing Cerberus on the floor but he'd smelt the lobster and was now wide awake.

"Here, I cooked the chicken for Cerberus." Handing me a huge plate of chicken, my eyes nearly as big as the plate, I passed it down to Cerberus, whose tail went frantic.

His shoulders dropped, brows knitted as he seemed to relax. I felt it, too, a tension in the room, so I tried to break it.

"So, did you grow up here in Bath?"

He finished his mouthful, tore some bread from the basket and dipped it in the olive oil. Leaning back in his chair, a half-smile on his face, he answered me, "No I didn't. Where I grew up, raised... it was Hell." He eyed me as the words almost whispered out of his mouth.

I nodded, swallowed. "So, your parents?"

Licking his lips, he picked up his glass, running his index finger around the rim. "My father abandoned me and my mother before I was born, Lucifer. My mother lives, she's not very... maternal. So I suppose we have that in common, our father's deserting us. I don't wish to talk about my upbringing, it was violent to say the least. You like Eva, don't you?"

Puckering my lips in a half grin, I nodded. "It doesn't matter. I *am* attracted to her. She's a strong woman, and compassionate. I haven't met many women, Joash, more before I fell. But with people, regardless of their mortality, I often found the strong, cold and scathing. No level of self-awareness in their soul. Plus, she's beautiful, in my eyes, but you feel the same way, too. As much as it pains me, she'd be better off with a human. I am only here to rescue my brothers, after that..." My mind trailed off as my eye fixed on a painting on the wall. I wasn't really looking at it, thinking about her, her scent, her lips, her body...

"You're thinking about her now. Humans and immortals don't mix and in fact, it's forbidden. Forbidden to have a relationship as it complicates everything. That's how wars start. Of course, a few mortals know about supes, but generally..." His elbow resting on the table, he indicated with his fork, "It's not accepted. And because of that-"

"I know, I should stop thinking about her."

He placed his fork down and sat back, his nose wrinkled. "No, you should date her if you want her. You are the Devil, that alone...You could have anyone you want, and not by using some glamour, some spell. Immortals in the city and beyond have heard of your being here, even now they'll be queuing up to have you, but as the Devil, you can have who you want. Screw the rules." He chuckled, "Anything else is weak. Are you, are you weak, Lucifer?"

He sounded like Cain, testing me. "Joash, I appreciate your help but I don't know why you're so concerned with Eva. I know you like her, so why are you pressing me? I am no angel now, I have the Mark."

Pointing with his fork, he leaned forward, his face close to mine. His breath smelt of grapes, as he talked his eyes slowly scanned my face. "Our shadow side exposes the radiance of our divine self... in darkness there is always a light. If you cannot find it, Lucifer, if you cannot find the light, that is because you must become it..." Sinking back, his voice became lighter, "I'm just saying. I see a man, a powerful man, the father of demons, fallen angel who has been denied existence by his father for all eternity. Now you're hellbent on saving your brothers who couldn't give a shit about you and still you deny yourself pleasure. Because that's all you know. All you've been taught. You have become a martyr. Now answer this, is that what you want to be, was that why your father, God, created you? To be a martyr?" Then sitting up, he placed his fork back down and pushed the plate away, his fingers twisting his long hair. Eyes animated, a smile wrapped on his lips. "You should take a time out. Sex is, in itself, a divine act. Powerful, life enhancing, magnetic. You might be an angel, or were but you are a man first."

I chuckled. "Thanks, but I'm kind of busy right now." And I continued eating, leaning back in my chair.

His voice raised slightly. "That's the problem, isn't it? How long since you have known intimacy? Had flesh on flesh contact with another, and I don't mean fighting."

Talking with my mouth half-full, as he wasn't letting up, "Joash, I am not sure why you're so concerned. But as you're such a gracious, if inappropriate host, I haven't been with a woman since Lilith."

At the sound of her name, a little gasp escaped his lips. His eyes darted around, then he composed himself. "Lilith, tell me about her? Was she your first love?"

I finished the lobster and salad. Cerberus had miraculously stayed on the floor, so I pushed the chair back, grabbed my glass and sat back.

"Lilith, she was more than a first love, Joash. She was... well she changed me. Before her I knew little of sex, carnal love, desire. She was powerful, strong but also cruel at times. My dad had treated her badly, to say the least but I don't know. She always seemed, no, I don't kiss and tell. That said, it was with reluctance that I left her, I needed some space. I tried, of course, to get back to her. And every time I did, I was caught and tortured in Hell. I wish I knew if she was alright, though." I shrugged. "So, yeah, I was a little shocked when you channelled her during your ritual. And you, you seem like a regular Casanova?"

He eyed me closely. "I'm not dating, Lucifer, if that's what you're asking. I like sex as much as the next person. But I'm careful, I don't want just anyone. You can lose part of your soul when you climax, so I am choosy about who I am intimate with. Their energy will blend with mine. They don't have to be chaste, in fact I'd rather they weren't. But Eva, that's why I like her, too. If I was going to choose a mate, it would be her. Or Austin. That doesn't surprise you?"

I shrugged then finished my wine. "As you said, I am the Devil. I'm not hindered by human inhibitions. I've seen things in Hell that would make a sadist blush." I chuckled. He was trying to be serious, I was tired of that. "So, if you like her and you are careful not to pollute your power, your energy, then how is it you have an Incubus upstairs in your bedroom, Joash?"

He never missed a beat. I'd felt its presence. Casually pouring us both more wine, he said, "Easy, Lucifer. He's a plaything, a toy. I use his energy. I don't have sex with it. Why, would you like to try him?"

I spluttered a laugh. "Thanks but no. I've fallen far enough for now. Sleeping with a demon, hey, seen enough of them in Hell."

"Ah, so you'll save yourself for her? *If* she waits for you?"

"Goodnight, Joash. Stay safe. Come on, Cerberus..."

As I got up to leave, his voice throaty, "Anyhow, what will you do once you've rescued Michael and Gabriel? I can't imagine you'll want to return to Hell?"

Sleep was wearing me down. "I need to go to bed, Joash. Alone. I don't know. One day at a time."

The bed was better than I could have imagined. I hadn't had much necessity to sleep in Hell, but when I had rested it was always on stone. And then I'd used my wings to soften the surface. In Heaven we had rarely slept, and I couldn't really remember but the beds there, well, Joash's furniture would certainly fit. I put Cerberus next to me, my body seemed to melt into the mattress and closing my eyes I had the most luxurious sleep I'd had since I'd fallen. Unfortunately, it seemed only minutes had passed when I heard a knocking at the bedroom door.

"Lucifer, they're here. Austin, Xaphan, Anthony and Eva. Breakfast is ready, Maddie has it in the dining room. I'll join you shortly, she's left you some clothes..." Joash opened the door and peered around.

Raising his eyebrows, he muttered, "You slept alright I see?"

"Yes."

He came in and placed the clothes on the bed, sitting up I stretched, noticing a slight glower as he eyed my dog on the bed, tail wagging. Cerberus's tail that is.

"Thank you, Joash. I guess you're not used to serving people, having staff yourself?"

A small smile crept up on his lips, inclining his head, his voice quiet, "On the contrary, Lucifer. Leaders serve, if serving is beneath you, then so is leading. Anyway," he glanced around, his chin up, "It's not every day the Devil comes to stay. Must make a good impression and all that."

I laughed. "I'm sorry if I'm not all that theology made me out to be, you know, horns and tail."

He turned on his heels, swiftly walking towards the door, then hesitated and glanced back. "Ah, but you are, aren't you?" Then he left with me wondering how he knew about the beast.

The smell of fresh bread wafted upstairs. I dressed after a quick wash. "Come on, Cerberus. Time for you to go out."

As we bounded down the stairs a lightness embraced my heart, I would find my brothers. The snow was still settled outside, but spring looked to be fighting back, it had started to melt.

Eva almost sprung out on me from the living room. "Trying to get away from the snakes?" I laughed.

Rolling her eyes, she said, "Well, I prefer dogs, but I got you these, and this. Ali, my boss has let me take a few days to help you. Her and Rez wanted to help, but I figured too many cooks and all that."

"Too many who, what?"

"It means we probably won't be successful if too many people are helping at the same time. Otherwise it gets confusing, cluttered."

"I see. Thank you. I think you would be better off at your job, Eva, Cain…"

"Cain whatever, well I'm helping. With Austin. So, how was your night?"

Rolling my lips, I remembered Joash's words. My gaze fell to her face, her lips. "It was fine. Joash made a feast. Look, I have to take Cerberus out, will you join us?"

"Sure."

I made my way through the kitchen, the smell of bread and pastries making my stomach rumble. As the backdoor opened a bitter chill nipped at my fingers. Waiting a moment as Eva grabbed her coat, I thought about his words. In the last few days I had had more contact with people than I'd had previously in over a thousand years.

I could smell her coming back. Lilacs and sandalwood. Her smile lit up my heart.

Cerberus raced outside, sniffing the plants and finding somewhere to wee. I turned to look at the objects she had given me.

"Ah, that's poop bags- for your dog. The other is a collar, but you knew that. You probably want to get him de-wormed and de-flead. Ali said to bring him by when you can."

"You look rested, Eva. I'm so glad you're okay." I turned away, I wanted to hold her, to kiss her. But I couldn't. My brothers came first. After that, well, I only needed to focus on my brothers right now. Joash had expressed an interest in her. As much as I liked her, I was a monster even if it had gone into shadow for the time being.

After my dog had finished, we went back in, I rubbed my hands to warm them up.

"Beautiful isn't it, the snow? Come Lucifer, we'll have breakfast together. Then we'll rescue Michael and Gabriel. But we have a surprise for you, after you've eaten

I fed Cerberus more chicken that Maddie had prepared. She bustled around silently like a ghost, averting her eyes and even when I tried making conversation, it was ignored. It was kind of weird. Like the Incubus Joash had hidden last night, but it wasn't my place to voice my opinion. I guessed everyone had their quirks, and who was I to judge anyway?

I ate with Cerberus in the dining room whilst the others chatted busily in the living room, grateful for some time to collect my thoughts. Regardless now I would find my brothers, and by this time tomorrow, they would be free. My stomach knotted knowing I wouldn't be accepted into Heaven, unless perhaps... maybe they would restore my grace in payment for me saving Michael and Gabriel. No lightning, no thunder for a day or so meant Cain had stopped torturing them. Unless... I gulped.

Startled, my dog I leapt up, unless I was too late. A sudden sweat broke on my forehead. I had been too busy sleeping, taking showers, I needed to get there now. Pain clamped a tight band around my chest. I rushed into the other room, feeling the weight of their stares on me. "Look, thank you for helping me. But I must go now. Something dreadful..."

Eva's voice, high and startled, "What's happened, Lucifer? You don't know where you're going."

"I, I have to go. Now."

"No. We will all go, Lucifer. Give us half an hour, we have a prepared a spell for you, to empower you. Then we'll transport to the caves," Joash answered.

A wry smile as all eyes were on him, Joash's hands by his side he slowly lifted them up, his smooth voice, palms facing forward but he was interrupted by a blinding golden flash.

Cerberus whimpered, I picked him up and pulled him close, but I wasn't worried. Well, not for him, maybe for me.

There before us, a warm glow of heat radiated out. Joash startled, brows meeting, forehead creasing, he stepped back. Appearing in front of Joash, a face with soft features, deep eyes, and golden hair that fell just beneath his ears. Plump lips pressed together radiating a resolute and regal power as he waited.

Golden wings tucked behind him, a sheen of silver at their tips matched his armour. He rarely left Heaven. Scribe to my father, Metatron was considerate, meticulous, and if he was here, it was serious. And he was furious.

However, my heart lifted. I hadn't seen him in eons except in the crystal.

Metatron stood in front of Joash and silently eyed each and every one of us, his eyes narrowing as his gaze fell upon Xaphan. Then looking at Cerberus, me, back to my dog, his eyebrows arched in shock. Composing himself, a cold stare. "Why did you leave Hell, who gave you permission?" He cocked his head, waiting patiently for his answer.

"I don't need per—"

Holding up his hand, he stated, "Stop right there, brother. Your punishment is not at an end. Or did I miss something? You must return immediately."

I stood up and passed Cerberus to Austin, then stepped before my brother. We were of equal height. As I did this, Joash walked from behind my brother, who almost scowled at the witch but then hid his emotion. "Have you been there... brother? Hell? Until you stay there a few thousand years, I for one will not return. I will save Michael and Gabriel."

He huffed, Joash stood a little to Metatron's side and cast him a veiled glance.

Metatron's voice boomed, "No, you will return until our lord father—"

"I will not. You'll have to kill me. I will not return to Hell."

He nodded. "I see, so we'll have to force you back there, again. Michael and Gabriel do not need nor require your help. Heaven will rescue them in time. For now, you are to leave them."

"What? Are you mad? They—"

"We know, Lucifer. All of Heaven knows, but these things take time. There is more to this situation than meets the eye."

Now I was angry. Clenching my fists by my sides, my voice raised, "So you knew they were captured and are being tortured, and yet you have done nothing. And to think I wanted to go home, you're a cold lot in Heaven. They are in pain."

Like a soft breeze, he responded, "Yes. Yes, they are, but nothing they cannot withstand. We don't believe Cain is behind this, he is merely... a pawn. So, there is no need for you to be involved, and we insist you go back to Hell and continue with your punishment."

Now Joash stepped forward, he could smell the Mark scorching on my arm, he touched it lightly, his silky voice carrying through the room, head cocked he eyed my brother over slowly until his eyes rested on my brother's face. "And tell us, Metatron, *who* is behind this? Who could be so powerful to control Cain, and...?" He glanced at me, then back to my brother, "And capture two archangels? Why, it is not possible, surely?"

Metatron eyed Joash. "We don't know. But we will." My brother looked at Joash with disgust in his face, then nodding to himself, his eyes sliced into mine. "Lucifer! Surrounding yourself with witches, vampires, warlocks! Underworlders, all. The dog, though?"

In the tension, such a left-field question, I withheld a splutter of a laugh. "That's my dog. I found him when I left Hell."

Metatron walked over to Cerberus, who was in Austin's arms. He went to touch my dog's head, then pulled away but was transfixed. I breathed relief Cerberus didn't try to bite him. The mood Metatron was in, he'd likely smite Cerberus and Austin.

Turning back to me, my brother drew out the words. "Yes, father's favourite animal. I wasn't informed. So, you found the dog after you escaped Hell," he peered at Cerberus from his distance, "An earthbound creature. I see. I will then allow you one chance to avenge your brothers, but you have to follow my instructions to the letter. We still don't know who controls Cain. You will find the blade, or rather spearhead, that Cain used to kill Abel. You must remove the Mark from your arm using the spearhead, then thrust the spearhead through Cain's heart. Then you will leave him in the Lake of Betrayal in Hell. He will be in purgatory, reliving his nightmare, which is fair as he is the first murderer. Then, and only then, will we even consider allowing you here on Earth.

But..." He held up his index finger, "Any deviation from this, any at all, and I will personally drag you back to Hell, and your friends here... Including your dog."

"You cannot do that! You have no right!" I demanded.

"Ah, but I can and I will."

Eva, who had been watching everything but had said nothing now cleared her throat, came and stood by my side. I noticed Joash watching as she brushed her hand against mine. Metatron, however, flinched, a look of repulsion on his face.

"Where will we find this spearhead?"

Metatron stared at me. "Not you, too?" He glanced at her hand, the back of which touched the back of my fist, but her presence, her flesh on mine soothing me like a warm breeze. "Carnal sins are prohibited amongst angels. Your brother," then realising he'd said too much as Austin and Joash laughed, his eyes became dark. "You'll find it in a sacred place, obviously. Protected by the Knights of Blood. Good luck with that, I'm sure I'll see you again soon when I send you all to Hell."

Lifting his hand, a brilliant burst of gilded light and my brother was gone.

"So uptight. I think he needs some carnal sin." Austin spluttered laughing running his free hand through his hair. "Saying that, so do I." He smirked at us. "It's not an easy life, is it, being a mage, all blood and magic. Still Lucifer, your brother taught me something. If I don't get laid soon, I could turn that cranky. Geez, I'm glad you're not as miserable as your brother, Lucifer. Still, we'll scry for the blade, or spearhead, or whatever it is."

Even Joash's lips were slightly upturned. "Well, *the might of Heaven*. I wonder who they think is controlling Cain. The spearhead, however, is easy." He flicked his wrist, and we all turned to stare at him, I added, "How would you know?"

He shrugged slightly. "Many in the craft know where it is. Getting it is an entirely different matter. It's on Glastonbury Tor, but it's hidden in the mists of Avalon and..." he sighed. "As your bad-tempered brother mentioned, guarded by The Knights of Blood. Deadly wraiths, hard to kill, no, not hard, impossible. It is on the Tor, though it's precise location is a mystery."

I cleared my throat. "No, nothing's impossible, not for an immortal."

Joash played with his lip. "If we had the spearhead that would kill The Knights of Blood. But therein lies the irony, how to get it before they kill you, us?"

"I would like to find it first. Can we not scry for it? I alone will go and get it. You, all of you, have done enough. This has to be done by me. We know where Cain is, in those caves." I exhaled.

"Not quite, I will come with you. I am the most powerful witch, these knights intrigue me, the spearhead even more. Its power... I will join you, Lucifer. And Lucifer..."

My stomach flipped as I anticipated what Joash would say next. I eyed him, frowning.

His head jerked. "Metatron, see what I told you last night about being a martyr. I was right. You need to start owning your title, your dark side, your power. And... well," he glanced at Eva, then back to me, "You remember the rest."

I nodded, relieved he didn't share my lack of intimacy with the group.

Anthony muttered, I'd forgotten he was sat behind us. He'd been sitting as still as a statue, as vampires do, his face like stone. "Look, you two, go get the thing, as for us, we'll scry, check out the caves. Cain caught Eva and Austin." He looked at them and they nodded. "Did you get any of his blood on your clothes, any of his hair?" He lifted his brows.

"Of course we did, we're not amateurs." Austin cast him a wicked grin.

I stepped over to them. "Cain's blood, hair, whatever, that could be very good for helping us get the exact location of the spearhead, surely?"

The vampire curled up his lips, his stone face like a mask with illuminated eyes. "That's the spirit. Plus, there are a ton of spells you can use against these Knights of Blood. It often depends on the weapon, doesn't it?"

I rolled my lips, then glanced at Joash whilst rubbing Cerberus's head. Austin lunged back, thinking I was going to rub his head. "Of course, swords... blades forged in Hell."

"Lucifer, Joash, I will join you." Xaphan had, like the vampire been standing behind the others. Now he pulled himself up, his hand on his sword hilt. Xaphan was a sight to behold, like me he stood taller than mortals, lithe and his wings that were furled behind, him reached up above his head.

"What do we need?" Austin chirped in.

"Well, I still have some of your blood, Lucifer, from the spell to find Cain. And if Eva and Austin can retrieve Cain's blood- that could be useful to locate the spearhead." Anthony strode over.

Hum, so the bloodsucker kept my blood.

"Yes, blood magic is the most powerful. We can use this to find the exact location of the spearhead and to strengthen us against The Knights of Blood, we will need it." Joash lifted his chin. "I know of a few powerful sorcerers who have tried to gain the spearhead and all met with a brutal end. So, I think it wise if we use your sword, Lucifer, and Xaphan's, infuse those as they were forged in Hell. And for me, I can be your weapon against these wraiths. Your fire of God." He flicked his wrist. "These lesser underworlders won't know what they're up against... as your brother would say. We should go upstairs to my den where I spell cast. Austin, Eva, you go collect the blood with Anthony. We'll wait for you up there."

Anthony made me jerk, clicking his fingers, Cerberus barked, and the three of them disappeared. Austin had taken him with him.

"Shall we?" Joash indicated to Xaphan and me.

Up in his den, the floor had been thankfully cleaned of blood and now the scent of wood and earth hung in the air. Glaring morning sunlight spilled through the huge arched windows, casting weird shadows from the huge sculptures across the walls. Joash moved quickly, pulling the drapes to block it out, whilst Xaphan and I stood waiting.

"So, did you sleep last night or did Austin drill you with questions?"

Xaphan smirked. "I did sleep, in a bed. It was heavenly, but yes, he asked me questions well into the night. Then he gave me some strange tea that took away the nightmares, I am grateful, Lucifer. I had, if I'm honest, been dreading sleeping." He watched Joash, his eyes lost in thought. "Nightmares of... well, what about you?"

I nodded. "About the same. And I agree, the beds are divine. What an invention. I had, thankfully, a dreamless sleep, too. But then I had Cerberus with me." On those last few words Joash shot me a cold stare. I nudged Xaphan. "I don't think he likes my dog sleeping on his bed, but in Hell, you could sleep next to much worse."

"So, they won't be long now. Have you thought what you'll do, Lucifer, once your brothers are safe? Get a house, money? Take my advice?"

As soon as Joash had finished speaking, Austin and Eva appeared with Anthony.

"Here, some remnants of the clothing we had on when Cain the pain kidnapped us, and... Anthony has the Devil's blood," Austin spluttered loudly and wide eyed. "God, that sounded awesome. *I have the Devil's blood...*"

Anthony's shoulders dropped and reverently he placed the golden bowl, containing my blood no less, on Joash's desk.

With a scornful look, he said, "Lucifer, see, I located the Tecpatl. When we saw you in Hell, I noticed it wasn't there. I scryed, of course, and found it on top of the abbey." Joash held it up then placed it on the desk alongside my blood.

I shuddered. A ritual dagger and a bowl of my blood. I didn't know what that meant, but if I believed in omens, it wasn't a good sign.

I strode over to Eva. "I know you want to help, you and Austin, but I'd rather, if you agree, neither of you will come with us to find the spearhead." I looked at Joash who nodded, then back to her. "These Knights of Blood or whatever they are, I need to know you and Austin are safe. And after your exertion in Hell, I'd say you need to rest. That experience..." I shook my head, "Horrific."

"And look out for Cerberus. If you three can find out where Cain is hiding in those caves, I don't know," I glanced away then looked at her then Austin, "Find me an advantage? But do not put yourselves in danger. We'll have our backs against the wall with these Knights of Blood, so I won't be able to help you, none of us will. Once I have the spearhead, we will regroup."

"What about Heaven? Will you follow their instructions?" She clasped her hands around mine, and I could feel Austin's and Joash's eyes boring into me. Then I did something crazy. Compulsion perhaps. Maybe Joash putting all those ideas into my head.

Scanning her face, I stepped in, my gaze resting on her lips. For a moment I could hear her heart thumping faster, see her pupils dilate as passion stormed through me like a tempest. Passion that had been dead for centuries. I noticed the lines around her eyes, her mouth, and I hoped she'd gained this from laughter, not from sorrow. But Eva, from what I already knew, found good in the darkest of places. She was the star to my darkness, I was drawn to her, to her illuminating spirit that shone brighter than any angels. Leaning in, she didn't step away. Instead, making my heart skip a beat, she let go of my hands, placing hers around my face and pulled me into her.

As our lips touched, hers soft on mine, my head swooned and desire gripped my body. As we touched, her energy washed into mine, cleansing, calming. Ardent. Lost in the moment I forgot everything, my hands pulling her into me, she shuddered with a force that seemed to thrum through me and her, shivers of bliss, tantalising, longing sparked through us. Breathless, caught up in the moment, in her. But then the moment was lost, gone as Austin cleared his throat and brought me back into that room.

We pulled away, her eyes reaching deep into mine, soothing my broken soul. Our fingers interlinked, then let go. Catching my breath, I turned around to find Austin beaming at me and Eva.

I avoided Joash's eye contact, I could feel the burn of his stare. We don't choose who we love. Love chooses us.

Blood & Magic

Then all eyes locked on me, I swallowed hard but it was Xaphan who spoke. "Good, two fallen angels and a witch. These Knights won't even see us coming."

"Well then, Lucifer..." Joash smiled, his voice oozing charm. "It's time then I showed you what I'm capable of. It's time for you and your fallen friend here to see some real magic..."

No one spoke as they prepared. Austin handed me Cerberus, and I noticed from the corner of my eye the flashes of amusement from Joash as I spoke to Cerberus, lifting him up, then down and rubbing his head with my chin. "Have you been a good boy, have you? Did you teleport against my wishes with uncle Austin?"

As Austin, Eva, Joash and Anthony set about readying for their magic, Xaphan strolled over, his arms out and pleading eyes. I smacked a kiss on my dog's head. "Go to uncle Xaphan. Be good."

"Are you talking to me or the dog?" Xaphan laughed.

I looked him in the eye. "Both."

He held my dog, unsure, his eyes small as he studied the creature. "I have never held a dog before, in fact I have never been close to any other species, except angels or demons. I've seen them, of course, but as that... *thing*... well, my mind was mashed. Demented. Why do you have it?"

I sniggered, unable to hold back a chortle. "It? Him. People have animals, dogs, well, for the companionship. Joash there," Joash glanced quickly as I said his name, "He keeps snakes."

"Yes, but why? What do you get out of it?"

"A friend, Xaphan. They love, so I'm told, unconditionally."

He frowned hard, then gently, I noticed, put Cerberus on the floor where he proceeded to run around and yap in his puppy voice, following Austin especially who spoke to him in a silly voice, encouraging him. "Come on, Cerby, Daddy being mean, is he? Come to uncle Austin, yes, that's right. Your dad is Satan, that's why he's grumpy. Your dad is lord Satan, Cerby."

Still with brows meeting, Xaphan muttered, "Unconditionally. Humans can't do that? Oh I see. Love... We, as Metatron said, were not designed to feel emotions. But..." he looked hard into my eyes, "I have had feelings?" Then shaking his head. "Pah, maybe because I fell. Your brother certainly seems the perfect angel."

Taking a breath, I patted Xaphan on the shoulder, stepping forwards to play with Cerberus. "He was lying. Metatron used to cry like a baby when we teased him when we were first made. We all felt things, Xaphan, I felt anger, and you know," I winked at him, "I still feel that."

He rolled his bottom lip, brow furrowed. "I see. So why do they, like your brother, say we cannot love?"

"Control. If we love, and that's the most powerful force, they cannot control us. Though I noticed Metatron was about to mention my brother, regarding sex. I wonder which one has followed his heart?"

Austin spluttered a loud laugh. "Heart? Maybe just his dick. It's not always love, guys, c'mon. Get with the programme."

Eva slapped Austin's back. "Don't you believe him. Austin is no ladies man. I know, I helped him set up his romantic dates." She nudged Joash, helping mix some herbs. His face was stoic, but the faintest grin battled on his lips. "As for Joash, his dates are legendary, so I hear." She turned and winked.

Joash stared at her, his face expressionless, then smiled. "My dates are extraordinary. I have a reputation, Eva, as you seem all too aware."

Xaphan piped up, "Humph, Metatron was probably talking about Raphael, he was always lecherous."

Shocked, my mouth curved down. But Austin chortled out loud, "Stop throwing Xaphan shade, Lucifer, he's right. Raphael is a tart."

Joash stepped inside the circle, lowered his head, his hands by his side. Then lifting his head, "We are ready."

Indicating with his hand, Joash looked at me and Xaphan. "Please, enter the circle and place your swords in the middle."

I picked up Cerberus and placed him on a chair where he settled down, his head resting on his paws.

Eva and Austin had put a smattering of torn clothing in the middle, clothing splattered with Cain's dried blood. My blood gleamed, Anthony had placed it into a bowl, the silver shards inside it caught the candlelight, sparkling. The four of them stood at each endpoint of the pentacle that was painted inside the circle with Eva offering. "Xaphan, if you would stand at this point, you can represent spirit."

Nodding, he stood at the edge of the circle, his feet on the point from the pentagram. I saw now, each one would represent an element of the earth.

"And what about me?" I asked.

She smiled, Austin yelled, excited, "You'll need the most energy, so you stand in the middle. We will direct the power into you, and the swords." His voice dropped, "Relax, we got this."

I couldn't, I was tense. Having all four magicians and an angel staring at me was unsettling, knowing some kind of weird power would be directed straight at me, I took a deep breath, shrugged my shoulders to loosen them and flexed my arms and neck.

As their chanting began, a warm breeze picked up and brushed my face and hair, almost caressing, lulling me into complete calm.

For a moment I closed my eyes, the urge to drift into sleep almost forcing my eyelids shut, but as I fought against that I noticed Eva, her palms facing the middle, muttering the chant, her hair blowing lightly towards me. A scent of cleanliness filled my nose, like rain on leaves, sweet and fresh. Invigorating. I trembled, remembering back to a time when I was young and everything held a fascination, a beauty that was bold, big and bright. The first time I came to Earth, I smelt the breeze it filled me with energy, with awe. Air. Eva was channelling air.

I widened my stance slightly, leg muscles engaged but not tense as a rumble echoed through the floor, almost

grounding my feet. It was light, benign, and an almost soothing sensation beneath my boots. Turning my head to see Anthony, his eyes closed, chanted in whispers. Stone, soil and
leaves. Rich scents stirred my senses, reminding me of the
times I had picked up the dirt, watched in wonder as it ran
through my fingers. Such a simple substance, yet it held so
much potential. The potential for life. I smiled, that scent,
that wonder at the plants, the rough feeling of bark beneath
my hands when I first came here thousands of years ago. The
reverberating seemed to come from him. Anthony was har-
nessing the power of earth then.

Revolving around, Austin grinned. His eyes were wide
open. Slowly he lifted his arms, palms facing the ceiling. His
eyes grew wider and from above large drops of rain fell in
slow motion. Each drop shone like a tiny bauble of glass. It
showered down over the circle edge, Cerberus barked, his
eyes following the cascade of rain from his chair, but just before the water hit them it disintegrated. Rain that's not wet!
Mesmerized, like crystal beads, they shone, gleaming, and
I noticed Austin flick his hand suddenly and they changed
into large snowflakes. Each one had a myriad of crystalline
needles that sparkled silver flecks, dappling shadows that
bounced around the ceiling, the walls before vanishing as
they fell on this tiny coven. Inside me, rising up from my
feet, a force surged up, whipping through my legs, my muscles warming, powerful.

Heat touched my back, spinning around Joash with his
palms up as flames flared steadily from them. Amber, orange,
black, then they seemed to intensify and turned blue, the

tips of the flames arctic white. Again a bark from Cerberus. He wagged his tail as he led on the chair.

So this was elemental magic. I looked at Xaphan. As far as I knew he held no magic, a wild look in his eyes, his wings tucked in behind him, but I noticed a golden glow radiating from their edges, and then through him. His skin turned to a bronze sheen like a statue, almost reflecting in the bobbing and flickering candlelight.

Raising his chin, he opened his mouth to the shape of an O. A cool energy swept through me, grew stronger like a current and changed from wind to what felt like diaphanous angles.

As they swept through me, the shock sent me doubling over, almost painful, but inside I felt lit up, stronger, and a slight feeling of the divine presence that I had had before Cain had stolen that from me. More poured out of him, a glint of silver, a hint of bronze, a golden illumination as these spectral angels in a torrent. They shot into me, through me, leaving me breathless. As I stood up from my crouched position, the air from Eva blew into me, Austin's snow now rain poured over me. I felt heat lick fast and furious from the hands of Joash as that fired into me, and finally a rumble from the earth resonated throughout my entire body.

My gaze clouded, my hand clasped the back of my neck. I staggered, disorientated, awash with power and shock.

Rasping, my hands fell to my thighs, supporting me to stay upright until I felt a familiar hand on my back, her calming presence and voice that whispered my name.

"Lucifer, are you alright? You look a bit... *green*."

More hands met my shoulders, I tried to push myself up but the energy still crashed through me in an unstoppable force, unable to find my balance. It was like navigating a small boat on a stormy ocean; they guided me to a chair; I heard Cerberus barking as a glass of water appeared before my face.

"Drink this, it's a tonic, it'll help."

Shaking, my fingers grasped at the glass, desperate to find myself some semblance of normality and clumsily I drank the liquid. It wasn't water, and it wasn't pleasant, but I chugged it down, willing it to help.

Slowly my vision cleared, my breathing slowed, and I sat back in the chair. Austin took the glass from me, gawking.

"So, how do you feel now?"

"He'll feel stronger, not angelic strong but able to take on the Blood Knights." Joash's voice, smooth, lilting cadence.

"The colours. I see them all now, reds, yellows, blues and purples and all the hidden entities. I'd only been able to see a few of these since Cain." It was like a wonder. Being able to see more in the colour spectrum took my breath away for an instant. Tiny specks of light darted about the place, leaving glittering trails, like miniscule seraphim. The energy around Austin, Eva, Joash was a hue of violets, scarlets and amber. The colours were darker, denser around the vampire. Looking at Cerberus, green and orange. I scooped him up from my feet as his tail wagged like crazy.

Goosebumps dotted my arms, a yearning to stretch my limbs was overwhelming, I stood up clutching my dog, and a force thrummed through my limbs. Cerberus trembled slightly. Don't think I ever did that before, I guessed that was from Joash's and Eva's human side, from fusing with their energy. My muscles relaxed, for a moment I forgot my mission, as my body drank up the magic these five had bestowed onto me.

"Better, ready to go?" Joash asked.

"Indeed. These Blood Knights, what can you tell me?"

He glanced at Austin, who raised his brows. "Not much. Wraiths, more like the Voror, wraiths from Norse mythology who are guardians. We have little information on them because, well," Austin's lips curled down as he shrugged, "no one's lived to tell. Some have reportedly seen them but ran away. They are attracted to negative energy, so with the Mark you'll have no trouble finding them. They say cutting off the head of wraiths works."

I hugged my dog; I hated leaving him again. I hoped that after this nonsense, after jailing Cain in Hell and setting my brothers free, I might spend some time with Cerberus, with Eva and Aaron and explore this world, this world that I had perhaps been so wrong about.

Eva's arms were out. "I'll take him Lucifer, he is adorable. Whilst you fight these ghosts we'll scry, see what Cain has hidden. And Lucifer..."

"Yes?"

"Don't lose your head."

Rolling my lips, I nodded, holding her gaze. The urge to kiss her strong within me, but this was not the time.

I handed Cerberus to her; he licked her face, making her splutter and twist her head away. Then Xaphan and I picked up our swords. Thrumming with power, we sheathed them.

"Before I go, thank you, each of you. I don't know, maybe you've all proved me wrong, maybe Earth isn't so terrible…" That was all I would say. It was one thing to admit it to myself, but I'm not the open type.

"So, you're not all going to fit into Joash's car, are you? Want a spell to get you there faster?" Austin chirped.

"Yes, thanks."

His lids lowered, and the mage whispered an incantation, I stole a last glance at Eva holding Cerberus, my lips curved into a smile as her eyes met mine, then blackness engulfed me and in the next instant a harsh wind whipped around me.

Austin had sent us to the side of Glastonbury Tor, I had heard of it obviously. It was steeped in British legends. From tales of Jesus visiting Glastonbury, to Merlin, King Arthur and the famous mists of Avalon that cloaked the Tor, revealing secret paths to those enlightened enough to view them. Glastonbury Tor then was steeped in magic from the forging of Excalibur, to Morgan Le Fay.

We circled around the place; the mist rising to our shoulders. Only then I realised how long we'd been in that vampire's basement. I shivered as the sound of crows' and rooks' caws echoed throughout the land, and the delicate song of birds fell sweetly on our ears. In the distance an amber glow edged lazily, partially hidden in the mists as the sun pushed slowly up.

Unsheathing my sword, I breathed in the air, crisp and clean this place held a power that resonated through me. Xaphan grinned, the tower above us peeped out, jutted above the haze and without instruction we quietly made our way up and around following the path that was cut into this natural hill. The Tor stood vigil across hundreds of acres, rising high above the land. The Somerset levels that sit below were in ancient times, flooded as the Tor stood high above, a beacon to the people in the Dark Ages. According to legend, the Isle of Avalon, Glastonbury Tor is the burial site of King Arthur who will one day, when needed, rise again to save his people.

Joash whispered over the bird calls and song, "According to legend, Joseph of Arimathea visited here with the Holy Grail and thrust his staff into the hill, from this place where his staff struck the ground grew a thorn tree, a symbol of Christianity. Now the spear is said to be located in direct correlation to the thorn tree, up the top, so we must find the thorn tree, which is easy without the mist."

"Hum, we may end up-"

As the mists started receding, figures emerged but instead of being masked in black cloaks, their pewter skin, stained with pale blue, limbs cracked as if they were statues come alive. Ablaze with a smattering of brilliant luminescence before them, faces of young warriors clothed only in ancient shenti's, a type of skirt gathered at the waist, alongside a sword belt, their lids down, they materialized above us at the top of the Tor.

The hazy amber and orange rays of the sunrise peeked around the hill, Joash stepped alongside me, his voice hoarse as he grabbed at my arm, "They look more like the Voror, Norse wraiths. Not usually malevolent, they've obviously been cursed. I will muster some magic, be careful Lucifer."

My sword drawn alongside Xaphan, we strode up, then took to the wing to land on top of the hill. No point in trying to fight from below. Eight of them stood around the perimeter, stoic faces with swords before them, waiting.

My skin burned, I needed this spearhead, Joash hadn't said exactly where it was located here but once these knights had fallen, it was believed the spearhead would be visible. For a moment. So were they knights of God, my father? Certainly, they couldn't be Norse, though they were dressed primitively. One thing was for sure, they couldn't kill me. Not whilst the Mark was scorched into my skin.

As we landed, they turned to face us, walking like corpses, their feet thudding on the ground. Rays of golden light lit up behind them, an eerie chill blew across the Tor, Xaphan and I stood back to back.

Twisting my wrist, I spun my sword around to feel the new power these people had given me, and as I did the wraiths looked up, mouths in an O and a silent screaming pierced through my body, cutting like glass on flesh. Swallowing hard, I tensed my muscles as an icy trickle oozed out of my ears. With my free hand I touched it, but I knew it was blood before I looked at my fingers. They continued, and it took all my concentration to block it out, reminding me of the first fall into Hell where the agonizing screams of the damned had haunted my mind, and had clung and ripped at my sanity for the longest time. But not now. Now I was used to it, almost blanked it out. Now I was going to kill them.

As they edged closer, I heard Xaphan's breathing. He shifted back slightly, whispering, "Are you afraid, Lucifer?"

"Of course, only a fool feels no fear. But use that fear, wield it, don't let it hinder you. Embrace it and push forward with it."

Four faced me, four faced him. Joash was cooking up a spell somewhere. Although I couldn't die, I could be injured and pain, especially from such macabre magic, is likely to be bad. Really bad. And where I can be happy inflicting it on those that deserve it, I'm less happy receiving it.

For a second, a standoff, they assessed us; we eyed them. This would be hard. As if wanting to burst from my chest, my heart pounded, I noticed their nostrils flare slightly. Ah, the Mark.

Unfortunately, it didn't deter them...

Swords sweeping, some high, some low, they charged with such grace I was breathless. From the stone-like, heavy-footed warrior, their movements were feline. "Jump!" I yelled. My plan was to fly above them with Xaphan pressed up behind me, my wings pressed into his back, abut with four fighters before me, I was distracted instantly as Xaphan winced, a yell, as blade clashed with blade before me, it was too late to fly. I crouched, swung my sword up to block one, a flick of my wrist to block another on my right, but too late for the one before me. I felt the icy kiss of his blade as it touched my neck and in that instant as steel licked flesh, I could not move my limbs.

Spluttering at the shock, at the ease of my defeat, I watched as the blade before me, like ink on paper their colour spread up it, my limbs became stiffer. Breathing stilted and behind me, nothing. No sound. Sweat poured from my neck and back. "Xaphan?" The word was hard to say as my lips became rigid and the realisation was these knights had no intention of killing us. Instead, they wanted us to join them.

I was becoming a wraith.

"Lucifer! Lucifer!" I heard his voice, I knew it was Joash, but I could no longer speak.

Weapons of God

My eyes fixed open and watered as the chill wind thrashed around me up on this Tor. Stepping closer, the knights lowered their swords and reached out towards me. I was becoming one of them.

Is that what had happened to the others they'd encountered? In the distance, just beyond them, a small cluster of daisies caught my attention. More so because as one of these wraiths stopped on them, they died, as had the grass beneath their feet. They seemed to leave a trail of death.

And I would join them. No more brothers, no more Cerberus, no more Eva. I pushed my lungs to breathe, keep breathing. They stopped as the smell of burning flesh from my arm caught their attention. I would not lie down and take this shit. I would have gritted my teeth, but I couldn't bloody move my mouth, grunting I forced all my power, all my energy to move.

Joash's voice was muffled. My legs hardened as I watched in horror as my hand turned to anthracite. Just like these wraiths, an icy sensation crept up my arm.

I groaned, trying to push past it, the devastating ice freezing my elbow, my biceps, my shoulder and oozed across my chest.

From the corner of my eye, I could just see Joash appear at the edge of the Tor, arms up chanting, and alongside him Austin, whilst the knights turned slowly, walking towards them.

In his hands, Austin held a plastic bottle filled with water. He caught my eye and called to me, "Lucifer, I can smell the Mark. They feed on anger, on hate. Focus on something good! Focus on Eva, on Cerberus!"

Unable to see her, I heard Eva call, "Xaphan, you must do the same, please. Remember something good and put your heart there! Do not think about vengeance! That's the trick!"

Their words were muted in my ears, but I understood enough. Damn hard though, I felt the blood run from my face as my gut tightened and my limbs became frigid. Lowering my lids, I concentrated on Eva. Still, the icy sensation gripped me, the memory of her touch, her lips on mine. But my mind flipped to the present, the inability to move, shivering as a cold chill whisked through me as if my blood had turned to ice.

But it was my dog that saved the day.

Barking, running up the hill. Cerberus. I moved my eyes to see my dog bounding towards me. Melting, my limbs softened immediately as if thawing, and my breathing slowed. I felt my chest move up, then down, and slowly I pulled myself up. Cerberus! My tiny dog was enough for me to break this spell. His tiny tail in a frenzy, his bravery, or madness depending on your mindset, he charged forwards. Growling at the feet of the knights who I don't think knew what to make of him.

Flashing a glance, Austin was still chanting and scattering the water from the bottle onto the knights but as they backed away, their limbs cracked like frost on glass, it left their limbs crumbling as they fell to the ground until only a pile of dust remained. Cerberus yapped and raced around them, his tail swishing madly before running to me. Standing at my feet he barked shrilly, I took a deep breath.

"Look!" Austin shouted. I turned to see what he was pointing at. From the front of the tower rising up out of the ground, a small worn wooden box pushed up by some unseen force.

"Come on, boy..." I stumbled forwards, as I did it seeped back down into the earth. Falling to my knees, I snatched at the box. But it tumbled deeper, the hole grew wider, and the box fell further away until I was led on my belly, reaching in. I grabbed it, it slipped, muddy, moist. I yelled as I felt the others grab at my ankles so I lowered myself down.

Cerberus yelped alongside me, Austin shouted at him to stay back, but he barked and chirped. Now getting deeper again, the box was just, only just within my reach when my dog somehow tumbled into it, scrabbling and still the hole grew larger. As if it was tunnelling into Hell itself.

I grabbed at Cerberus, his little front legs scrabbling up the earthen hole, which was still getting deeper as Austin yelled above me. I heard Eva. "Oh God, Lucifer, quick!"

Opening my mouth to answer through a mouthful of dirt, I wrapped my hands around my dog as suddenly the bottom of this pit fell open. A faint smell of sulphur hit me and a glow of embers from underneath. Cerberus wriggled, terrified, he yelped. I was holding him too hard, but rather that then too loose. I pulled him to my neck, now upside down as I was, and through a mouthful of muck, I yelled, "Pull us up! Quick!"

"I have you Lucifer, hold him tight," Xaphan yelled, his hands around my ankles, dragging me and Cerberus back to safety, and an easing of energy. Only then did I realise Joash stood on the opposite side peering down into the hole, his face racked with anger, flicking his wrist with narrow, mean eyes. He pointed below.

The box hurtled up; he snatched it, and in the next moment flicked his wrist again, covering the hole.

Panting, I laid on the ground, unable to let go of Cerberus who shivered in my hands, my arms locking him to me. A well of emotion threatened to flood out, I forced it back. But for the moment, I wouldn't let him go.

They fussed and spoke. Trembling from the shock, I rolled onto my knees and forced myself up, still holding my dog. Slowly Cerberus calmed, and I with him.

"Our stuff is over here, come on. Oh, thank God, Lucifer, thank God you saved Cerby!" Eva panted.

Yes, *thank God indeed...*

"Thank Xaphan actually," I corrected her.

Still mud in my mouth, I wasn't impressed back there. It didn't bear thinking about. I was grateful to Xaphan, Austin and Eva, but what the hell with Joash? And Dad? Was that a test I wondered, if it was it really, really angered me.

We slowly trudged down the Tor, and at the bottom found a bench. Eva opened her back pack, I placed Cerberus on the seat, then turned aside to spit out the rest of the mud that still clung to my cheeks.

"Here, swill it out with this." She handed me some water. I nodded and did that as she filled a bowl of water, sprinkled a few herbs in it and gave it to Cerberus. Lapping it up, he sploshed water around, but he looked calmer. "Don't suppose you have any of those herbs for me?" I asked.

She grinned and looked back at Cerberus.

"Austin..."

He bounded over. Like me and Xaphan, mud and grass stains covered our tops, our jeans. Cerberus's white patches were brown. Only Joash looked immaculate, holding the box reverently in his hands. He hadn't said a word.

"Holy water, from Wookey Hole! We were scrying, as you know, and Eva was chasing down the history of the place on the net. Anyhow, it turns out that the calcified witch, the witch of Wookey Hole, was thus so..."

"Thus?" I chided him.

"Sod off Lucifer, yes, *thus* calcified because a priest blessed the water in the caves." He shrugged. "It was just a hunch, but we scryed to see you two and well, you obviously needed our help. *Thus,* our lord Satan, we saved you. Again."

"And I am grateful, truly. Thus, otherwise I'd be a wraith."

He stuck out his tongue.

"But what, you transported here?"

He shrugged. "Bring it on. I'm not known as the best mage for nothing old Nick, you know."

"Okay. And Cerberus, you?"

"He's fine. Eva and I whipped up a protection spell so he wouldn't be harmed by being transported by magic. Mind you, I hadn't counted on him falling into Hell, that's your job. You're still Hell's guardian, I guess? Still, yes, back to the legend. It is said, thus... that there was an evil witch who tormented villagers of Wookey hundreds of years ago. The villagers pleaded with a local priest to save them from her wickedness..."

I frowned, wiping off the dirt from my face with the back of my arm in between glaring at Joash. Eva perched on the bench. "This witch, she was, well evil, so legend has it. Killing people, children. Who knows what is true or whether it was discrimination- I suspect the latter? But the water in Wookey Hole is blessed. Now, as for your wraiths, we knew they feed on anger, on hatred, so, well you with the Mark, it's not surprising, but, hey, we warned you."

I nodded, feeling almost myself. "You did and without your magic I would no doubt have been lost before you arrived. You saved me, my life. I won't forget that. It's hard sometimes facing death, remembering all the advice, this doesn't help." I raised my arm.

Clearing his throat, Joash glided over. "I wasn't just watching Lucifer, I was actually tapping into your soul, trying to fend off the curse of the wraiths. But I told you, none have lived who have fought them. Bravo to the younger generation. Without them, we would be lost."

"But they didn't touch you? Why is that, Joash?"

His brows flickered up, a small smirk. "Probably because I kept my distance, I wasn't the one brandishing a sword. And although my magic is strong, it was the holy water that stopped them, wasn't it?"

I rubbed Cerberus's head. I don't know, I mean, really? But I didn't have to like him. He was helping, I was grateful for that. And maybe this was Joash at his best. After all, he was used to the luxurious house in Bath, fraternizing with his 'followers' and hanging out with snakes. Austin and Eva seemed more the type to get their hands dirty. They were more grounded.

"So, let me see inside the box." I held out my hand to Joash. For a split second a frown knitted on his brows, his lips pressed together. Then lowering his lashes, his smile like a cat grinning, he extended his hand. "Be careful, Lucifer, I sense..." His eyes cast up to the heavens, "I sense immense power inside here and there is no telling..."

"I hope so, Joash." Ignoring him I held out my hand.

A curt smile on his lips, he tilted his head, his voice smooth, "Of course."

As I took it, Austin yelled, "Wait! It might be... you know, jinxed?"

I sighed. "No, I don't think so. It feels powerful though, and, um, not in a good way."

Eva patted Cerberus's head, her voice grating, anxious, "Maybe we should wait then, you know until we find Cain?"

I narrowed my eyes at her. "Still no. I need to make sure this is the real thing, the spearhead that Cain used to kill his brother."

As I pulled the box open, a gush of foul-smelling air blew out, along with dust and a torrent of energy. I grasped it, my knuckles white as I seemed to fight some invisible force that had the Mark on my arm burning like the infernos in Hell.

Clenching my teeth, I groaned, grabbing up the spearhead in my hand, which seared my palm. I didn't let go. Then as fast as it started, all the energy stopped.

"It's gone into you; the spearhead power has seeped into you, Lucifer!" Eva gasped, leaning back, keeping Cerberus out of the way as he barked and barked.

My head swam for a moment. When I'd picked up the spearhead, a flash of visions had penetrated my mind. An acrid landscape, two men, anger... hostility. In that instant my skin felt hot as a blazing sun beat down on me and the woody scent of frankincense had filled my senses.

I shook it off.

I lied. "Well then, I'm ready. It's now or never." I bottled down the shock, a sheen of sweat on my forehead. "It's nothing, it was just a surprise. I am fine. And if I'm not, too bad. I want to meet Cain, rescue my brothers before anything else happens to me."

Ave Satanas

"Eva, Austin, thank you. Please, when you get us to the caves, you must leave. It is too dangerous. Somehow Cain has amassed too much power."

"No Lucifer, we're coming, you need us. And don't worry, we'll keep Cerby safe. But we're coming and you can't stop us," Austin piped up.

My heart sank. "This is no joke Austin, this isn't the Blood Knights. Cain has my brothers, he took your magic once before. There won't be a second chance."

Austin shrugged. "Look man, we're a team. Xaphan-"

"Xaphan is a demon from Hell. And even he-"

Eva reached for my hand. "We're coming, we will help. The six of us, working together, we got this. That's what I believe."

"Six?"

"Sure. Cerberus. Never underestimate a dog, right?"

"Look, I appreciate your help, without you I would be a wraith right now, but you must leave. This is dangerous, even for a mage, Austin. Cain has my brothers, they are archangels. Look around you. Those falling stars you see, they're not stars!" I pointed heavenwards.

"They're angels. Lucifer, it is you who underestimates us. Some of us may be merely human to you, but Eva is right. We are more powerful if we work together." Joash stepped forward, his voice caught the breeze, rising, as he sucked in air. "The apocalypse has already begun. A blood-red moon, storms, angels falling from heaven. Only together will we stop this immortal."

I feigned a smile. Their belief was foolish, romantic, and I couldn't help the nagging at my heart that by the end of the day they would all be dead. All of them. My shoulders sagged at the thought, my heart heavy but none the less, Austin lowered his eyes, a whisper from his lips.

A swirl of black fog before me, my head spun and as the stars cleared before my eyes, dotted, bright I saw that Austin had used his gifts and transported us all near the cave entrance.

Soaring limestone cliffs lined the twisted country road down towards the gorge where the Wookey Hole caves were located. Moss flecked the walls, breaking up the blinding white cliffs whilst on the opposite side of the road the countryside was abundant with life, trees and shrubs and the sounds of owls, their cries haunting and echoing around the gorge. But even in this beauty, my heart was heavy. Storms wrecked the sky, angels fell sporadically from heaven, and as the lightning ripped across the earth, it signalled that my brothers were near their end.

My skin chilled as the moon shone crimson shadows over the cliff face, the tempests, and now from a few spots of the earth's crust, demons spewed from Hell. This was the beginning of the end. If my brothers fell, if Cain succeeded in killing them, there would be no way back. Even Metatron and the archangels, the seraphim, none could stop this. And I was armed with a paltry spearhead which, despite its power, didn't fill me with confidence.

Cerberus barked at my feet. I pulled my dog up, hugging him and cursing myself for bringing him here. Eva gripped my arm, then smoothed Cerberus's back, a small smile on her lips. I could taste her fear. All of them. Except Joash.

Austin had transported us just a short walk from the main cave where they assured me Cain held my brothers. The village was deserted. With each heavy footfall, my soul grew heavier. I couldn't fail. But what if I did?

The entrance was pitch black, and I'd assumed Austin or Joash would use magic, but strolling in casually, Austin flicked switches which lit up the caves. Like a grotto, the lighting inside was coloured, reds and greens which bounced and dappled off stalactites which clung to the cave roof like majestic spears. Fissures in the cave face shone like diamonds, glittering amongst the lights, a briny smell heavy in the air and the twinkling from calcified water. Stalagmites and stalactites gave the caves a presence of a prehistoric cathedral.

I passed Cerberus to Austin and drew my sword as Xaphan and I led the way over a rickety rope bridge where emerald spotlights bounced and reflected off the cave walls.

Holding our breath as the walls opened, a huge cavern lay before us, the doomed roof covering a large lake which under the lighting had hues of purple and violet. Crystalline water on the roof and walls sparkled like stars in an inky sky, alongside stalagmites that rose majestically from the ground like obelisks from another realm.

Her voice low, Eva whispered, "Just follow the path along. You'll come to a small cove, from there we have to take the boat."

Then what? I had not counted on that...

As we walked on in wonder and trepidation, pinks, blues of lights enchanting this cave, we came to the witch. I shuddered. A menacing presence left my spine tingling, but contrasted with the beauty, the wonder of the place. Austin walked up to join me.

The calcified witch was perched at the bottom of the cave wall, separately. Layers of crystallised limestone had built up over her remains over eons of time, so that only a rough outline remained. Perhaps more disturbing was the crystalline structure of the witch's dog at her feet.

"Shudder indeed, so that's the witch, but more than that it was written that covens met here and the church hanged them all in these very caves."

Well, thanks for that.

"Indeed. It feels... unsettling."

The silence was heavy; we walked reverently by, only Joash stopped to touch the petrified witch and her dog. I cast a look back, seeing him tremble as he perhaps picked up an energy, a power... something.

The walls narrowed and climbed up, as we stood at the top of a small incline below a smaller cavern lit again with hues of emerald with vast towering walls around a smaller lake. The water had a sheen on its surface like green leather. It's crystal clear and clean water showed the bottom wasn't deep, and beside it the boat Eva had mentioned.

I turned to Austin, who held my dog tightly. "Austin, whatever happens—"

"I know, I'll stay safe with Eva and Cerby. Don't panic, Lucifer. We killed the wraiths where others failed."

Eva shot me a grin. "He's a millennial, they're pretty smart as it turns out."

Austin shot her a lopsided grin. "That means a lot coming from Generation X."

I had an idea what they were on about, but I let it go. What the bloody hell would that make me.

We climbed into the boat and set off. Sparse lighting lit the waterway, the tunnels narrowed and Xaphan and I took the oars, rowing as quietly as we could.

The deeper into the caves we travelled, the colder it became, until I felt a few of my companions' shiver. Aside from the dripping of water on the cave surfaces, dripping into the lakes, everything was still. I felt bound up, the dread and anticipation of what I would find.

Gleaming clusters of stalagmites adorned the walls, reflecting incandescent shafts of light that bounced on the skin of the water. A primeval beauty, raw, dangerous and cold.

As we spied a shore, Eva leaned forward into me, pointing to it. She whispered in my ear. Her sweet scent of lilacs filling me, and for a moment I wondered how I'd got here. How had I, after escaping Hell, arrived to take down the world's first murderer with an angel, two witches, a dog and a mage? Instantly, I regretted bringing them here. I should be here alone, or with the might of Heaven at my back. Why were they risking their lives? They should not, and I worried that through my actions their fate was now in my hands. I worried they could die, or worse... be sent to Hell.

I pushed the oars into the pool bed, pushing the boat in, then leapt out with Xaphan as we pulled the row boat ashore.

Before us a slight hill, the cave arched and a glittering bronze light radiated from the distance. Swallowing hard, I knew this was it. Cain was here.

As they got out of the boat, my voice hoarse, I whispered, "Stay behind me. Do not be tempted to be a hero, whatever happens. If I die, get out. Joash, Austin, use your magic and get out of here. Is that understood?"

All eyes on me. Eva's eyes pleaded, I hardened my face. Joash was silent, his expression resolute.

"I'll go first. Wait!"

Stealthily, I crept up the slope, a golden light growing brighter before me until I came to a chamber. Unlike the main cavern this place was smaller, its low ceiling glistening with crystallised water, a few stalactites smattering the roof.

Bracing, I saw Michael and Gabriel tied up, their hands stretched high above their heads, their bones almost protruding from their skin. Faces etched with dark circles around their eyes, motionless, they resembled husks of the angels I had known. Revulsion welled up in my throat, my stomach in a knot. The Mark seared as my limbs tensed, anger fermenting in me. Michael was on the right-hand side of the cavern, Gabe on the left and sitting before me, at the back on a stone dais, his foot bobbing over his knee, Cain grinned. A cigar in the corner of his mouth, Michael's sword in his hand tapping the flat blade against his leg. Anger flooded inside me, thrashing, my arm seared and grinding my teeth I bit all the hate, the rage down.

For now.

Through gritted teeth, I spat, my voice echoing around the cave, "I will flay your skin from your body as you watch.

You crossed the wrong angel, Cain. You took my brothers, stole my grace and you left me with evil, with hatred. I am the manifestation of man's terror, I am the beast that lesser beings fear... I am your darkness. Say your goodbyes Cain, it's time to meet your maker. I am taking you to Hell."

"I am meant to be scared that the cavalry's arrived. I'm honoured boys, seeing you all here. Touched, even." Cain placed his hand over his heart, smirking, then extended it. "Please all of you, don't be afraid, too late for that. See, I'm quaking in my boots. You can come out of hiding, that won't help you."

The air was thick with stale smoke and copper. Joash and the others walked slowly until I could feel their presence behind me.

Cain eyed every one of us. "Why, Satan himself graces me with his presence and he's kindly brought my hostages back, though thanks, I don't need them anymore. Joash though, the *mighty witch*. You two will make this whole plan go down with a bang." He indicated with his hand. "Please take a seat. Before I end world."

"Give it up, Cain. I have orders from Heaven, you are mine."

"You, Satan, orders from Heaven? Fantastic!" He switched his legs placing his feet on the floor, now leaning forward on the makeshift seat he was on, his face lit up. "I'm all ears, Luci, tell me? How does Satan, the Devil, get to 'take orders' from the very place that cast him into Hell, of all places? I'm as eager as a beaver to know, ya know?" Smiling, he leaned back and puffed hard on his cigar.

"You're pretty conceited for a man who's about to spend eternity in purgatory. Where did you get this power?"

He shook his head. "Since when did you take orders from Heaven, Satan?"

I pulled the spearhead from my jacket pocket. "See this Cain, remember this?" I held it up. Only now I noticed runes etched onto its blade edge, which glowed faintly amongst the bronze and gilded light.

It took all my strength not to lunge at him and shove it in his heart. Grinding my teeth, I stared into his eyes, reading his actions. I had to concentrate, the compulsion to rush to my brothers, to untie them battled with the will to sever his big, fat head and boot it across the caves but I had to somehow maintain control.

Kill... tear him to pieces, shred off his skin...the Mark hungered for murder. Thoughts flooded my mind, glancing at Michael, Gabriel, it burned deeply, scorching my skin.

Cain leapt up and strode over, reaching to grab the spearhead. I moved it away, extending my sword to meet him. "Give up my brothers."

His sword met mine, a clank of steel on steel. "Aw, Luci, I thought that was a gift? I have something for you and your friends."

"I'll take my brothers, thanks."

His lips turned down at the edges. "Really, I got something better than that. But first let me tell you, you know what I really hate about the twenty-first century?" His cigar bobbed in the corner of his mouth as he spoke. Extending his free arm, palm splayed he stepped back. "Now I know what you're going to say Luci, I do, they weren't technically invented in the twenty-first century, they've been around as long as us, but humans," he shot a wink at Eva then gazed back at me. "Humans have only written about them for a while. Zombies, Lucifer, I really, really hate zombies." Cain waved his free arm, his voice piercing, "I mean I almost hate them as much as I hate angels, I don't know. It's a tough call, you know to choose between the two. Look at your species. You're like zombies, right? All you do is follow orders, act without emotion. It's like you're dead inside." He leered forwards. "I mean, were you ever alive, I mean truly alive? I don't know. These questions keep me up at night. Still, an army of the undead. I'll give you a clue, what's white and silver, falls from the sky and splatters on the ground when it impacts?"

I shook my head.

No... just no...

He shouted, "Angels Luci! Like beautifully crafted automatons. Except," he shrugged, "I don't know, not as useful? It's a tough call, ain't it?"

I turned as I heard a zipper behind me. Austin was tucking Cerberus into his jacket, his face quite pale. I could see my dog shivering. Eva stood closer to Austin, a hint of green on her face.

Then, distracted as the sound of feet stomping on the ground marching towards us, I turned on my boot heels to look. In the entrance to this torchlit cavern, shadows appeared on the walls, growing larger. They moved like a shadow puppet show, getting bigger and bigger. A trickle of sweat ran down my back, my heart speeding up. My hand ached from gripping my sword hilt, I took a deep breath.

Marching up from the cavern entrance like machines, fallen angels, contorted, broken, marched carrying an array of swords. That's why they were falling, Cain was using them as an army?

I shivered as they dragged the tips of their blades along the ground, steel on stone it grated right through me piercingly loud. Their heavy limbs plodding towards us. An icy shiver ran down my back, their beauty, sculptured faces, high cheek bones, lithe warrior figures clashed with the death that lingered around them like a smog. Angels are created to symbolize perfection, their skin once luminous now dull, their dead eyes stared right through me. Lips slightly parted, their armour was the only thing that looked vivid as the flames of the cavern reflected on it. Silver, bronze and gold, their breastplates glimmered, their long hair swayed with each footfall.

Echoing around the chamber, as they walked towards us, their dark shadows swelled up on the walls as if consuming us.

Growling, I looked at the others, "Eva, Austin, Joash. Get the hell out of here."

Now these marionette angels were almost upon us. Twisting my sword to flex my wrist, I stood sideways, sword at the ready.

There had been dozens of my kin fallen. Why had Cain only used six? That made little sense, not that I was complaining. But to kill your own kind, to slaughter your brothers. The temptation gripped at my heart, clawed at my soul to throw down my sword and refuse. Point blank. But I knew, from their sombre stare, their ice-cold eyes and their scent that they would stop at nothing. Glancing at Xaphan, a thick sheen of sweat glistened on his face, I noticed his white knuckles seizing his sword hilt, a look of terror. Yes, they hit close to home.

We stepped closer; they raised their swords, the scraping noise stopping and their scent of death engulfed us. They were dead, but living. Cain's undead army. He'd been right, the end was coming. It was already here...

Their arms limp at their sides, they continued to drag their swords on the ground. The sound of steel on stone rasping. Swallowing hard as bile rose in my throat at having to fight my kin.

But their eyes, dry and dead, looked right through me. A hollowness in their movements, they marched in unison, pawns to the puppet-master controlling them they massed six to our five. I wasn't counting Cerberus.

Broken and torn, wings were bent out of shape, one had a wing hanging off in a twisted contortion that would be blindingly painful. But he moved without a spark of life in his face, unceasing. Unable to curl back their wings, it distorted them. These lifeless atrocities had been made to fall for the pleasure of Cain.

Skin that was once glistening, was pallid, grey, rotting, the shimmering flecks from their wings dirty and caked in their own blood. The mercy of Heaven, fallen... Where the hell was Metatron?

As they edged slowly, the gilded light fell onto their stony faces, a shadow danced over them, menacing I felt the sweat trickle down my neck at this new horror.

We all edged back a little, I moved before Eva and Xaphan before Austin. Leaning forwards, Austin looked at Joash who smirked at the small war band coming toward us, their feet stomping on stone, hunched, unstoppable. How do you kill the dead?

Austin edged to the side of Xaphan and stole a look from Joash, both now on the outer edge. Joash issued a curt nod as both raised their hands, palms facing the angels and cast fire, whip-like that smacked the ground and flicked up on the angels nearest to them. I screamed, my voice echoing, "No! Do not kill them, they are my kin! Possessed or not."

Shouting back, his face wrinkled, Joash issued, "They're dead Lucifer, if we don't kill them, they will kill us!"

"No! Immobilise them, don't kill them!"

I shot a glare at Joash who stared back, mistrust in his eyes. He nodded, lips pressed tight together. Austin and Joash shut their eyes for a second, both muttering something, and the fire turned to ice, freezing the angels in their step.

A moment of relief, Cain cackled. "You never give up, do you? I mean all of Heaven wants you and your wayward friends here dead, Luci, and yet you protect these... *puppets*?"

Gritting my teeth, I had no time to answer him as the other four angels now lumbered forward.

"Xaphan, don't kill them," I whispered. He nodded.

Our swords met, the loud clash of metal on metal. Pushed back by their strength, I blocked the incoming sword, its blade catching the amber illuminations, it gleamed like a fiery torch.

Joash, Eva and Austin scrambled to the side, I heard Cain bark a warning to them not to touch Michael, but I had to push the two undead angels back. I knew that if we could subdue them, that Heaven, the Seraphs could heal them, I refused to kill my own kind.

Whacking the one on my right on his leg with the side of my blade, made him stumble, at the same time the one on my left's blade came hurtling towards me. I tumbled down to the ground, smacking my knees on the stone, scraping the skin off, falling too fast to put my hands down. My right wrist twisted as I held the sword and landed badly. Fury whipped through me like wildfire as my skin burned. The Mark wanted blood. Demanded it. But I would not give in. Shifting my knees, bloody and sore, I pushed myself up. As a blade came hurtling towards me, above me, Cain cackled again. "Just kill it for God's sake. It's dead anyways."

Burning acid from my muscles, I held up my sword blocking another lethal blow, then sprung forwards into the angel, my head in his chest driving him back, out of the cave down the incline. A clank of metal as his sword fell to the floor, we tumbled. He tried to kick and thrash, confused. I heard the footsteps of another, again using my knees as leverage, I pushed the angel around so I was on top of him. Grinding my teeth, I punched his once-beautiful face. Again and again, my knuckles sore, bruised, an intense stinging smarting my hands. The pain, though, was not as bad as that of my heart, which shattered every time my flesh pounded into his.

Yelling as he in turn punched into my sides, the sweat running down my face; I felt an cold breeze wash over us and as my fist went to drive harder, I braced to smash it into his face, my heart splitting, he froze. An icy frost appeared on his face, his hands before me, the freezing cold wafting up over me. He lay there motionless, crystalline, illuminated like thousands of diamonds sparkled from his blackened and bruised face.

Staggering up, I turned around with my arms out, finding my footing to see Joash standing over me. His small eyes stared through me before he gave a curt nod and his eyes scanned me, his brows arched, lips parted slightly. He cast me a veiled smile.

The second angel was standing, sword raised just behind me, frozen.

Then Joash eyed the frozen angel, closed his mouth and walked back towards Cain. Scrambling back up, I fished the spearhead from my pocket, my palm sweaty, trembling with adrenaline. Enough.

"Well, well, well, Joash is surely a mighty one. And you Luci, fist fighting, I'm impressed. Never knew you had it in you. Well boys, and," Cain winked at Eva. "Lady, I'm almost regretting having to kill you all, and by you all I mean us. But I'm determined, I've been on this path for nearly one hundred years and I've made up my mind. I'm stubborn like that see, but you know that. Meeting my zombie angels, ah, don't worry. There's plenty more where they come from. But hey, it's been great meeting you all. Who knows, maybe we'll meet each other on the other side?"

I lunged at Cain, the anger raged through my veins. My vision blurred replaced with a crimson mist. Austin shouted and I heard Cerberus barking. Cain dropped the sword, pointed to Eva and laughed harder. She screamed, as I turned around Cerberus lay before her, his tiny belly rising and falling.

"You hurt my dog? You fiend!" I lunged at him, gripping the spearhead.

He pushed me back with some invisible force. "We're going to die Luci, and no one can stop it."

I turned as Eva cried, thrust off the ground, up against the wall. Then Austin groaned as Cain thrust him on the wall on the opposite side. A brilliant amber radiance flooded the skin of my brothers, Joash fell to his knees, his face hidden as his hair curtained his face.

The cracking of ice, I shot a look behind me. Their spell had died, the angels were coming.

Unable to restrain any longer... I breathed deeply as the beast split, cracked, roared, broke free from my shell...Screaming as I felt my skin tear, falling to my knees the red haze before my eyes, my bones splintered.

It was my shadow that they saw first. Looming, horrifying, it engulfed the entire wall, walking half man, half beast, weird, perverse. Unnatural.

The sound of my cloven feet clunked on the stone floor. As I looked at my hands, there before me giant claws, raven black and legs of a creature, I towered above them all. I could see my muzzle, feel the fangs with this tongue, and on my head, I felt where my horns grew. Heavy.

And my wings, black, the tips clawed. They beat slowly as I edged forwards.

Even without seeing, I knew what this form was, what I looked like.

Without wanting, I bellowed, a powerful and sinister sound, half bawl, half roar lunging forwards, my instinct to thrust my head down I charged.

Cain's face was bleached white with horror. He froze, pee trickling down his leg as he dropped to his knees, then cried. Actually, cried as I, the beast Satan, towered over him, a threatening snarl and the Mark it burned as red as the fires of Hell. It would have blood. I was damned. I used to be beautiful but now I was this monster and with each kill, each act of evil this monstrosity would become permanent and the fallen angel would cease to be... I bit down a tear, instead roaring at my own disgust.

I glared at Cain. Then with my head down, the monster charged him, impaling him through the ribs. His bones cracked as my horns crunched into his body. His wail pierced, shrieked around the walls. Throwing my head up, tearing his flesh as he staggered, tried to shuffle back, fell on the floor, his face ghost white. His rich scent of blood filling my nostrils...

Another sound made me look up. Cain's magic had lessened with my friends as Eva and Austin fell to the ground.

Turning suddenly as Eva shouted at me, arms out, she reached, but the beast threatened blood. But the angel, the man, wanted something else. Angel and demon battling inside of me...

Her small hands gripped around my leg, sending a shiver of expectation through me. I was unable to control the animal's instincts. Slowly I bent towards her, gently placing my clawed hands on her shoulders, tilting my head. How could she look at me? This monster?

Tears streamed down her face, so fragile, so mortal. "Stop this! You must do what Metatron instructed. You are not this creature. Cut off the Mark, Lucifer! I am here for you. Always."

Always? She didn't know what she was saying. Offering herself to me, her soul? Forever...

I yelled, the roar that came from me, horrified me. But the anger, the rage was stronger than my fear of myself.

Staggering back, I wanted to break out of this form but it held me. The grip from the beast, I was trapped in its form, unable to break free.

As soon as his eyes opened, Austin's mouth fell open wide as he stepped back.

My demon eyes followed their sounds. Xaphan, his eyes wide with horror, he was pinned to the wall in shock. The beast...

Joash stepped forward, smiling, a crimson fire behind his eyes. "Hail Lucifer! All hail Satan!"

He had no fear of me. Something flashed, something in Joash's hand gleamed, but he closed his fingers. It was gone.

Joash rounded his shoulders, seemingly taking comfort in my brutish form. He studied me for a long time, a smirk on his lips. He gestured, an elegant flick of his wrists, then brushed my face with his hand. His smooth voice rippled through the cave, "Well, aren't you going to punish him? Cut off the Mark, Lucifer, and put Cain in Hell. You have to, otherwise, well, you'll stay like that, won't you?" An abrupt laugh erupted from him before he composed himself standing before me. My chest rose and fell as I surveyed him. Even in this state, as my mind battled the madness, turbulent, he was familiar to me. His scent, those eyes... Conflicted with the compulsion to kill them all battled with the desire to be... normal.

Runes illuminated a scarlet light from the spearhead in my clawed hand. Reaching over my chest the blade sliced the flesh around the Mark on my arm, a sharp gasp escaped Joash's lips as he watched, breath baited.

Distracted, I felt her hand on my side, a sea of warmth flooded my body, twisting my neck as Eva called my mind.

"Lucifer?" Her voice was shrill, like metal being scratched on glass. Everything in my mind played in a hazy slow motion as my brain, this thing, this beast battled to make sense of the situation. Neither man nor beast.

"Do it! Do it now or we'll all be damned, Lucifer!" Joash's words were biting.

Eva tugged at my arm, I towered over her. Turning around I bent down until my massive snout was before her. Her rage turned to fear, a flash of terror in her eyes. She stepped forwards, Joash yelled. Slowly a smile wrapped her face, she whispered, "Lucifer..." then she reached up and I felt her lips on my face, my cheek.

Noises bellowed all around me, but I couldn't distinguish them out as I felt her lips, her energy, her love and power surge through me. Lost in a haze of energy, my heart pounded loudly, my body heated, desire whipped through me. I gasped, making a weird wailing goat sound and stumbled, falling back. My huge mass tumbled over. As my head hit the rock, my body spasmed, and a screaming deafened my ears... Snapping and crackling as my bones tore apart in agony, my body shredded open, the beast disappearing. The yelling got louder, I found myself howling on all fours, and only then realised that the screaming was me.

I had a darkness inside of me. Consuming me...

Coming around, naked, cold as I found my head on her lap. "Lucifer!"

Swallowing hard, I groaned, my mouth a hot mess. "You kissed me, you kissed that, that thing?"

She bent over me, her hair soft on my skin. "I kissed you. Whatever you are. Lucifer, the light and the dark. The good and the bad. What will you do with Cain?"

I let her help me up, though I didn't need it. Still buzzing with desire, with fury, I shook my head, panting.

Looking from Austin to Joash, whose eyes were small with wonder and wore a catlike grin, I cleared my throat. "I need the spearhead."

"It's here, it's here, Luci... fer! Wow, man, that was bloody intense!" Austin rushed forwards handing me the spearhead but his eyes were wary.

A gush of relief as Xaphan peeled himself away from the wall, he eyed me from a distance.

Panting, I looked at Cain, and I saw... what did I see? Myself.

I walked towards Cain who, still on the floor, doubled over from his injury as blood seeped from his chest. He rasped violently, struggled to get away from me on his hands and knees.

I knelt before him; the stone pressing hard on my naked skin. "Brother, let me release you, I will not condemn you to Hell. I will keep the Mark, you," I looked skywards, "You, I will give you the only gift I have left. Redemption."

His face contorted, fighting through the sobbing. "Why?"

Waves of guilt drowned me, I gulped at the man before me, seeing the fear, the hopelessness gnawing at him.

Metatron was right. It wasn't Cain doing all of this. It couldn't be, he wasn't that powerful. Someone was controlling him. And even though his actions were heinous and the Mark drove me to flay the bastard, I could not. The Mark, this Mark on my arm... it had taken away any sanity he'd had. It had almost taken mine.

My hands fell to my side. My voice had lost its power in this vast cavern of torment.

I breathed deep, trying to ease the tightness in my chest, and to lessen the sinking feeling in my stomach. Cain knelt before me and the Mark burned with a fury, but my mind questioned my next actions.

"Lucifer, cut off the Mark, what are you waiting for?" Joash's voice had a ragged edge cutting through me.

"Lucifer, Lucifer, what's wrong?" Her voice caressed my ears, but the words sounded muffled to me in the haze I found myself in. They were all talking at me, pushing me. Get on, do it. *Punish him. Punish Cain.*

A tingle of cold sweat rippled down my back making me shiver, I looked at him. Hopeless eyes stared back.

How could I? How could I, Lucifer, punish him? After all I had seen, could I really cast him into purgatory to replay the horror of his mistake? In Hell he would relive the murder of his brother day after day, night after night in all its full and tormenting horror. Could *I* do that?

He had killed his brother, had let jealousy govern his heart and my father, God had punished him. Cain had been impetuous, he had made a choice, an impulsive decision that he regretted. Even with his bravado, that was a mask. His face, tired and worn, wrinkled. For an immortal, it was unusual. His old face, despite his cocky attitude and merciless arrogance, showed guilt, self-hatred. It was that self-loathing that was eating away at him on the inside, so now he was just a husk of who he once was...

Gripping the spearhead in my clammy hands, I didn't see a villain kneeling before me, I saw a victim. A broken man whose face reflected out the tragedy of his life, the horror of his existence. I would not, could not do what my brother had asked. I had to give Cain what I wanted for myself, even though in doing that I would lose it for myself the moment I gave it to him. I had to give him redemption. Even though... even though... I would never see home, Heaven again.

Like a knot tightened hard, my stomach twisted, my jaw slack as I knelt before him. My throat swallowed down the bile, forcing myself not to retch. Part of me felt like mourning, knowing I would lose the very thing that had defined my existence for so long.

I glanced at Cerberus. Tiny, weak, frail body, so innocent. We were all innocent once. Before our dreams shattered. Before we lost our hope, made mistakes. My hand shook violently, I bent over him, whispering, "Close your eyes." He shook fiercely, tears streaming down his face. His voice croaked, "Luci, I just need release. I... I don't know what happened to me?"

I brushed the hair and dirt from his face, I was aware of the other's voices in the background. Challenging, raised, screaming.

I waited until his body collapsed onto my lap. I murmured, "Remember your home Cain? Where your father, Adam, and your mother, Eve brought you up? I want you to picture it now, in your mind, close your eyes, feel the heat of the sun on your skin."

I waited a moment until his lids lowered, his body trembled then relaxed onto my knees as I sat back on my heels, his body on my legs, into me. Softly, I muttered, "It is I, Cain, it is Abel, your brother. Come, come with me. See how the sun shines bright and hot across the fields, feel the breeze, taste the air. Can you feel the heat of the sun on your face?"

A smile tugged at his lips as he took a deep breath. I felt their eyes boring into me as they stepped closer. Silence pulled at me, a warmth flooding my heart, my limbs but I looked only at the broken man before me.

I placed one hand on his shoulder, then with the other shaking hand I plunged the spear tip into his heart. He gulped fast, then sank back.

In those few seconds his face changed from pained, tormented, to peaceful, almost a smile.

I dropped back onto my heels, his blood on my hands, as the Mark burned with violence and glory. I was doomed... I am the beast. I am Satan.

Heaven would be out for my blood now, with their fleet of Seraphs, wielding the flaming sword no doubt.

I had given Cain redemption, where my father had failed, I had not.

Moving Cain's body aside, I pushed myself up and stumbled towards Cerberus, but Eva was there. Dark lines etched on her face as she weaved a spell, a brilliant arctic blue thread that spun from her hand into my dog. She whispered a chant over Cerberus, as the threaded light glowed brighter. His little body glowed, illuminated and then, behold, my tiny dog breathing got up. And barked.

Her smile, weary, it had cost her to do that but Eva, my Eva, had the gift of life within her.

I bit down my emotion, too overwhelmed but managed a ragged smile in thanks to her.

Then I turned to them. "Who will help me take them down?" Silence fell on them all as they busied themselves. Xaphan whose voice hadn't shouted in disagreement carefully cut the cords that bound Gabriel and carried him towards me, whilst Austin held Michael's limp frame as I cut the cords that bound him.

We placed them on the floor with their backs to the ledge where Cain had sat on his make shift throne. Immediately Cerberus bounced over, licking my brethren's hands. It was as if he, in his own way was trying to help. Maybe he was... Unconditional love *is* a powerful force.

Crouching before them I called softly, "Michael, Michael, can you hear me?" His face, bruised and blacked, his eyelids started to flicker. "How can I restore him?"

"With this? Look!" Eva cried.

"The Armadel, the angel's grimoire. Aaron tried to find it, so Cain stole it."

Austin's voice was weak, "That's how Cain caught two angels. He used their own grimoire against them. But I don't think he acted alone. I mean, my hunch..."

A faint sound, Michael croaked, "Lucifer, is that you?"

"Michael, yes, yes, it is! Brother." I grabbed his frail body and held him close.

I twisted to Gabriel, my heart breaking in a thousand pieces seeing his ravaged body, face. Holding his hand. "Gabe, Gabe can you hear me?"

His heart was faint, fading. I pulled him into me, tears streaming hot down my face.

I glanced at his bloody chest, under the shreds of his T- shirt a leather thong and pendant. Biting back the storm of emotions, I knew that pendant. I had made it for him when we were as children. A tiny wooden cross. Now feelings fought and battled, rage, grief, nostalgia. Inside me the monster roared...

Without notice, a familiar heat burned in the cold cavern, a brilliant gold illumination as Metatron appeared, his face a torrent of anger.

Lashing forwards, his voice like a raging storm, "Did I not tell you! You unholy, evil demon! You were not to kill him, now you have the Mark! Cain did not deserve redemption, he was to be punished. Angels have fallen, died and now their blood, all of this is on *your* hands! You were warned Lucifer, warned to do exactly as Heaven requested. Had you done so, had you put Cain into purgatory, we would have welcomed you home. We don't know who controlled Cain, you utter, evil, arrogant imbecile! Who are you to give forgiveness? The same, you never change! You, the mighty Lucifer gave Cain redemption! Led by your pride, your arrogance. Now all of Heaven will smite you and your vagabond friends, and your bloody dog, you will all go to Hell."

"That's not-"

Metatron cut Austin off, his voice twisted and spiteful, "Quiet witch! We've a *special place* for you in Hell, magician. You'll be seeing it, backwards, shortly! All you witches!" His narrow eyes filled with anger and glanced at Michael and Gabriel who sat limply against the wall.

Striding towards me, he glanced at Joash, the faintest of nods.

With a flick of his hand, a blazing light shone and my brothers were gone.

I stood uneasily, my will to fight growing. He wrinkled his nose as my skin burned, visible to all. Like the lava from Hell, red-black flames seared around the Mark.

"Michael and Gabriel are in Heaven and praise to the Seraphim's will be healed soon enough, but as for you, evil bastard... you are Father's mistake. A rebel, unable to comply for the good of all."

Gritting my teeth, I felt the wrath building, shaking my head.

He turned his back on me. "The rest of you will never see the light of day again, for helping the Devil. Vile creature, Satan!" Then turning back, he said, "Because of you, we cannot stop the apocalypse. Had you stayed in Hell where you belong... it is too late now."

Shaking violently, I pulled the spearhead from Cain's chest.

"Brother, hey?"

He turned, his downturned lips, he eyed my
hands, gasping, hatred stared back at me. Looking
him in the eye, I thrust it into his angry heart.

His mouth fell open in shock, in horror as his eyes grew
cruel, but before he could say any more, he gripped it and fell
back, thumping to the ground as his head smacked the stone.

I stood there shaking violently. My brother's blood on
my hands. What had I done?

Joash strolled over to me. "Look at the Mark. It's glowing... Like Cain, you killed your brother."

He touched it as I stood there, sweaty, my mind a hazy
mess, unable to think. Finally, I looked Joash in the eye. "He
was going to kill you, all of you, I couldn't... I couldn't..."

He narrowed his eyes, scanning my face, and nodded.

Silence blew cold around us for several seconds.

"What now?" Austin murmured.

I looked towards the cave entrance. "Out there all of
Heaven will be hunting us. Seraphims', Dominions, Virtues,
Authorities and even the Principalities. If they catch you,
you three at least will be sent, as Metatron said, to a special
place in Hell. Your bodies will be broken, twisted and your
heads, well... they will be on your body backwards. As for me,
I don't know, but it will be worse..."

"How?" Austin choked.

"I suggest we'd better hide, and there's only one place
that Heaven won't look for us. At least for now, I know of
some places we can be safe. For now," Xaphan's voice was a
comfort.

I cleared my throat. "Hell. We'll have to go to Hell. Just for a while."

I had killed my brother; just like Cain before me. I had been driven mad by this infernal Mark. *The Curse.* Its power to drive me to kill, to be evil. I had unleashed the beast.

I will stop the Apocalypse. And protect my friends from the wrath of Heaven.

Warmth and dread radiated through my body and a feeling that I was not used to, but it pulled at my heart, making it both empty and full. Both happy and sad.

Would I ever find redemption? I swallowed hard, biting back a tear.

I shall be a benevolent angel, where my father, where Heaven is not.

I shall be the light and the darkness.

I am Lucifer; I am unbound, and I demand redemption.

Ave Lucifer.

Be not afraid...

Thank you for reading Lucifer Unbound. I really hope you enjoyed it. Below you'll find a snippet from the next book, what happens next. If you enjoyed it, please post a review without spoilers!

The Devil's Redemption Legacies
Book II: Extract.

Mark.

The caves echoed with howls. The hairs on my arms stood on end. Joash grabbed the spearhead, pulling it roughly from Cain's corpse whilst Xaphan paced, hollow eyes shooting me a cold stare as I stood over the body of my brother.

Clenching and unclenching my fists, crumbling inside, unable to take my eyes from my dead brother, I blocked out the sounds, numbed.

Shaken by her touch, Eva came up beside me. She whispered, but I didn't hear her words. I knew two things.

I had killed my brother, just as Cain had killed Abel. And my brother was an archangel.

Scooping up Cerberus, I tucked my shivering dog into my jacket, zipping it up to keep him from harm, then snatched up Michael's sword. The blue flames cast their eerie light on the walls and rough ceiling. Stalactites and crystallised water glistened like ice blue diamonds around me, a surge of determination as my hand wrapped around the hilt.

In Metatron's haste, he had left behind the holy sword when he'd sent Michael and Gabriel back to Heaven, but that was where my luck ended. Fixated on Metatron's lifeless body.

And now as I stood in the caves, screeching from an unknown source resounded through the caves from outside.

My companions were talking. It took Eva shaking me for me to hear.

I held out my hand for her to take it. "What will I do? When Heaven realises I killed my brother...." my words trailed off, lost in the commotion, but I was the only one thinking of Metatron.

Xaphan bolted up the track that led out of the cavern, peered out and shot a glance back, his voice quiet and hurried. "We need to get a way out of here, Lucifer. Now! Whatever the hell is out there ... if it comes here, we're trapped!"

Eva gripped my hand tight, I could sense her whole-body tensing. Candles flickered in the cavern, enlarging the shadows as the shrieks and cries of werewolves washed through us. It sounded like a battlefield outside.

"Let me." Austin's lashes lowered as he muttered a spell to whisk us away. A faint glow of his tattoos, holding my breath as we all watched him. Could he get us out of here? But a churning in my belly made me realise I needed to see what was happening. And I had to ensure they were safe first.

Muttering quietly, Austin opened his eyes, his brows meeting.

Nothing.

Scrunching his eyes, Austin mumbled under his breath. And whilst he kept trying, I guided Eva with me, stepping to the back of this grotto.

The sounds got louder. My dog trembled inside my jacket. I gripped Eva's hand tighter. I could hear her panicked panting, feel her energy radiate through me. I wanted to hold her, to kiss her, to tell her she would be alright.

But even the crevices hidden in darkness at the back of the cave revealed no passageways. A trickle of sweat ran down my spine.

I jolted, startled, as a howl bellowed: a single shriek that intensified and pierced us, then a clamouring of metal on metal. My breathing quickened, and I felt a stabbing in my stomach as my eyes were drawn back to the corpse on the ground; to the murder I had committed. I battled with the urge to gag at my own disgust.

Blood and fear filled my senses. Sighing, I let go of her hand and unzipped my jacket. "Eva, take Cerberus. Xaphan, Joash," they gave me a cold stare. "Make sure Eva and Cerberus are safe. Austin, your magic isn't working here, that's clear."

He unscrewed his face, lifting his head away from the spell he was trying to force. "Austin, you can probably look after yourself, but, all of you, look for another way out. I think if you get closer to the surface, at least away from this hollow, your magic should work. And take the Armadel," I pointed to the heavy tome of a book on the floor. "It's the angel's grimoire. It's probably the only thing that will keep you alive right now. Xaphan will be able to read it."

Wetting his lips, Joash titled his head, "What about your brother's body?"

"Leave it!" I loped over to Xaphan to peer out into the inky shadows of the caves beyond. The fighting grew louder.

Huffing, Xaphan turned to them. "Do you know of another way out?"

Frowning, Eva nodded, her eyes full of fear. "Yes, if we follow the river in the boat, I think it comes out at the river Axe? But what will you do, you can't go out there, Lucifer!"

I nodded, ignoring her question. "Come, let's go."

We hurried out of the cavern, leaving both my brother and Cain's bodies, and scrambled into the rowboat. Cerberus barked, struggling to get away from Eva, so I leaned over him whispering, "Good boy. Stay with Eva, she'll keep you safe."

We could hear that somewhere outside the cave, a battle raged.

Swallowing my fear, I knew that whatever befell me, whatever horror I endured, I couldn't die. Now I was almost familiar to the stench of my flesh as the Mark burned, its curse coursing through my veins. Wanting, willing blood.

I waited until they were seated. The silence between us blanketed our fear as the fighting grew ever louder. Using the oars to row the vessel to the other side, I paddled as quietly as possible. Stalactites glistened from the roof, and fossilized water reflected like stars in the night's sky. A beauty devoid of life, empty, the emerald water rippling with light, its gleam crystal clear.

Passing the oars to Joash, I leapt off the boat and onto the ledge.

"Do as Eva said. Follow this underground river, get to safety. Joash, Xaphan will explain to you the Echonian text in the grimoire, though I know you already have some knowledge of it. Use it to shield yourselves from Heaven. Do not look for me. That is your only hope for surviving Heaven's wrath, and survive you must." Biting my lips, the weight of her stare burned through me. "Eva... I have to go out there. I don't know what's happening, only that, no doubt, it is because of me. If I never see you again, know that you are brave and compassionate. Use your gifts wisely."

She made a sound like she was going to speak, then cried out as my dog struggled free and bounded off the boat to follow me.

"No! No, you can't, Cerberus! You're not safe!" I ran to catch him, but Cerberus stubbornly ran off in front of me into the gloom. My heart in the back of my throat, I rasped as Cerberus leapt onwards. I ran to catch him as he dodged, edging just out of reach. Sweat poured from my forehead. My hound was running to his death! Gritting my teeth, I called quietly but sternly, "Cerberus, get back here! Heel!"

But he didn't. Bounding forwards as if it was a game, his tiny legs able to easily navigate every rock crevice, every cranny. My heart hammered through my chest.

Only a few lights remained on inside the caves. I was damned by Heaven, hated by Hell, and doomed on earth. And now my dog was running towards a battleground. Holy bloody hellfire.

Sprinting after Cerberus, the uproar grew louder, metal clashed, clanked and screeched. Then, a high piercing wail. Swallowing hard, I kept to the shadows running alongside the cave walls, my eyes wide, watching for anything waiting in the corners, in the darkness. But nothing leapt out to me. My hair blew back lightly off my face, and a speck of light appeared as the cave entrance was finally in sight. I ran lightly over the wooden bridge, sword held low, its arctic blue flames a sure sign to give me away to the hordes of enemies that waited outside. Knowing I was approaching a world of torture and pain, I stopped for a moment, allowing myself the one last thought of her. Lowering my lashes, I could taste her lips on mine, feel her skin brush against face, her scent...

And now the little soul Cerberus who had managed the impossible, turning my vicious, angry heart into something lighter.

But that was gone now. Brief though it was, a taste of love, of warmth maybe, had the power over me to last a thousand years in Hell. And I would suffer again to keep them safe. As my chest rose and fell, I stepped slowly towards the entrance to face the onslaught of war outside.

Heaven Hath No Fury.

I continued to the mouth of the cave, then stopped, my breath catching in my throat. Perched outside, on the ledges, on the cave walls and the surrounding gorge, blood dripping from their snouts, howling werewolves gathered.

Gargantuan claws ripped and shredded at an angel before me, the sword in my celestial kin's hand falling to the ground as his entrails spooled out. In the last second of his life his eye caught mine, his face wracked with shock, his eyes shot me a look of hate. Then he fell, tumbled to the ground like a sack of stones. The werewolf had already bounded off to another divine victim. I could see Cerberus shivering, hidden under a nook horribly close to the fighting. He yelped seeing me and bolted, tail between his legs standing behind me.

Like a marionette, my jaw fell open, but without time for shock, a gust of wind above me had me moving fast. My boots shuffled on the rock surface, edging back. My sword blocked an incoming sword from the white-winged angel who spat obscenities at me, fierce faced. He lunged in his anger, over stepping.

I crouched, then bounded to the side, shouting, "What is happening? Why do you want to kill me?"

A hoarse reply rang in my ears, "Satan, God's finest? This is all your fault, Lucifer! The apocalypse has begun, your progeny walks the earth. A reign of fire, a blood-red moon, it is already here. If we take your head, it will all stop. And Lucifer, we will kill you and your pathetic dog."

Yelling in my face as his sword clanged on mine, his fury mixed with mine as the Mark seared on my skin, "I do not want to kill you, you are my kin, my brothers!"

He didn't seem to hear, so consumed with wrath, his sword fast as he tried to whip a way around my weapon, to find a weakness.

Stay hidden, little hound!

Clashing, our weapons chimed. I stared into his eyes. But there was only anger and hate.

As he pulled his sword back, I lunged forward with all my force, gritting my teeth as my sword crunched through his ribs, taking his life and a part of my soul along with it. I had woken the monster inside me. It roared, willing me to take more, wanting blood.

Vengeance. The beast wanted out.

Something stirred behind the angel as he fell to ground face first. I withdrew my sword and stepped back.

An angel corpse behind him sprung to life, an amalgamation of angel and werewolf bolting upright. In a fit of gross mutation, feral eyes, scarlet orbs glanced feverishly around as a canine snout jutted out from the angel's bloody face.

His gashed body, the open fissure in his chest, entrails moving like snakes—it all healed before my eyes with supernatural speed, as his flesh knitted together fast, hiding them. His skin changed from glistening to leather, sprouting hair, his bones snapping. Jerking violently, in the grip of unbearable metamorphosis, the divine being morphed from angel to wolf. Standing perhaps nine feet tall, his blood smeared wings dropped to the ground, crumpled as he snarled. Rabid.

Talons extended, his glance savage, he lunged towards me at preternatural speed, the remnants of his armour clamoured to the ground as the half angel, half wolf's muscles expanded, he leapt forwards, the scent of blood fuelling him.

At the last moment I leapt to the side, crouched low and held my sword hard in my hand, extended, slicing through his ankles. Whipping my blade back, I paced behind him, reaching up high to thrust my blade between his shoulder blades as he rolled forwards from the laceration on his legs.

Falling to his knees, his head lolled. Drawing back my sword, he fell forwards, his roar curtailed by my blade's final goodbye.

The sound of heavy footsteps reached my ears. Another were-angel leapt in fast behind me. Cerberus yelped, unable to turn around quickly enough as the atrocity was upon me. I twisted the sword hilt in my hand, lunging my sword backwards. I felt the thrust of my sword crack through his bones, his howl cut short as he crumpled.

The thing fell into me; I stumbled away bloody, shocked and shaking with battle rage, with fear, feverishly looking for my hound.

The werewolves attacked the angels in numbers, but as fast as the werewolves brought them down, the corpses mutated and rose up, fighting the werewolves.

Insanity!

Some fought tooth and claw, brutal as the angels who were clad in bronze, silver and golden armour and fought them mercilessly.

Limbs were sliced as blades hacked. But the werewolves mutilated my species, tearing the angels to shreds their wings splayed in blood, angelic faces wrinkled in hate as underworlder and the divine destroyed each other.

Sweat poured from the back of my neck. I'd never seen anything like this. Gripping my hilt, I searched urgently for my hound.

Scurrying to hide, Cerberus growled, his tiny voice lost in the cacophony of howls and shouting. I went to scoop him up, but he dodged me again. I trembled violently, seeing my dog so perilously close to death.

White feathered wings spraying scarlet as the blood splattered. Climbing down walls: huge claw-like hands, vampires joined the fray. Fangs bared under the pale wisps of the morning light.

For seconds I was too dumbfounded to move.

I realised almost too late when the angel landed beside me, majestic and full of anger, boots thumping on the ground. I took in the sheen of his gilded armour. Blonde hair fell around his face, lips curved slightly in a sneer, sword poised at my heart.

As the blade touched my chest, his face crinkled, Cerberus jumped, biting his ankle. In a flash I raised my arm, swung my sword, taking his head. I had no choice in that. Their armour leaves little uncovered. I wouldn't risk Cerberus being killed.

Angel or not, I had vowed that I'd kill any that harmed my dog. Twice now my dog, still a puppy, had saved my life.

There was a heavy thud behind Cerberus. The leering werewolf cast his head back, roaring. Saliva drooled from his fangs as he howled. Dark wiry hair covered his leathery skin, standing unnaturally upright. Formidable limbs ragged with claws, each paw the size of my head. I twisted my sword in my hand, ready to impale, but despite his savage countenance I sensed no malice. This was a pure werewolf, not a wereangel. The angels were sent to kill me. But I couldn't be sure. Staring at the monster before me, it took all my willpower not to glance at my dog, lest the beast snatch Cerberus up and...

The fearful creature had a massive snout. His powerfully built body was an unnatural hybrid of man and wolf. Red eyes burned with a fire. Towering over me, blood matted fur its claws were now retracting, the mass of muscles shrinking before my eyes. He wasn't roaring in aggression or attack; the man inside the monster was battling to get out. Holding my breath as I watched, poised to kill, I could smell the stench of copper and flesh as his bones snapped and cracked, and he lurched over, screaming.

Bolting behind me with a sharp whine, Cerberus shivered as I held my sword before us, ready to kill any and all that dared to harm us.

With my back towards the cave entrance, I sized up the creature before me as its body burst violently, bones breaking, wailing from beast to man.

Lifting his tilted head, mid-scream, he opened his eyes, swallowed hard, and eyed me. His stare fell to Cerberus. His eyes twitched, locking his glance at me. "Lucifer? And this must be the famous Cerberus! He certainly has the Lupine spirit!" Holding out his bloody hand, "I am Conor, alpha of the Wychwood pack."

I narrowed my eyes. Staring at his hand and breathing deeply, I took it, shaking it firmly. Naked and bloody, he stepped closer. His lips curved into a grin. "Lucifer, an honour to meet you. I trust you will stand by us. Your kin, as you see, have started slaughtering us in your name!"

Werewolves, vampires, and angels were battling everywhere we looked. I nodded. I snatched up Cerberus and in one swoop and nestled him into my jacket, zipping him in without putting down my weapon.

"Your kind are not killing angels, they are turning them? That is madness!"

He nodded curtly, and shouted above the din, "An unfortunate side-effect. But the vampires can finish them off. Not every wolf has the power to create another."

"You cannot control a wereangel. They will wipe you out! Pull back your forces, or you'll all be slaughtered."

"You underestimate us, Lucifer."

Conor turned around and roared as he started transforming. Cerberus shivered against me.

I leapt up, my wings beating hard as the alpha metamorphosed back into his lupine form.

Landing on a ledge nearby, a Grigori angel rushed towards me with hate-filled eyes. He hesitated when he saw my dog. I'd put Cerberus into my jacket, facing me to ease his fear, but he shuddered nonetheless.

Spitting in anger, "Why have you brought a dog?"

"He is my dog, you fool! Why are you killing underworlders like this?"

His lips curled down, small eyes looked from Cerberus to me. "Orders, Satan, from Heaven! They will all be killed unless you give yourself up."

I laughed in his arrogant face. "Never." But I let him attack first. Parrying with him, his anger seemed to burn worse than mine, but I knew the trick of the Mark now. When I was last in Hell, in The Fields fighting those demons I had let the Mark drive me into a fury, a rage and it was only through luck that the demons I'd fought were not experienced sword fighters.

Now I let that wrath simmer, using its energy to sustain mine whilst I examined the angel's strengths and weaknesses. Radiating confidence, he was heavy-footed, and relied on his right hand. He carried no shield. Like most Grigori, they had taught him a system of fighting. A system I knew.

Blocking him, his sword clanking on mine, he scowled, "It is an abomination that you, the Devil, carry the holy sword! You are an affront to God!"

My face lit up. His fighting was clean. I'd learnt in Hell.

"Is it now? Are you sure you know what my father thinks? Why it was my father who placed this puppy before me when I left Hell to rescue Michael and Gabriel?" I edged back, fighting cautiously with mischievous Cerberus in my jacket. I'd sooner die myself than have him hurt, but all around me vampires tore and leapt at angels. Some held weapons: swords, lances, bows.

Claws extended, werewolves fought passionately. The angels, my kin, fought by the book. And, alas, the divine militia were winning.

He overstepped. I took the advantage and sliced his arm. Blood gushed, sparkling silver and red. His face contorted in pain, but he continued fighting, just as he was taught. Grigori fight to the death.

A hand landed on my shoulder. I spun around, almost impaling Joash with my weapon. A sly grin on etched on his lips. Extending his arm with his palm facing the angel, a wisp of flame fired from it and the soldier went hurtling backwards.

Sighing, Joash surveyed the battleground. The scent of blood, fear and guts were thick in the air. "Ah, so it has begun then. Heaven battling the earth. The tourists will arrive soon. I think this needs to end?"

Fear clenched my stomach. Joash was supposed to be guarding Eva. "Why are you here–?"

Rolling his eyes, he tutted, "She's safe, Lucifer. I told Xaphan to babysit your witch, he is an angel after all. No, I had to see... this. I called for back-up. Look, there he comes now. Blaise, an old acquaintance."

A deathly hush fell over the battle. Gasping at a sight of a rider on a horse made of flame and fire. The rider was untouched by the inferno.

I'd only heard whispers, rumours, but never believed fire horses to be real. The fighters stopped battling, weapons poised, waiting to see which side this fire-wielding rider would take. A scarlet cloak bellowed out behind him. His lustrous bronze armour caught the dim morning rays, and in his hand, he held a sword that wielded flames just like his steed.

The red rider.

"How is that even possible? I know magic can be powerful, but that?"

Joash merely grinned, watching his acquaintance as the horse galloped into the fray.

Angels crossed themselves, grouping themselves together. Some took to the wing, flying above the rider with arrows poised whilst the vampires and werewolves merely stopped to watch.

The rider hammered down into the fight, changing direction and charging straight into the line of fire of the angels. Swords ready, they stood in a circle, facing outwards. I watched, knuckles white from gripping my sword, my other hand resting on Cerberus's back.

The fire from the horse grew brighter, flames growing as he whooshed towards them. Restless werewolves took their cue, leaping, bounding forwards. I grimaced, gritting my teeth. Why had it come to this, Heaven in its arrogance had to inflict their rule on every underworlder and do that in my name?

Instinctively I shut my eyes as their beautiful, ice-white feathers caught alight, their swords not harming the horse as they plunged into a furnace of fire. A fire that licked up their blades and engulfed them. Angels were beautiful—and deadly if you fell on the wrong side of their ideology—but it tore me in two seeing my kin battle and kill, their hatred fuelled by their hatred of me. God's first.

But we couldn't stand and watch. Boots landed behind me. I whisked around, one hand over Cerberus's head as he buried his face into my chest, the other fingers strained around the hilt of my sword.

Joash joined me, his movements languid, wearing his smile like a menacing mask.

The angel eyed him. Joash held up his arm, his fingers moving as he muttered a spell. The angel shook his head as he stepped forward, hair blowing around him and the scent of death heavy around us. His wings were sprayed with blood, and his boots thick with battle guts. I stepped forward, hearing Joash mutter louder.

Staring at my foe, I tilted my head slightly back to the witch, "I told you, you should've brought the Armadel! Your magic won't be powerful enough to stop angels. Only the Armadel grimoire, the angel's grimoire has the power to ward you.

The angel spoke. "Give yourself up, Lucifer. See how many have died in your name already. Will you really condemn the rest to a fate of purgatory? Are you too weak to surrender?" He was bold, young, with ethereal pale eyes, the lightest blue. Puffing out his chest, his armour gleamed silver. Yes, a newer creation, still old, but not as old as me.

"I have wronged, certainly, but this," I glanced to my side, "This is your doing. If the apocalypse is coming..."

His voice throaty, "It has already begun, you fool! And you, Lucifer, are on the wrong side!"

I couldn't withhold a spluttered laugh, but I stopped moving. Not taking my eyes off him, the sounds of fighting restarted around us, each of us weighing the other up. Cerberus gave a low whine from inside my jacket. The angel's eyebrows shot up, and he sniggered. "A puppy, really? You think a puppy will stop me from slaying you?"

One more step. Cerberus shivered. Our swords clanked. He parried around me whilst I watched, eyeing his movements, his feet, looking for his weakness.

He had none.

I blocked the incoming blade. Teeth gritted, this angel was fast. I'll give him that.

We began thrusting blades. Each movement was controlled and careful as we studied each other's technique. Looking for a way past my sword, I could smell the ambition from him. The one who took down Lucifer.

Cerberus trembled. The ground was uneven and rocky, forcing me to widen my stance with each movement I blocked, watching his body rather than his weapon. Metal on metal clattering, I muttered soothing words to my dog as I looked for an opportunity to end my opponent.

It was a composed fight, unusually, but it bought me time. Joash disappeared, and in his place, another angel appeared, anger distorting his face. Blood smeared his cheeks, his hair tangled with crimson knots, his sneer full of fury. My mind slowed, heart racing as adrenalin coursed through my body.

"That smell," spat the angel. "So it's true. You have the Mark of Cain. Tell me, if I take your head, will you still live?"

Swallowing hard, my tongue stuck to my mouth. "I would. It is my father's curse, after all. You both defy me, his son?"

It was odd. I was in two battles. One facing these... *traitors*, and the other my anger at the abomination of angels turning against their own. Their sheer audacity. But I had to reign it in for Cerberus. Opening up my wings, they both snarled. But I wouldn't risk the life of my hound. I'd never run from anything, but I couldn't promise Cerberus would live if I was fighting two angels and trying to protect him. And losing face is fine, as long as I don't lose my dog.

Their wings mirrored mine. I stood back, appraising the situation as each angel approached. Gritting their teeth, as I looked behind their anger, I saw a sadness. So many would die today, never to be reborn, but forgotten. Whatever their opinion of me, their resentment, I was still underneath this, damned though I was, one of them. Created by God. And they could be me, if they fell...

A loud yell distracted me. Blaise, the red rider, came charging towards us, sword held aloft. My attackers' already pale faces grew even whiter. I sprung up fast, leaping into the air, my wing muscles burning as I forced them to beat with speed.

In one fell swoop, using surprise and fear for his weapons, Blaise cut them down, their snowy wings burning red and black.

Fear fired in their eyes, before they engulfed in flames. My soul dropped, choked, how had it come to this?

His horse edged backwards as Blaise nodded to me, his face hidden beneath a terrifying helmet. Long brown hair was all that I could see of the man behind the mask. His brilliant bronze helmet was demon shape with two massive gold incisors over the grinning mouthpiece. I had assumed Blaise was mortal, a witch but the eyeholes in the helmet were dark, his eyes hidden and the horse? I wasn't so sure. Could a mortal ride a horse of fire? If it was magic, it was the strongest I had ever witnessed

Shielding his sword, he cantered towards me, lifting the mouth piece up. He shouted over the din, and I saw the face of a man. Black brows framed an angular face, dark eyes, and golden skin. He looked human, though I doubted he was mortal.

Shouting, and evil grin on his face, "No point in fighting if our Lord Lucifer has fallen, is there?" Still seated on his flaming horse, he bowed, clenched hand over his chest and then disappeared back into the thick of the battle that raged below.

With Cerberus in my jacket, I was weary to join him and loathed to kill any more of my kin. Caught in the middle, I wanted to roar but the pup that shivered by my chest stopped me. A deep emptiness in my core. My heart was tormented.

Joash shot me a grin from the battlefield. I thought him insane until I saw the glinting dagger that he clutched in his hands. A black sheen under a hazy sunrise, I could see it was the obsidian Tecpatl. Why hadn't he used that earlier, I had said his magic would be useless against my kin. He laughed boisterously before striding into an oncoming angel, dodging in a heartbeat the blade that threatened his life, then plunged the sacrificial dagger into the angel's heart. His back was to me, but he was ruthless. That was the least of it. Spinning the angel around, my kin's face wrought with horror as Joash pulled the angel to him, snuck the dagger into his belt, then ripped out the heart.

And as the celestial man watched, Joash drank his blood from the still beating heart. The witch was brutally enjoying his savage nature. Instinctively repulsed, I would watch him closer now. Killing should never give you pleasure, brutality, even less.

My wings still open, I flew upwards. My mind, my heart, waged its own private war, drawn from this side to that, but foremost protecting the hound who had put his life in my hands, and saved mine twice over.

I had to fight, loathed as I was to slay my kin but my friends' lives were in danger. As I started to descend, Cerberus's shrill bark a cloud of darkness covered the dim light. A fast glance over my shoulder, a fleet of angels, their armour, swords glinted on the horizon. It seemed that Heaven was destined to slaughter us all.

Maybe hundreds...There was no way in hell we could fight them all off. Not even with the incredible fire horse rider.

"Lucifer! Down here, come!" Joash's yell echoed through the air.

As I descended lower his eyes flashed scarlet. "The blood Lucifer, it has empowered me. But I hear them, Heaven has sent an army! We need to leave! I can get us out of here now."

"We cannot leave the others here to fight alone! But I agree, there are too many. And I need to collect Metatron's body! What we need is a miracle."

But we had none.

I heard them on the wind, faint at first. A rustle in the distance, growing noisier the light waning clouded by their numbers. A rhythmic whooshing grew louder and louder.

A tempest, it surely was.

Wading through the fray, smacking angles out of his path with his massive clawed hands, the werewolf stood before us, transforming. Bellowing through the glade, his roar rumbled through us, and there before us stood Conor, looking up with defeat in his eyes. Panting, his chest heaved, "We cannot fight all of them. We need an escape!"

Spinning around, his head tilted back as he cried across the battle, he shouted, "Tilbaketog!"

I edged back and saw before me what his word meant. Without hesitation his pack flew at the speed of light, it seemed into the forest, the vampires realising the meaning scattered like a murder of crows. He spun around, "Lucifer, go. We will meet soon enough." I nodded, as he ran, he changed into the monster as I grabbed hold of Joash's arm and flew up fast to find Eva, Austin and Xaphan. I knew they were somewhere alongside the river, and I scoured the land below searching as Cerberus whimpered, nestling inside my jacket, Joash clinging to my arm.

Joash it seemed wasn't keen on flying, a pale shade of green on his face, but that was preferable I guessed than facing a hundred swords from Heaven.

The boat they'd taken was partially hidden under a tree near the shoreline, but I could see no sign of them. Landing swiftly, Joash wobbled, his arms splayed, I placed my free hand on my dog, my right hand gripped my sword ready. The sky above darkened. Shouts and cries from my kin above, taunting me as they started to rain down on us like plumes of fire had my mind, my limbs freeze in terror, I screamed, then I fell to my knees...

Book 2 release follow: jnmoon.com

About Lucifer Unbound & JN Moon...

Hello reader,

Well, I started writing Lucifer Unbound in February 2020. My first draft was messy, I think subconsciously with the lockdowns and uncertainty no amount of CBD oil seemed to help. Much.

In October 2020, I sought a coach who, aside from monthly coaching sessions, also assessed and commented on my book. She has tons of experience and I then re-wrote the entire book.

The idea... I bought the covers in 2019 after seeing them for sale and it was the artwork that inspired the story. I knew I wanted Cain in it, a cocky villain but with a somewhat sad story, his eternal punishment adding to his madness, a punishment and remorse that he cannot escape.

Reading theology, I was keen to make some of Lucifer's traits, pride, arrogance and sprinkle these into the book exaggerating these, but also dropping him into new situations.

There are a lot of symbolisms in the book regarding the Apocalypse- did you spot them?

Cerberus. Originally, I was going to make him a Xolos breed. They look really beautiful, but as an advocate of rescue animals, I thought it more important that Cerberus be a lovable mixed breed. I love how animals teach us valuable lessons just by being.

It was my brother that pointed out the dog was God backwards! Like everyone knows that!

Eva's character grows throughout the series. Some kick-ass heroines in vampire and sci-fi movies especially inspired me, so you'll enjoy that.

Joash. Really loved developing his character. You'll see more of him later. The Influencer.

I have six planned and might do more if there is a demand.

How did I translate Enochian? Aha, that would be telling, lol! OMG. I found an online translator, it says it's rough. It probably is, but as a huge Supernatural fan I always think these spells sound great in Latin or Enochian, neither of which I speak btw!

Yes, Dante's Inferno definitely inspired my visions of Hell. Creepy and horrifying aren't they!

We're allowed to use references, I checked.

Snow in Spring in the UK? Oh yeah, except in 2021 we had snow in January. We very often get it at Easter! But mostly we get rain. Never travel here without an umbrella!

That's all for now. To reach out or find out more, it's all here: www.jnmoon.com

Don't forget to grab your free book.

Wolf Moon.
A lone alpha. A community shattered by a bloodbath.
A love born from the ashes...
www.jnmoon.com

All Books. JN MOON

Always Dark Angel Series
Vampires, werewolves and Nephilim battle it out on the streets with a taste of romance.
Get FREE Always Dark Angel Prequel @ jnmoon.com
Book 1 Immortal Curse
Book 2 Dark Nephilim
Book 3 Children of the Fallen
Book 4 Prince of Hell
Book 5 King of Hell
Boxset
The Blood Moon Series
Smoking hot Alphas, werewolves, demons & a kickass heroine.
Wolf Born
Dragon Born
Shadow Born
Boxset
The Blood Oath Series.
Gritty urban fantasy with a kickass heroine and sizzling paranormal males smattered with a bite of romance.
Immortal Creatures
Immortal Secrets
Immortal Obsession
The Blood Oath Boxset
Newsletter: www.jnmoon.com

About the Author.

What got me hooked into vampires, as a kid, I secretly watched Hammer Horror films on my tv, then reading the classics, Dracula and Frankenstein. I was always more interested in the vampires than Van Helsing. Inspiring movies, Underworld, The Lost Boys, and Blade.

My books are gritty and action-packed, taking you into the underbelly of the world of the damned, who live alongside the world of the living.

I base my stories where I live, the beautiful Georgian city of Bath, UK is minutes from my home.

The Cotswolds is where my wolves are based and Bristol my other urban fantasy series.

Being in the South West of England there are a lot of interesting sacred sites, Stonehenge, Glastonbury, Stanton Drew Stone Circle to name a few.

Vampires, werewolves, demons along with mythological creatures are all mixed into my stories. A balance of fantasy and reality, a world that takes you, the reader away from the mundane stresses of life. And sometimes a smattering of the philosophical...

Dark, Sublime, Gripping Stories.

If you want to connect, I like talking to like-minded souls so get in touch.

When not writing, I love reading. Surprise! I do aerial arts and have a thing for hanging upside down, I don't know, maybe I was a bat in a last life? Also enjoy snowboarding. But not at the same time as aerial arts. Love animals, nature and science alongside studying the occult and metaphysical studies. I always wanted Peter Cushing's study from the Hammer Horror films. Have yet to get a crystal skull for my desk! I do have an Anubis skull however...That's Glastonbury town for you.

Where Am I?

Email: author@jnmoon.com
Twitter: alwaysdarkangel
Facebook: Author JN Moon
Web: jnmoon.com
IG: instagram.com/authorjnmoon71/
Pinterest: taoistjo

Feel free to connect! Thanks for reading, stay weird. JO x

Printed in Great Britain
by Amazon